... The man backed off—wary now, plainly surprised at his opponent's agility and speed. Ki watched his eyes, the tendons in his neck. He let a right catch him gently on the shoulder, tossed a left aside, and went in fast. His fists moved in a blur, punishing the man with hard, savage blows to the face, driving him back on his heels. Blood fountained from cuts and a broken nose. Ki hit him again, peeling back flesh on his cheek. The man's eyes glazed, and Ki hit him once more across the temple, swinging the base of his fist like a club. Red Vest dropped like a sack. The whole thing was over almost before it had started.

# WESLEY ELLIS

# LONE STAR

## AND THE SCHOOL FOR OUTLAWS

A JOVE BOOK

LONE STAR AND THE SCHOOL FOR OUTLAWS

A Jove Book / published by arrangement with
the author

PRINTING HISTORY
Jove edition / February 1985

ISBN: 0-515-08110-8

# Chapter 1

Paso del Norte baked in the sullen, oppressive heat of the afternoon. The molten sky drank every shadow and sucked color out of the earth. Ki left the Hotel Alberto and walked north, down the narrow cobbled street past a dry stone fountain and the flat expanse of the open market. The shops and stalls were empty; buyers and sellers alike had fled behind thick adobe walls until evening. Only the odor of rotten vegetables remained. A washboard-ribbed dog spotted Ki and skulked quickly away with some prize.

Cutting across the plaza, Ki walked into a street of brown adobes butted one against the other. There were four cantinas in the block; he ignored the first three and walked through the batwing doors of the Azteca. The bar seemed cool and dark after the harsh light of the street. Every eye looked up to take him in. Then, just as quickly, the drinkers turned back to their business. They'd seen Ki before, in one cantina or another. He was a tall, angular man in a black leather vest, faded denims, and rough-out boots worn at the heels. His striped shirt was buttoned at the collar and the cuffs. Hard muscle in his shoulders and upper arms stretched the fabric. A battered black Stetson covered thick black hair and shaded eyes slightly tilted at the corners. His features were hard to fathom, the planes of his face blurred by a six-day growth of beard. A .44 Colt in a double-loop Mexican holster hung from his waist. As long as he kept his peace, he was a man of no interest to any other.

Ki ordered a beer, and the fat bartender set it before him with a yawn. Bringing the glass to his lips, Ki turned and set his elbows on the bar, using the motion to quickly check the room. There were four cardplayers at a table. Ki knew the men by sight. Farther back in shadow, three young

Mexicans shared a bottle of mescal. Two Lincoln County hands in dusty clothes lounged at the bar. A young Mexican girl stood between them, flattering the pair for a drink or something more.

Ki looked at the girl with interest. He hadn't noticed her in town, and she was worth a second glance. She was slim and high-breasted, taller than most Mexican women he'd seen. Her frilly red dress clung to her figure, molding the pinch of her waist and a firmly rounded bottom. Her hair was raven-black, swept up tightly from her cheeks and pinned atop her head. Dark eyes flashed with pleasure when she laughed. Ki figured that the smooth, honey-brown flesh, high cheeks, and full mouth bespoke Indian blood as well as Spanish.

The girl saw him looking and offered a lazy smile. Moments later she left the two hands and moved up beside him, letting the pressure of her shoulder find his arm.

"Hey, I don't see you before, do I?" she said brightly. "You want to buy Juanita a drink?"

"Sure," said Ki. "What'll it be?"

The girl caught the bartender's eye and a glass appeared quickly on the water-stained wood. She cupped it between her hands but didn't drink. It was rotgut whiskey or colored water or some of both; Ki didn't care and was glad to pay. Having her there was a pleasure to the eye. More than that, it was a natural thing to do and showed he belonged.

"Hey, what's your name, huh? You goin' to tell Juanita or not?"

"Marcus," said Ki. "Mark'll do fine."

"Mar-quas. Hey, tha's a real good name. I like it."

"You do, huh?"

"Oh, sure. Is *muy* fine name."

Ki repressed a grin. If he'd told her he was Cowchip Charlie Bumpas, she'd have liked that just as well.

Juanita pressed closer and let her breast touch his arm. "You like me pretty good, Mar-quas?"

"Oh yeah. I sure do."

"Those—*burros*"—she glanced scornfully to her right— "They tell Juanita they don' have money. Don' buy her any drink. Pretty cheap, huh?"

"Well there's no accountin' for taste."

"*You* got money, I think."

2

"Some, maybe."

"Don' take a whole lot, you know? You unnerstan' this?" She pressed a little closer in case he didn't. "Just a little bit of money, we get a good bottle of whiskey and go wherever you like. Nice hotel, maybe?"

"Might just do that," said Ki.

"Yes?" Juanita's eyes flashed. "Right now, huh?"

"Want to do a little drinkin' here first. Don't get anxious, girl."

Juanita started to pout. Ki flipped a coin down on the bar and told the bartender to bring her another. She hadn't yet touched the first. Juanita grinned and gripped his arm. An extra drink was certainly a token of good faith.

"Where you from?" she asked. "Where you live, Mar-quas?"

"Up north. Over the border."

"Well, sure," she scolded. "I know *that*. Where, though? Where you from in *Estados Unidos?* Texas? California, maybe?"

"Some of all over."

"I bet you from California. I know this man from California one time. He is very nice man. Treat Juanita real fine . . ."

Ki wasn't listening. Shadow blocked the harsh glare of the street and two men walked through the batwing doors, followed quickly by a third. Ki let out a breath. A hot week in Paso del Norte, talking to men he didn't like and drinking whiskey he didn't want, had paid off. The third, older man had to be Gaylord Brown, the other two the gunmen he kept at his side. And right on time, to boot. Ki's careful questions and double eagles had bought him that. If Brown was in town, he'd likely visit the Azteca after six.

Ki's eyes followed the three to a table, showing no more interest or no less than the other patrons. The bartender woke up fast, beating his customers to a table and wiping it vigorously with a well-soiled rag. Moments later, he was back with a bottle of fine Herradura Añejo the color of straw. Clean glasses followed, along with hot tortillas, a fiery red sauce, and wedges of white goat cheese.

The younger men looked near enough alike to be brothers. Each sported a plain black suit, string tie, and black derby. One wore a blue checkered vest, the other a red.

3

Both carried short-barreled Colts in their belts. Ki sized them up at a glance. They were lean, quiet men who walked with animal grace. Men much like himself, yet not the same at all. The flat, expressionless eyes told him that. Ki was trained to kill in a dozen different ways. He could do what had to be done, but never relished taking a life. These two, though, clearly enjoyed their work.

Gaylord Brown took him completely by surprise. Tall, lean, close to his early fifties, he carried himself like a man used to getting his way. A thick mane of silver hair and a matching full mustache complemented deeply tanned flesh and blue eyes. His bearing said banker, old cattle money, a man with a couple of railroads under his belt. And yet, thought Ki, if you judged the man by his clothes, he was a dandy or a fool. Was *this* the man he and Jessie had come clear across Texas to find? He wore a fringed leather jacket that George Custer would have envied, English-cut trousers, a cream-colored shirt, and a vest of jaguar skin. The black sombrero that topped his head was studded with conchos and tassels. His boots were hand-tooled, and on his heels he wore heavy Chihuahua spurs, the sharp spoked rowels inlaid with silver. The spurs looked comical off a horse, yet Ki had an idea no one *ever* laughed at Gaylord Brown.

"We get a bottle and go, *sí?*" Juanita's fingers clutched his arm. "Is good idea, I think. Now, huh?"

Ki caught the change in the girl's voice. The bright smile had vanished, and small lines of tension framed her lips.

"Something bother you about that bunch?"

"Le's go, okay?" A small hand worried at his shirt. "Look, we have real good time. I—" Her dark eyes suddenly widened in alarm. Ki turned and saw the man in the red vest coming toward him. He looked straight at the girl and didn't bother to glance at Ki.

"Juanita, get on over to Mr. Brown's table," he said plainly. "He'd like to buy you a drink."

"I—*sí*, yes, Señor . . ."

"Lady's already got a drink," Ki broke in. "You must not have noticed."

The man glanced curiously at Ki, surprised to find him taking up space. "Juanita, get on over there. Now."

"You're not listening," said Ki.

"No, please . . ." Juanita shook her head in desperation.

4

"Is okay. I go for a while, yes?"

"Sure," said Ki, "that'll be fine." His fist struck out without warning, found the man's belly, and lifted him off the floor. He smashed a chair to kindling and hit the floor hard. Then, too soon for Ki's liking, he came up in a crouch, sucking air and shaking off the blow. The quick recovery told Ki a lot. The fellow should have crawled off and tossed his supper.

Ki risked a glance at Brown's table. Blue Vest was out of his chair. Brown shook his head and motioned him back. Red Vest came straight at him, bent at the waist in a fighting stance. Ki let him come, ducked to the left, and landed two hard blows to the chest. The man backed off—wary now, plainly surprised at his opponent's agility and speed. Ki watched his eyes, the tendons in his neck. He let a right catch him lightly on the shoulder, tossed a left aside, and went in fast. His fists moved in a blur, punishing the man with hard, savage blows to the face, driving him back on his heels. Blood fountained from cuts and a broken nose. Ki hit him again, peeling back flesh on his cheek. The man's eyes glazed, and Ki hit him once more across the temple, swinging the base of his fist like a club. Red Vest dropped like a sack. The whole thing was over almost before it had started.

Juanita shouted a warning. Ki turned, already aware of the other man's presence. He'd tossed his coat aside and laid his Colt on the table. He faced Ki now with a blade held loosely in his hand, a bowie knife nearly a foot long. An easy grin creased his features, pure pleasure in his eyes. Ki bent and drew a slim-bladed knife from his boot. The man looked startled, then laughed aloud. The blade was much shorter and lacked the bowie knife's weight and awesome power. It looked for all the world like a California dirk, an ivory-handled gambler's knife and no match for the bigger weapon. Ki had fashioned the knife himself, shaping it from a slim *tanto* blade. The seemingly fragile dirk was made of the finest Japanese steel, honed to an incredibly keen edge.

"You're a plain fool, mister," a voice said from behind him. "I seen this feller cut before. I'd back off if I was you."

Ki nodded his thanks without looking. The man circled

wide, moving like a cat, on the balls of his feet. Ki kept his eyes on the big blade. Blue Vest knew his weapon. He had the style and likely the speed to do the job. Ki watched and let him come. The man lowered his shoulders and let the knife swing free, probing the air like a snake. Suddenly he feinted to the left, twisted his knees, and slashed savagely to the right. Ki sucked in his belly, letting the blade whip by and come back for a second try. The solid weight of the bar nudged his back and he slid away. The man stalked him again, stabbed out twice to get his attention, then jerked the blade up with lightning speed. The knife passed inches under his chin. It was a fast, wicked strike that could have ripped him from belly to throat.

Ki backed off, staying on the defensive. He'd managed the man's companion, beating him barroom-style and letting speed take the place of practiced moves with his hands and feet. The man with the knife would be harder. With a blade in his hand, Ki's mind and body worked instinctively in a classic *kenjutsu* manner. It took a conscious effort of will to set his samurai training aside, to beat the larger weapon without betraying what he knew. Likely no one else would notice—but Gaylord Brown would spot him in a second.

Ki's action bothered his foe. Ki could see it in his eyes. The man with the slim-bladed dirk should be dead. Instead, he was very much alive and hadn't yet given a hint as to how he fought.

Ki waited, holding back. When it happened, it had to look right. Speed, the way he'd handled the other. And if he was wrong, if he held off and gave the man a chance . . .

The heavy knife flashed, nearly catching Ki in thought. Juanita screamed as the blade slashed Ki's vest, ripped his shirt, and stung his flesh. The man grinned and pressed on, whipping the knife at Ki's face. Again, Ki retreated, let the blade brush his shirt, flash past him again, and jerk back for another pass.

In that instant, Ki struck. In and out before anyone watching could see. The man cried out, staggered back, and stared at the dark red line across his chest. He gripped the knife in his fist and came in low, the bowie knife hard against his thigh. Ki feinted, slammed his foot to the floor, and stabbed out. The man lashed back in response, the blood on his chest doing the thinking instead of his head. Ki wasn't there. The razor edge of the dirk slashed left, right, and left again, scarcely touching flesh at all. The man bellowed and stumbled back. His face was suddenly white, eyes wide with fear. Ki knew the look, saw what Blue Vest was thinking: the blade that had painted a pattern up his arm could easily have cut his throat. The man with the fragile-looking dirk was only playing with him now. He could kill him whenever he liked. It was a truth that brought bright beads of moisture to his face.

"That's all," Ki said quietly. "It's over."

"Goddamn you!" the man raged. "Don't tell me it's over, you bastard!"

"Sit down, Henry," Brown spoke from the table. "The man's right and you know it."

In answer, Henry shook his head and switched the knife to his good arm. He came at Ki like a bull, all the style he'd shown before now buried in anger. Ki stepped aside; the man was still a danger, and the blade came alarmingly close to his chest. The dirk flashed once. Blood covered the man's hand above his knuckles. He dropped the knife like a hot iron, grabbed his hand, and swore. Ki stepped in, kicked the knife aside, and stuck the dirk just below the other's chin.

"You try to pick that up, I'll cut off your head," he said softly. "You got that, mister?"

The man nodded, shame flooding his features. Ki let him back away. The man he'd beaten with his fists sat up and shook his head. Ki reached down and got the man's Colt and threw it outside into the street.

"I'd like a word with you, sir, if you don't mind."

Ki turned quickly to Brown, his hand resting just above his own weapon. "I'm not looking for more trouble. Wasn't looking for it with them."

"I fully understand," said Brown. He shook his head and grinned, making a show of bringing his hands up in surrender. "Would you let me buy you a drink?"

"Why? Those two belong to you, don't they?"

"I'll answer," said Brown, "if you'll do the same. You hurt those boys real bad. I've seldom seen it done any better. Any reason you didn't kill them?"

Ki shrugged, sat down, and accepted the glass of tequila. It went down warm, filling the pit of his stomach. "A fight's

7

a fight," he said simply. "Killing brings the law. I told you I wasn't looking for trouble."

"Well said. Makes good sense, it does." Brown nodded approval and touched the tips of his mustache. The light blue eyes studied Ki intently. "You answered my question, and now I'll answer yours. Sometimes I can find good employment for a man who can handle himself. It appears to me that you can. Think maybe you'd be interested in something like that?"

Ki had spent a week in Paso del Norte with a single purpose in mind: to find Gaylord Brown and get him to offer such a job. Jessie Starbuck was waiting across the line in El Paso to see if it worked.

"Thanks kindly," said Ki, standing and setting his glass back on the table. "I'm obliged for the drink. Thing is, I'm not much looking for work."

Brown raised a brow. "Pay's real good. You might be sorry you passed it up." His eyes told Ki what he already knew—Brown wasn't used to being refused.

"Like I said, *amigo*, I'm grateful." He nodded in the girl's direction and grinned. "Working isn't what I'm after at the moment. At least nothing too tiring." He turned and walked away before Brown could speak again. He passed the two gunmen without looking and slid his hand around Juanita's slim waist. "You ready for that party we were talking about, girl?"

Juanita stared in open wonder. "*Sí*, Mar-quas."

"Well, come on, then, let's get at it."

# Chapter 2

The room was simple and clean, with whitewashed walls and a clay tile floor. In one corner stood a roughly fashioned wooden bed painted blue, and a table close by with a kerosene lamp. Across the room was a dresser with a pitcher and a washbowl. The single window was barred with wrought iron, shaded now with fiber matting against the last rays of the sun.

The girl stood by the window, light and shadow striping her face. It was hot and still in the room, yet she hugged her arms tightly over her breasts. Ki took off his belt, folded it over the holster, and laid the rig across the dresser.

"You don't have to stay, you know that, don't you?" he said gently. "If you figure they'll cause you any trouble over me—"

"Ha! Them?" Juanita's mouth curled in disdain. "They won' do nothing. Not to me. *You*, maybe. Tha's something else, you know?"

"I'll worry about that tomorrow." He yawned and scratched his head, working to make the words sound easy. "That fellow in the fancy duds is sure something. Who'd you say he was?"

"Señor Brown."

"A pretty big man around here, is he?"

"I don' know," she said stiffly. "I don' know *nothin'* about him, okay?" She caught herself and smiled, crossed the room, and snaked her arms around his neck. "Hey, is too much talking, *sí*? More fun we do something else."

"Well, I won't argue with that."

She closed her eyes and brought her lips to his. Her mouth was soft and willing, opening at once to his touch. He slid his arms about her waist, caressing the small of her

9

back. The slender form flowed easily against him, finding the places that fit. Her hands trailed up his shoulders to cup his face. She gave a little cry and thrust her tongue into his mouth. The pink tip probed and teased, setting a lazy rhythm that flowed the length of her body. Ki held her closer, his hands pressing her belly against his rapidly swelling member.

Juanita grinned and pushed him away, retreating quickly to the window. Holding him with her eyes, she reached up to take the combs from her hair. Black tresses tumbled freely over her shoulders, a thick veil reaching nearly to her waist. Lowering her head shyly, she loosened the buttons of her bodice. One sleeve fell provocatively over her shoulder, then the other. She faced him through a mist of tousled hair, then brought her shoulders together and let the dress whisper softly past her breasts. As Ki had imagined, she was naked underneath. His throat went dry at the sight of the full, swollen breasts, the hard and dusky nipples.

"You like, yes?" she asked softly. "You like the way Juanita look?"

"I like the way Juanita looks just fine."

"You want to see more I think, *sí?*"

Ki didn't answer. His hunger was clear enough to the girl's discerning eye. She grinned and let her tongue dart quickly about her lips. Releasing a hook at her waist, she slid her palms slowly down her sides, peeling the dress past her hips until it fell in a froth about he ankles. Hooking one toe in the dress, she flung it playfully in Ki's direction. Then, stepping back, she clamped her hands behind her; the motion gave her breasts a saucy tilt and hollowed her belly.

"What do you think now, Mar-quas?"

Ki grinned. "You can *see* what I think, if you're looking."

"Oh, Juanita don' miss that." She rolled her eyes in mock alarm at the bulge in his pants. "You won' hurt me now, promise?" The little-girl voice, full of wonder and a slight touch of fear, was clearly designed to arouse a man further. But Ki didn't need any help. The sight of the willowy young girl was all he needed. She was a dark-eyed beauty, surely no more than eighteen. Her lovely skin was pale olive and wild honey. Ki let his eyes feast on the long stretch of her legs, the soft swell of her belly, and the dark promise of pleasure between her thighs. For an instant the day lingered at the edge of darkness and light. The girl's naked flesh seemed to glow, the supple curves half lost in shadow. The hair that fell past her shoulders seemed made of smoke. Ki took a step forward and she came into his arms without a word. The softness of her skin against his clothing made him shudder. He lifted her in his arms and carried her to the bed. She watched him take off his shirt and throw it aside, pull off his boots and step out of his denims. Her eyes were smoldering circles in shadow. He came to her then, and she raised her arms to greet him. The sudden heat of her body, the fragile texture of her flesh, filled him with wonder. She whispered quick pleasures in his ear, offered sweet young breasts to his mouth. She sighed as he caressed the nipples with his tongue. Her hands snaked between them to grasp his member. She stroked it with practiced fingers, teasing the tip against the satin of her thighs. Ki slid his hands beneath her hips and pressed her close. She responded to his touch, arching her back and thrusting her feathery mound hard against him.

"Ai, yes, *yes!*" she cried softly, her breath a hot fire against his throat. Her legs opened wide and she guided him into her warmth. Her fingers found his back and raked his flesh. Ki plunged inside her and she opened like a flower to welcome him in. He ground himself against her, hungry for the treasure she had to offer. Her legs scissored about him, strong calves pounding him even deeper into her body. Juanita threw back her head, shouting her delight in bursts of Spanish too fast for him to follow. He wrapped his arms around her, her breasts flattened against his chest. She trembled and held him tight, matching the pulse of his pleasure with her own. Her breath came in short bursts. Moisture slicked her flesh, and Ki savored the taste of her body.

He could feel the swelling now deep within him, a storm that threatened to pick him up and toss him roughly aside. He fought against the pleasure, the sudden surge that would tremble through his loins and bring release. Holding back wasn't easy. He was schooled in the Oriental arts of love, but she was a challenge that took all the will he could muster. Juanita's fiery young body sought to draw him over the edge and drain him dry. The practiced little nest between her legs knew every trick in the book. Her silken flesh was a hungry mouth, pulling him toward a moment he couldn't control. Soft velvet walls teased his member, daring him to stop and pull away.

She laughed against his throat. "Right now, Señor—right *now!*"

Ki sucked in a breath as honeyed warmth spasmed around him. It squeezed him again and again like wicked fingers, loosing a flood inside her with a force that made her gasp—one fierce explosion following the next and then the next. Juanita gave a ragged cry of pleasure, gripped his back, and jerked uncontrollably against him. Her body shuddered, trembling with sweet release. She flung her arms to her sides and laughed aloud.

Ki shook his head in wonder. "I didn't think I was going to stop."

"Oh yes?" She tried to show concern, but Ki's expression threw her into laughter again. She twisted into his arms and covered his face with kisses. Ki's hands found the soft swell of her belly, the unblemished flesh of her thigh.

"You want a drink, maybe?" she asked. "I get you whiskey or something?"

"No. I don't need a thing."

"You wan' me to go now? I go if you like."

"No. I don't want you to go at all."

"Okay, then." Her eyes flashed with delight. "I stay with you, Mar-quas. Long as you like, *sí?*"

"*Sí*, it is. You do that, *conejita.*"

She gave him a sleepy smile and nestled in his arms. The room was dark now. He turned on his side and she snuggled into the hollow of his belly. Her hand found his and cupped it over her breast. In a moment her breath came slow and easy. Ki looked past the curve of her shoulder, into the darkness broken only dimly by slivers of moonlight through the fiber matting over the window.

The flat adobe roof of the hotel was still warm from the heat of the day. The night was sultry and quiet, low clouds scudding over the moon. Ki guessed it was close to ten, or maybe later. Moving silently to the edge of the roof, he peered over and studied the street below. Halfway down

12

the block, lemon-colored light spilled from a small cantina into the street. Two sleepy mounts were hitched to a rail. A quick burst of laughter filled the night. He watched the street for a long while and finally found him: one man, standing in the doorway of a darkened *panadería*. From there the man could see the front of the hotel and anyone coming and going. There could be a man out back, but Ki doubted that they'd bother. The girl in his room was their assurance that he'd be busy for the night.

Backing away from the edge, Ki moved in a crouch across the building, carrying his boots in one hand. The passageway beside the hotel was only a four-foot jump. He made it without effort, landing without a sound. Swiftly he worked his way north, running silently across the darkened roofs until he was well away from the hotel. Finally he dropped to the ground and pulled on his boots. Past the alley and down the street he found exactly what he wanted. Half a dozen horses waited before a small cafe, in a pool of light. The heady aroma of roasting *cabrito* assailed his senses, reminding him he hadn't eaten for some time.

Ki gathered the reins of a flinty-eyed mare and walked it casually out of the light. Once in shadow, he mounted up and moved the horse north through narrow streets. Stealing a horse was a bad idea—on either side of the border. Still, he couldn't risk the livery near the hotel.

For a while he rode northwest, leaving Paso del Norte and paralleling the border. A few miles out, he turned and crossed the muddy shallows of the Rio Grande. The amber lights of El Paso appeared to the east. He rode for another quarter-hour, circled back, and came into town from the north.

At night it was hard to tell the difference between this border town and the one he'd left behind. Ki kept to back streets, rousing a barking dog now and then and bringing a curious face to a window.

It was close to midnight, he guessed, but El Paso's liveliest saloons were going strong. Keeping Jessie's map in mind, he found the place he wanted, three blocks south of the main street. A good dozen horses were hitched outside the big two-story house. High-pitched laughter blended with a tinny piano. The shades were all drawn, but every room

13

glowed with life. Ki found an alley nearby, left his mount, and walked. A large bull of a man sat on the darkened front porch.

"No weapons inside," he said quietly. Ki stopped. The man stood, and Ki handed over his pistol and belt. "What else you got?" the man asked.

"Knife in the boot," said Ki.

The man bent to retrieve it, brushing practiced hands down his leg and over his chest. "All right, you're fine."

Ki knocked on the door. A man even bigger than the first opened up, gave him a quick inspection, and stepped aside.

Ki blinked against the light to get his bearings. Crystal chandeliers graced the ceiling. The textured walls were a rich wine red, hung with gilt-framed paintings and diamond-dust mirrors. Ornate, hand-carved European furniture filled every corner of the room.

Ki dismissed the fine decor in an instant. Gilt and crystal paled before the room's main attraction. There were raven-haired girls with smoky eyes, amber-haired beauties with long legs and creamy flesh, pert young girls with cornflower eyes and yellow hair. The gowns were silk and satin, Chinese red and emerald green and burnished gold. The dresses were as varied as the ladies fitted snugly inside them, yet each managed to show more lovely flesh than it concealed.

The girls looked up from sofas and chairs and granted him polished smiles. The men, held by the charms of their companions, scarcely gave him a glance.

Ki watched the woman approach him across the carpet. She was tall, slender, a lady of regal bearing. Her hair was as dark as night, swept atop her head and crowned with a tuft of ivory feathers. Her gown was black satin, and whispered as she walked. Ki couldn't guess her age—forty, maybe, or older. It didn't seem to matter; she was still a striking woman.

"Hope you have lots of time, mister," she said with a smile. "We're pretty busy tonight." Ki didn't miss the disapproving glance at his worn, dusty clothing.

"I've got time," he told her. "I'd guess you're Miss Lorna, am I right?"

The lady wasn't surprised. "I am," she told him. "Now what can I do for you?"

14

"I'm looking for someone special."

Miss Lorna gave him a tired, understanding smile. "Most everyone is, friend. Just what kind of 'special' you got in mind? We have all different kinds, you might say."

"I'd like to see Maureen. Maureen Kelly."

The woman's expression didn't change. "Sorry. I think you have the wrong place. We don't have a Maureen."

"You're sure?"

"Now I'd likely know, wouldn't I?" She studied Ki a moment, then bit her lip in thought. *"Had* a Maureen once. Pretty little yellow-haired girl about so high."

"This one's as tall as you are, ma'am," Ki told her. "Green eyes, strawberry-blond hair down to her shoulders."

Miss Lorna looked right at him. "You have a name of some kind, mister?"

"Marcus. Marcus Villon. From San Francisco," he added.

Lorna nodded. "Why don't we go on back through here?" she suggested. "Just follow me, if you will."

She led him through the brightly lit parlor into a smaller room and through a door she unlocked with a key, then down a dim hall and up a narrow flight of stairs. Ki could tell at once that this part of the house was near the back, separate from the long row of bedrooms he'd find up front.

Miss Lorna stopped before a door and knocked twice. In a moment a key turned and the door opened a crack. "You've got company," she said dryly. "Doesn't look like much to me, but he's got the right name."

A bright burst of laughter came from the room and the door flew open wide. Jessica Starbuck grinned at Ki, pulling a white dressing gown about her shoulders.

"My Lord," she exclaimed, "thought for a second it was William Bonney himself coming to call!" She threw her arms around him and kissed his cheek. "Smells like Bonney, too. It's all right, Lorna. You got the right man."

"Huh," Lorna said doubtfully. "If you say so, Jessie." She turned and disappeared down the hall. Jessie closed the door behind her.

"I'm so glad you're here," she said softly. "I was getting worried, Ki."

"So was I." He dropped into a chair and gave her a weary grin. "I found him, Jessie. I found Gaylord Brown, and he's the one!"

# Chapter 3

A week before, Jessie and Ki had stepped off the stage into the deeply rutted main street of Sweetwater, Texas. This, at least, was the name that had been lettered on the sign hanging above the door of the clapboard stagecoach line building, though someone who apparently knew the place better had crossed out the second *e* and replaced it with an *a*, so the sign now read SWEATWATER. It was even more telling, perhaps, that no one had bothered to change it back.

Jessie let her eyes sweep the street toward the center of town. "I don't see anyone who looks like he knows us," she sighed. "Guess *we're* going to have to find *him*."

Ki picked up their two leather valises and followed Jessie across the street. Two young men rode by, and a gray-headed teamster atop a wagonload of timber. All three stopped to watch Jessie. Wherever she happened to be, in Denver or a small Texas town, Jessie Starbuck never failed to turn men's eyes. She was tall for a woman, and slim as a willow. The cream-colored blouse and light green jacket and skirt failed to hide the proud lines of her body, the long stride of her legs. Sun caught the tumble of blond hair and turned it to burnished copper under her Stetson. The hair framed startling green eyes, a classically straight nose, and a full, sensuous mouth. The young riders looked at each other and grinned. The old man on the wagon remembered things he figured he'd forgotten.

"Jessie? Jessie Starbuck?"

Jessie stopped as a rawboned man with a balding head and heavy brows stepped off the board sidewalk to greet her. "By damn, it *is* you, too," he said, his weathered features splitting in a grin. "Ain't seen you since you was twelve, but you're the image of your mother, rest her soul."

16

Jessie answered his smile. "And you've just got to be Sheriff Art Hamill. My father said once, 'Just walk till you find the handsomest man in West Texas. When you stop, that'll be Art Hamill.'"

Hamill threw back his head and laughed. "Goddamn, that's the truth. I never knew Alex Starbuck to lie!" His eyes darkened with sadness and the broad smile faded. "I'm sorry as hell about what happened," he said soberly. "I'm sure goin' to miss him."

"Thank you." Jessie lowered her eyes. "He had a lot of good friends. I know you were one of the best." She looked away quickly and introduced Ki. Art Hamill gripped his hand firmly and turned to Jessie.

"We'd best be going," he said flatly. "I'd offer you somethin' to eat and a chance to rest, but I don't figure we got the time."

"Then the man's still alive?"

Hamill nodded. "He ain't dead, but I can't figure why. 'Cept he's determined to talk to you."

The boardinghouse was two doors down from the sheriff's office. The room on the second floor was dark and already smelled of death. A middle-aged woman stood up from a chair, and Jessie saw what lay behind her. She drew in a breath, her fingers tightening instinctively on Ki's arm.

"Why, he's only a boy!"

"Closer to twenty," Hamill said quietly. "A man's features soften when he's dyin'."

The slight figure scarcely disturbed the blanket pulled up to his chest. He had once been a fine-looking man, Jessie could see. His proud Spanish features were still clear, but his skin was waxen. A tight bandage covered his chest and stretched over his left shoulder. Jessie looked questioning at Hamill.

"His name's Vargas. Miguel Vargas."

Jessie lowered herself to the straight-backed chair beside the bed. As if he somehow sensed her presence, Miguel Vargas opened his eyes. Jessie laid a hand on his arm. The flesh was hot with fever.

"Miguel," she said gently, "I'm here. I'm Jessica Starbuck."

17

The flat black eyes seemed to brighten. "You came. Yes?"

"Yes, I'm here."

Vargas tried to raise his head. Jessie pressed a palm against his brow. "You just take it easy, you hear? You don't have to move."

"You are a . . . very beautiful lady . . . *muy bonita* . . ."

"Thank you. That's nice of you to say."

Vargas winced as pain caught him. "Did he . . . did he tell you?"

"Left that up to you, son," Hamill said from behind Jessie.

Vargas gave a faint, almost imperceptible nod. *"Sí.* This is so." His eyes found Jessie. "You . . . must forgive me for what I have to say. Please. You will do this?"

"Of course," said Jessie. "But what is it I have to forgive?"

For an instant the man's eyes seemed to mirror a hurt far greater than the pain that racked his body. "When I . . . when I was shot, I was on my way to Sarah, Texas. To the Circle Star Ranch."

"Yes?"

"I was coming to kill you, Señorita. This is the task I was given. To kill Señorita Jessie Starbuck."

Jessie started to draw in a breath. "Miguel . . . why would you want to harm me? Why?"

Miguel's dark, hollow eyes met hers and held them. "You give me a promise," he said intently. "You swear —by the blood of the baby *Cristo* . . ."

"I'll promise if it's something I can," Jessie said gently.

"I have a mother and a sister . . . in Hermosillo, in Sonora. You see they come to *Estados Unidos.* You see they come to no harm."

"Yes. I could do that, Miguel."

Miguel seemed to find a moment of peace. "You swear this?"

"Yes I do, Miguel."

He closed his eyes for a moment. "There is . . . I had a place. Down the street. A room." He glanced at the sheriff. "In back of the Abilene Cafe. You look under the floor there. You will find this thing. Then I . . . I tell you the rest."

Jessie raised a brow at Art Hamill.

"I know the place. You wait here."

Jessie nodded and stood. Hamill left quickly; Vargas closed his eyes, all the strength suddenly drained out of his face. Jessie followed Ki into the hall, and the woman went back to sit by the bed.

"Sheriff Hamill's right," Jessie sighed. "He isn't going to last much longer."

"You think he's telling the truth? Someone sent him to kill you?"

"He knows he's dying, Ki. What's a lie going to do for him now?"

Ki didn't answer. Jessie leaned against the wall and ran a hand across her face. Art Hamill's Western Union message had told her little—simply to get to Sweetwater as soon as possible if she could, that the matter was most urgent and wouldn't wait. Jessie trusted her father's old friend and had caught the first stage west from Sarah, Texas.

What was it all about? she wondered. It was clear that Hamill was right, Miguel Vargas was clinging to life for one reason: to talk to the woman he was supposed to hunt down and kill. Hamill had told them little on the way to the boardinghouse, only that Vargas's story had come out strictly by chance. He hadn't even been involved in the shootout that would soon take his life. Two drunken cowhands were having it out in a saloon, and Vargas got in the way and caught a bullet.

"Things happen for a reason sometimes," Hamill had muttered. "Maybe this is one of 'em."

Jessie turned as the sheriff puffed up the stairs, a small packet in his hand. "He wasn't lyin' about this," he said darkly. "Found it right under the floor, where he said."

Jessie took the packet and turned it over curiously in her hands. She untied the leather thong that bound it, and tore away the oilcloth wrapping. Inside was a stiff brown folder. She opened it and removed the thick fold of papers inside.

"My God, Ki!" she breathed as she stared in disbelief at the item on top. It was a sepia photograph, a studio cabinet card. It pictured Jessie and several friends posed under a large oak tree before a white-columned house. Her hand trembled slightly as she thrust the photograph at Ki and Hamill. "That was taken last spring in St. Louis," she exclaimed. "Look, there's Mary Lynn and Jack, and Senator

19

Gray and—damn it all, what's Miguel Vargas doing with this!"

She leafed quickly through the packet. There was another photograph, taken at a gathering in San Francisco. There was a map of the Circle Star Ranch, a fairly good sketch of the main house. The papers in the packet were the most astonishing items of all. Everything was there: her background, her habits, her friends, where she went and who she knew. Jessie drew in a breath and passed the papers along. "Sheriff Hamill," she said tightly, "how much has Vargas told you? You didn't know about this, obviously."

"He told me enough to get you here, Jessie. Enough to convince me he sure as hell knew who you were." He hesitated and nodded at the papers. "I reckon he's got more to say, if he can manage."

"Yes," Jessie said thoughtfully. "I'm certain he figures these papers are his credentials. He's right, too. They've made a believer out of me." She turned, then, and walked quickly back into the room. The woman stood and shook her head, a message that needed no words. Miguel Vargas was fading fast. Jessie sat and touched his brow. Vargas opened his eyes.

"You . . . find the things?"

"Yes. I have them." Jessie leaned closer to his lips. "Now. What is it you want to tell me, Miguel? I promise, you have my word. I'll take care of your family in Sonora. I'll send a Western Union message to friends in Mexico today. Do you understand me?"

"Yes. I understand. Come closer, Señorita, please. The talking is . . . not so easy." Vargas's thin lips creased in a painful smile. "Besides, you smell like a lady. This is a nice thing for Miguel."

Miguel Vargas told his story. Jessie listened, her ear nearly brushing his lips as his voice grew weaker with the strain. Some of the words were clear; others she pieced together as he talked, not daring to interrupt the flow. Vargas had left his home in Sonora, Mexico, as a boy scarcely more than fifteen. He had fallen in with a group of *bandidos*, and risen to become their leader three years later. He was known for his daring, his uncanny talent with a gun. Wanted all over Mexico for a string of robberies and killings, he had finally been trapped by the law and sentenced to death. A girl had helped him escape, and he'd made his way north toward the border.

Here the story became confused as Miguel's fevered mind began to wander. He'd met a man, been hired, recruited, and sent...somewhere. Vargas wasn't certain where this might be. Mexico, or maybe South Texas. No one knew for sure, for the men who were taken there never saw where they were going. It was a school, Miguel explained. A school in a mountain canyon.

"A *school?*" Jessie asked. "Is that what you're saying, Miguel?"

"*Sí, escuela,*" Vargas said weakly. "But...a school of a different kind. Not the *escuela* for children, Señorita. This is a school for men. A school for men who kill..."

A chill touched the base of Jessie's spine. She glanced at Ki, standing above her in shadow.

It was a school for assassins, Vargas explained. There were men there from all over the world—teachers and students alike. Miguel had met Englishmen, Germans, *norteamericanos*. There was even a man from the Japans. The teachers were masters of killing, experts with guns, knives, or simply their bare hands.

The chill that had touched her moments ago spread quickly through her body. *Whom* did these men kill, was what she wanted to know. Who was behind this school for assassins?

Vargas didn't know. Each man was told his own role and nothing more. The money for these tasks was more than any man there had ever earned or stolen.

"The leader, the man who ran the school. Did you see him, Miguel?"

"Yes," Vargas told her. "A tall man...strong...eyes like broken glass. A man with a ring...a gold ring with a crown..."

At Vargas's words, Jessie jerked straight up in her chair. *There, there it was!* Somehow she'd guessed it from the start. Who else could it be? Who else could put together such a tight, detailed account of her life? Find pictures that couldn't possibly disappear from the homes of her closest friends? Vargas's story suddenly explained a great deal— much more than he knew, Jessie was certain. The other killings—Melton, King, Hatfield, and the rest....

"How can I find this place, Miguel?" Jessie whispered.

21

"How, Miguel? Who *took* you there?"

Miguel's eyelids fluttered. His lips moved with silent words.

"He's going," said Ki.

"Miguel, how? Tell me." Her cheek touched the pallid face.

*"Paso del Norte. Brow' . . . brow' . . ."*

"What? What, Miguel?"

Art Hamill's hand gently squeezed her shoulder. "That's it, Jessie. It's over."

"No. No, he—" She sat up, saw the sightless eyes and parted lips. "Yes. Yes, of course, you're right."

Hamill grasped her arm and helped her up. Jessie stared at the drawn features until Ki pressed the eyelids shut and raised the blanket to cover the young man's face.

Jessie's stomach was empty but she couldn't bring herself to eat. She and Ki drank bitter coffee while Hamill finished off a steak and peach pie.

"Meanin' no disrespect for the dead," he said plainly, "but a person's got to eat. You all ought to try an' get somethin' down."

"It's all right," Jessie replied, "we'll have something later."

"Suit yourself, then." Hamill wiped his mouth and set his napkin aside. He leaned back in his chair and studied Jessie and Ki a long moment. "I got somethin' to say, and this is as good a time as any," he began. "I heard some stuff up there that isn't real easy for a man like me to swallow. I guess I got to, considerin' the circumstances. Awful big tale for a dyin' man."

"It wasn't a tale, Sheriff," Jessie assured him. "All of it was true."

"Yeah, that's what I figured you'd say. Which don't give me the kinda answer I need."

"What answer is that?" asked Ki.

Hamill ran a hand through thinning hair. "I'm a lawman, and not too bad at the job, I don't mind saying. Only what I heard up there sounds to me some stronger'n what we get in Nolan County. Horse stealin' and drunks and maybe a shootin' now and then." He looked straight at Jessie, one eye nearly closed. "This . . . *killin'* school, now. Not even

22

sure how I'd re-port a story like that. Or who'd believe it if I did. An' the peculiar thing is, I get the idea neither of you two was real surprised to hear it. You was, at first, and then you weren't."

Jessie forced a smile. "I can't lie to you, Sheriff. You talk too much like my father. And you're right. It isn't too big a surprise. We've run across these people before."

Hamill looked at Jessie, not sure what he was trying to find. "God Almighty, girl..." He pushed his plate aside, eased back his chair, and stood. "I got some things to do 'round town. I'll check you all in at the hotel, and this evenin' you'll have supper with me and the missus. That all right with you?"

"That would be real nice," said Jessie.

"Well, then..." Hamill nodded, stuck his Stetson atop his head, and walked out into the street.

"He won't tell anyone what he saw, will he?" said Ki. It was more of a statement than a question.

"No. And he won't ask us about it again, either. He isn't going to mix in it, Ki." She sipped her coffee and found it cold. "Lord, Ki, it fits too well to be anyone else. Look at what's happened in the last three months. Senator Melton; King, of the Union Pacific; that banker, Hatfield, in San Francisco. And Gaiter, Jay Gould's friend. Every one of them was murdered. Real professional jobs, too."

"Yes, it fits."

"But what?"

"Did I say 'but'?"

"Didn't have to. I heard it plain enough."

Ki let out a breath. "All right. But it doesn't have to be the cartel. It could be someone else."

"You heard Vargas. A man with a gold ring. A gold ring with a *crown?* Come on, Ki." She pursed her lips in thought. "He said Brown. I'm sure that was it. Brown, in Paso del Norte. That's not much, but it's a start."

"Now look, Jessie, they sent a man after *you*. Have you forgotten that already?"

"God, what do you think?" Her green eyes flashed and she tossed a strand of hair off her cheek. "Far as I'm concerned, I've got the best reason in the world to chase this thing down. I can't very well go back to the ranch right now. Look, I'm not talking about *doing* anything, just a little asking around. We'll go down to El Paso, but first we'll get some Western Union messages off from here. Get some friends on the newspapers to say I'm—what?" She thought for a moment, then said, "Traveling back East. New York, Baltimore, Boston—that ought to keep the cartel busy. And while they're doing that—"

"You'll be wandering around south of the river," Ki said soberly, "knocking on doors and asking questions. 'Excuse me, Señor, I'm looking for a Mr. Brown who runs a school for killers hereabouts. If you see him, tell him Jessie Starbuck's asking about him.'"

Jessie laughed, leaned across the table, and squeezed his hand. "Ki, I'm a *little* more discreet than that."

"No." Ki shook his head. "They've got *photographs* of you, Jessie. And even if they didn't, some of those people would remember you. Besides, you're . . . not a woman who exactly goes unnoticed on the street."

"I can if I try," she said stubbornly.

Ki grinned, stretching the skin tightly over the sharp planes of his face.

"Now what's that supposed to mean?"

"I'm trying to picture you going unnoticed in Paso del Norte. Please, Jessie, don't try it."

"Ki . . ."

"I'll do it" he said flatly. "I'll find out what there is to know, and we can get some help tracking the place down. The army, U.S. marshals, the Mexican law."

"I don't like it. Some of those characters have seen you, too. People we've run across before."

"That's not likely," Ki argued. "Besides, they don't have pictures of me, and I'm not that easy to remember. A week's growth of beard, my hair cut short—"

Jessie blinked. "You'd cut your *hair?* I don't believe it."

Ki looked glumly past his loose-fitting cotton shirt and denims to his feet in their comfortable rope-soled slippers. "I'll even wear boots. I can stand anything for a couple of days."

Jessie bit her lip. "You grow a beard and cut your hair and wear boots, you're going to *get* your picture taken, mister. I want one for myself."

# Chapter 4

Jessie found one of Miss Lorna's maids in the hall and arranged for several large beef sandwiches for Ki. Ki pulled off his boots and relaxed. Jessie wouldn't let him talk until he'd wolfed down the food.

She sat on the sofa and watched, still a little in awe of his appearance. The Ki she knew was a fine-looking man, the sharp planes of his face matching a full head of burnished black hair. This man was bearded and unshaven. His hair was cropped short and his features weren't his own. Even the upward tilt of his eyes, a gift from his Japanese mother, seemed lost in a stranger's face. All to the good, she supposed, considering. Still, she missed the familiar features.

Ki caught her looking, and grinned. "William Bonney, huh?"

"Or worse," said Jessie. "You sure aren't the man who left me in Sweetwater."

"He's under here somewhere, I guess." He stood and washed his face in Jessie's pitcher, looked about the room, and sat again. He started at the beginning, telling her how he'd gone west from Sweetwater to New Mexico Territory, then headed southwest of the Pecos. He'd spend a week traveling, taking time to let the beard change his appearance. Finally he'd headed for Paso del Norte.

"Brown's got a place outside of town," he told her. "Didn't take long to find it. Big house with white walls, riders all over the place in the day, and no way to get close to it at night. The land's cleared all around, so you can't even watch people come and go."

He told her about the Azteca and what had happened, leaving out the parts that included Juanita. He saw no reason to go into that.

"When you turned down his offer of a job," Jessie asked, "how did Brown feel about that?"

"He didn't like it at all. People don't say no to Gaylord Brown."

Jessie thought about Miguel Vargas. More than likely, Brown had recruited him in much the same manner, at the Azteca or somewhere else. A man who funneled killers into the cartel's operation would have more than one listening post.

"All right," she said finally, "you've done about all you can. We know who he is and what he does. Now we've got to get a little help. I think I know the deputy U.S. marshal in El Paso. He's a friend of Custis Long's. He'll know who we can trust in Mexico, in case the cartel's base is across the border. We—" Jessie stopped, suddenly aware of Ki's peculiar expression. "What is it? Did I miss something?"

Ki shook his head. "Jessie, it won't work that way."

"What won't work?"

"Marshals and Mexican law. We don't have the slightest idea where Brown sends his recruits. You think the cartel hasn't thought about this? Someone may be trying to track them down? You heard Vargas. Even the people they send to this place don't know where they're going."

Jessie frowned. "I know that, Ki. But we do know who Brown is, thanks to you. That's a start."

"No, *I'm* the start," Ki said plainly. "I'm already there and Brown wants me."

"What?" Jessie stared, then stood abruptly and shook her head. "Oh no. That wasn't part of it, Ki. We never talked about something like this. You've gone as far as you're going."

"Jessie—"

She turned on him, her green eyes mirrors of defiance. "Besides, you turned down the job, remember?"

"That was deliberate. I didn't want to scare him away. He's not through with me, Jessie. I told you Brown gets what he wants. He's had a man on me since I left the Azteca. He thinks I'm still in my room at the hotel."

Jessie stuck out her chin. "You didn't tell me about that."

"I was getting around to it."

"Sure you were. No, Ki. I don't like it. It's too risky.

26

You didn't want *me* in it. I don't want *you* in it. For all the same reasons."

"I didn't figure on joining the school, Jessie," he said dryly. "All I'll do is get in close, learn where they send the recruits."

"Uh-huh. All right," she said calmly. "He draws you a map and you tell him, 'Sorry, I don't guess I want to go after all.'"

"That's not what I meant, and you know it."

"Oh, Ki!" She sat down quickly beside him and grasped his hands tightly in hers. "You're right, damn it. Getting someone inside's the thing to do. I just don't want it to be you!"

"I'm not going inside."

"Anywhere's too close." She gripped his shoulders hard. "Just be careful. Promise you won't do anything foolish."

"I'll be back in a couple of days with what I've learned."

Jessie stuck out her chin. "You'd better. You've got to think of me, you know. Lorna owes me a real big favor, and this is a good place to keep out of sight. But I don't figure on camping here all summer."

Ki glanced at the ceiling. "Depends on your point of view, I guess. I saw those ladies in the parlor . . ."

"Ki!" Jessie made a face and punched his arm. "You wouldn't *last* the summer with those gals, friend. And don't say it—I know your answer to that!"

Long after he'd left, Jessie stood in the darkened room, watching the night through her window. A few dim lights winked in the darkness. Past them, she imagined the broad river, and Paso del Norte beyond. There was a hard little knot in her stomach and she wanted to call him back, to tell him that she'd been wrong to give in, that whatever he might learn wasn't worth what it could cost. *Damn you,* she said silently across the miles, *don't you do anything stupid, friend!*

Finally she let the white dressing gown slip from her shoulders. The air was too still for nightwear, and she crossed the room naked to her bed. For an instant, pale light from the window caught the full swell of her breasts, the creamy curves of her legs. She perched on the bed and slipped the red garter holster down her thigh, laid the holster and its

27

ivory-handled derringer by her pillow. Leaning back with a sigh, she crossed her hands behind her head and stared at the ceiling. High-pitched laughter reached her from the front of the big house. *At least someone's having fun,* she thought grimly.

Her arm touched the metal of the weapon. In spite of the hot night, the steel seemed oppressively cold. *Is this the way it's always going to be? Sleeping with a gun on your pillow because there are people out there who want you dead?*

A sudden image flashed before her eyes, so real she jerked up and cried out. The harsh staccato of gunfire, and then her father falling limply to the ground. The terrible look of anger and surprise in his eyes. Then the all-too-short vigil, as life faded from a man she'd never imagined would ever die.

She had already known part of the story, and learned the rest before Alex Starbuck closed his eyes upon the world. As a young man, he'd built a trading empire, opening the doors of the Orient to the West. It was in those early days that he had come face to face with a powerful group of Europeans determined to take the rich market for themselves. They struck out savagely, and Alex Starbuck struck back. Ships were sunk, and men died in a secret war. Jessie's mother, Sarah, became a victim, and in the end, Alex Starbuck himself. Jessie inherited the Starbuck holdings—and the wrath of the men who'd murdered her father. She learned soon enough, that the cartel of faceless men wanted a great deal more than Alex Starbuck's wealth. They were determined to seize control of the United States of America—or as much of its riches as possible.

She didn't question the truth of the scheme that had been revealed with the death of Miguel Vargas. She faced it with calm acceptance. A school for assassins, the coldblooded murder of prominent men in key positions—it seemed unreal, a horror too great to imagine, unless one knew what the cartel could do. Jessie had faced them more than once, and knew them only too well.

*And now it's happening again,* she thought. *Good God, it's starting all over!*

* * *

She sat up in the dark, eyes still blurry from sleep. "What you do, huh? Juanita wake up and you are gone."

Ki wearily pulled off his boots, stripped off his clothes, and sank down on the bed beside her. "Couldn't sleep. Had to get out for a while."

"Get out where? Is no place to go in the dark!"

"I took a walk, Juanita, all right?"

She sensed his irritation and came to him quickly. Her young breasts pressed against his chest. She swept tousled hair from her cheeks and kissed him gently. Her lips tasted faintly of their love hours before. "Why you go," she whispered, "when Juanita is here? I got ever'thing you want, sí?"

"Can't argue with that," said Ki. Her body stirred lazily against him. He was tired, but it was a feeling too pleasant to ignore. The hard mound of her pubis kneaded his thigh in slow circles. The sleek line of her legs probed his own. In spite of the weariness that pulled him down, his body began to respond. Juanita felt him against her and sighed approval. He reached for her, touched the hard peaks of her breasts, and felt her slip nimbly from his grasp.

"You don' move," she whispered. "You very tired with stupid walkin' in the dark. Juanita help you sleep real good."

A thick tumble of hair shivered lightly against his chest. He felt it move and settle over his thighs, felt her fingers find him, and then the familiar but ever-new shock of a small pink tongue. Her back was gold and shadow, indistinct in the pale light of the window. Her face was lost between his thighs. Ki imagined black water flowed from her head and past her shoulders to tease his flesh.

At her touch, his shaft grew as rigid as iron. He closed his eyes and gave a long and pleasurable sigh. Her tongue stroked him gently, like a kitten lapping cream. Ki felt the warmth between his legs begin to grow, and spread to every part of his body. Her kisses, slow and tender at first, quickened until he could no longer tell one stroke from another. It was unbelievable, something truly magic, like nothing he'd felt before from a woman's lips.

A sudden, half-forgotten thought touched his mind. Once, as a boy, he'd bathed in a pool in Japan where a swift flow of naturally heated water coursed up from the depths of the earth. He'd held his body against the rush of surging water, felt his member harden and finally explode against the intense, warm vibrations. He was young, and had felt a boy's mixed emotions of secret pleasure and shame. Now, somehow, he experienced that hot, throbbing sensation again through a young girl's practiced touch. And when the storm churned up within him, thundering through his loins, he made no effort to hold it back or make it last. He let the warm current take him and sweep him away, bellowing out his delight . . .

When he opened his eyes and gasped for breath, she was looking into his face, her hands folded under her chin on his chest.

"See wha' you miss?" she said smugly. "No more crazy walkin' in the dark, yes?"

"*Sí*," Ki told her with a smile. "How did you learn to do that?"

Juanita gave him an impish wink. "I don' ask how you fight a man so fas' he don' see nothin'. You don' ask Juanita this thing, hah?"

"Fair enough," Ki agreed.


In the morning she walked with him down to the hotel lobby. He offered to buy her breakfast, but she pleaded some errands for a sister who somehow produced more babies than God had ever intended a woman to have. Ki gave her a gold eagle and told her to buy herself something nice. Juanita squealed with pleasure and gave him a probing good-bye kiss. He knew the money was easily five or six times what she'd expect, and was glad to see her delight. He followed her out of the Alberto, squinting against the harsh morning light. A well-dressed Mexican boy was sitting atop a buggy out front. He looked Ki over and tipped his small sombrero.

"If you are the Señor Marcus Villon, please to get in, Señor."

Ki smiled. "And where do you figure on taking me, *amigo?*"

"The Señor Brown," the boy said politely. "He tell me— bring the Señor Villon to breakfast. He say you will be some hungry after very busy night . . ."

# ★
# Chapter 5

Ki's easy manner masked his concern. What exactly did Brown know about his "very busy night"? Was he talking about Juanita or something else? For an instant he was tempted to say no, to tell the boy he had no stomach for breakfast.

"Well, that's real nice," he said instead. Stepping aboard the rig, he leaned back easily and tipped his Stetson over his eyes, the picture of a man without a care.

The ride took a good quarter-hour, south and east of Paso del Norte. Ki already knew the way; he'd ridden the road twice, learning each time that there was no way to get close to Brown's place. Now he was passing through the heavy wrought-iron gates in a comfortable carriage, a guest expected for breakfast. He hoped that leaving would prove to be as easy.

A servant in cool white cottons met the rig. He greeted Ki with a nod and walked away. Ki decided the idea was to follow. Tall cottonwoods lined the neatly kept drive next to the sprawling white house. Glancing to his left, he saw the outside wall that surrounded the spacious grounds. It was easily forty yards from the house to the wall itself. Ki noted that there was a narrow, secondary portion of the wall some five feet lower than the first. Large earthen pots filled with lush green succulents were spaced along this shelflike space. The top of the main wall was notched with gracefully fashioned crenellations in the old Moorish manner. It was a very pleasant picture, thought Ki, and you could say it was decoration if you liked. Still, the shelf for plants was also a sentry walk, and the walls offered a perfect vantage for firing rifles from cover. It was a big, sleepy Mexican *hacienda*, but Ki had seen frontier forts less ably protected.

31

The servant led Ki through an archway of glazed blue tiles and out into the open again. The house was built in the classic Mexican fashion, living quarters surrounding a central patio. A fountain splashed in a brightly tiled pool. Gaylord Brown sat in the shaded gallery at a big wooden table. He half rose when Ki entered, and offered his hand.

"Glad you decided to come, Mr. Villon," he said heartily. "Sit down. Make yourself at home."

As if some silent signal had reached their ears, three young Mexican girls emerged from the shadow of the house. In less than a minute, Ki's place was set with a cool green melon half, neatly quartered limes, hot fried ham and scrambled eggs, freshly baked bread, and the ever-present bowl of hot sauce. One of the girls poured steaming Mexican coffee into a heavy earthen mug, then all three disappeared as quickly as they'd come.

Ki felt Brown's eyes upon him, waiting for some reaction. "Well, this looks real nice," he said, and smiled. Polite, but not overwhelmed, as he was sure Brown expected.

"Enjoy your meal," said Brown. He leaned back and watched across the tent of his fingers. "If you don't mind, I'll talk while you eat."

"Sure. Go right ahead." Ki fortified himself with hot coffee and squeezed a lime on his melon. Brown's attire today was slightly less startling than that of the day before: a white linen suit, and a citrus-yellow shirt open at the collar. Ki guessed he hadn't figured a way to wear the Chihuahua spurs on his *huaraches*.

"Have you thought any more about my offer, Mr. Villon?"

"Some." Ki wolfed down a bite of ham.

"You gave me a rather emphatic 'no' last night," Brown said coolly.

"Didn't mean to offend," Ki shrugged. "A man asks me a question, I figure he wants an honest answer."

"All right, fair enough." Brown leaned forward and sipped his coffee. "That was last night. What about today?"

"Now's now, like you say." Ki offered a sheepish grin. "Had that hot little chili pepper on my mind last night. I reckon I'm quit of that need for a spell."

"Juanita's a very . . . enticing young lady."

"Oh yeah. She's that, all right."

Brown set down his coffee. "Mr. Villion—do you mind too much telling me a little about yourself? Who a man is and where he's from is his concern, of course. But the kind of job we'd be talking about, the pay involved—I'd like to know a little about the man I'm talking to."

"Your privilege," Ki agreed. "Isn't all that much to tell. I grew up in Canada. Little place on the Milk River."

"Yes, stands to reason, considering the name. Villon's French, isn't it?"

"I guess," said Ki. "I don't speak it or anything. My pa got it from his, and on back. Family came west from Hudson Bay." He glanced up at Brown. "Got some Cree blood in the family, they say."

Brown offered a gracious smile. "Well, we are all the same under the skin, aren't we?"

*Yes, I'm sure you believe that, too,* thought Ki.

"And your mother's family?"

"Her people came from Alaska. Fur traders and, before that, seafaring folks. Roosians. Came from somewhere on the Pacific." Ki shook his head. "I don't know a whole lot about where."

"I see," Brown said thoughtfully. "Very colorful background, Villon."

Ki figured it was surely all of that. He'd spent some time getting it just the way he wanted. Brown was an educated man, and he'd write off Ki's bronze-toned skin and slightly tilted eyes to Asiatic-Russian grandparents on one side of the fence, Indians on the other. The cartel knew a man named Ki worked for Jessie, a man with a Japanese mother and an American father. The story he'd just presented didn't even come close to that.

"You fight well," Brown went on. "Incredibly fast with your hands and with a knife. Where'd you learn to do that?"

"North woods, cutting timber. A man learns to handle himself if he wants to be around for supper."

"And that was in Canada?"

"Canada. And Montana Territory, some."

"Whereabouts in Montana?"

"Up near the Bitterroot Range."

"And what brings you down here? You're pretty far from home."

"I like to keep moving."

33

"You get into some kind of trouble?"

"Isn't that enough questions?" Ki edged his words with irritation. Brown would expect him to have something to hide, and think him a fool if he laid it out.

"As you say, *amigo*. No offense intended," Brown said with a smile. "Your family—your folks still living? Brothers, sisters?"

"No," Ki said shortly, "they're not. Got a no-account sister in Oregon or California. Don't know where and don't give a shit, either."

"Ah, that's too bad. A man needs family."

Ki figured he meant it. Even while dying, Miguel Vargas had been anxious to make sure his people were safe. Knowing where a man's family might be found gave Brown's organization an extra edge.

The trio of servants appeared again and silently cleared the table, bringing hot coffee in clean cups.

"That was fine," said Ki. "Good breakfast."

Brown nodded and squinted across the bright patio. "This employment, if you accept it, is . . . conditional, Mr. Villon."

"I'm not sure what that means."

"It means that I will tell you three things and nothing more. One, the task will utilize your fighting skills. Two, the pay is excellent. I guarantee you'll be pleased. Three, some risk is involved, but I would think very little for a man of your ability."

Ki waited. "That's it?"

"That's it. If you accept, you'll be told what you need to know, when you need to know it. And you'll be expected to do exactly as you're told. Nothing you'll find unpleasant, I assure you. Just rules we have to follow."

Ki sipped his coffee and pretended to ponder the offer. "Good money, huh?"

"You won't find better."

"Would you like to pin that down some?"

"That's sort of a number four, Mr. Villon. If you agree on employment, I'll tell you the sum."

Ki laughed aloud. "Goddamnedest thing I ever heard!"

Brown didn't smile. "That's part of the conditions, *amigo*."

"Yeah, all right," Ki told him. "I guess you got yourself a man."

"Good, good!" Brown leaned over to shake his hand.

"Now—how much do I get?"

Brown held his eyes. "Five thousand dollars a year. Fifty-percent bonus if you complete your job successfully. You won't work more than a few days a year."

Ki gave a low, appreciative whistle. "What do I have to do?"

"Ah, now . . ." Brown raised a finger. "That's conditions one and three, isn't it? Maria—brandy and two glasses, please. Let's seal the bargain with a drink, Mr. Villon. It's early in the day, but brandy's right for the occasion."

"Suits me," said Ki. The girl brought a tray, heavy golden liquid in a crystal decanter, and two gracefully formed snifters. Brown poured, raised his glass to Ki, and drank.

"Ah yes . . ." He licked his lips and grinned.

"Hits the spot," said Ki. "So when do I get started?"

"Why, you've started already, Mr. Villon." He caught Ki's expression and laughed. "Just enjoy yourself. You're my guest for now. I'll have a room prepared for you in the house."

"Sounds good enough. I'd like to run into town and pick up my bag at the hotel sometime, if that's all right with you."

"No, no." Brown waved him off. "I'll have your belongings brought here, see you're checked out of the hotel."

"That's real considerate," said Ki. He forced a grin and sipped his drink. It was just as he'd feared; Brown didn't like his recruits wandering off. Which meant he'd have to figure some way to get out and get word back to Jessie, before they shipped him off to their damn school.

He'd decided, even before he saw her in El Paso, that he'd go if he got the chance. It was the only way they'd ever get inside. Maybe Jessie knew it was in his head, and maybe she didn't. One thing was sure—she'd be madder than a hornet when he told her he was determined to go.

*First, though, you must get out of this fortress for a couple of hours,* he thought grimly. *Which isn't going to be easy. These people run a pretty tight—*

Ki stopped, the brandy halfway to his lips. The woman

35

walked toward them over the broad, sunlit patio. She was a tall, rangy girl with silver-blond hair framing a long and angular face, a near-perfect nose, and wide-set eyes the color of ice. The bones in her cheeks were pronounced, lending the corners of her mouth a stubborn air. She walked straight and proud, carrying herself with style. Her white blouse was open at the neck, the fabric below taut against her breasts. She wore men's riding breeches flared at the calves, and highly polished, knee-length riding boots. She was a breathtaking beauty, so lovely it took Ki a moment to notice something else that set her apart. Around her waist she wore a leather cartridge belt and a slim California holster molded to fit a Colt .44 with an extra-long barrel. Ki sensed at once that the girl wasn't wearing a revolver for fun. It was a no-nonsense rig, and it hugged the curve of her hip as though it belonged there.

"Ellie, I couldn't be more pleased," Brown said smoothly. He stood and gestured toward a chair. "Sit down and join us for coffee."

"Yes, all right." The girl showed half a smile. Her blue eyes quickly inspected Ki.

"Ellie Slate, meet Marcus Villon. Mr. Villon's joining our employ."

"Oh?" Again she managed a polite, disinterested smile, as if moving the muscles around her mouth called for an effort she didn't really care to expend.

"Pleased," said Ki. He rose from his chair for an instant and nodded.

"Ellie, I think perhaps Marcus here will be traveling with you," said Brown.

"I see." Ellie's brow rose in a hint of disapproval. Then, for the first time, the astonishingly beautiful face turned fully in Ki's direction. The beginning of a smile creased her lips, a hint of wicked pleasure. "You are the man who fought Henry and Will?"

"I guess I am," said Ki, "if that's who they were."

"Well . . ." Ellie gave a throaty little laugh. "A point in your favor, Mr. Villon."

"Now, Ellie," Brown scolded.

Ellie didn't bother to notice. The intense blue eyes fastened on Ki and held him. There was nothing remotely sexual or inviting about the look. Ki had seen more personal interest in a doctor lancing a boil. Ellie's gaze was cool and detached; she was probing, trying to figure out what was there.

"That's a fine-looking pistol you have there," said Ki, shifting uncomfortably in his chair. "Don't think I've seen one like it."

"I had it made," she said evenly, "for me."

"Special, huh?"

"Yes. Very special."

"You must shoot well, then."

"I do."

"Ellie," Brown broke in, and cleared his throat. It was obvious he didn't care for the conversation. Ki wondered why talk about the girl's shooting prowess made him nervous. "Ellie, when you go inside, stop and tell Carlos to fix a room for Mr. Villon, will you? I'd appreciate that."

"Yes—of course." Ellie flushed slightly and stood. Brown's voice had clearly said *now,* and Ellie apparently didn't care for that at all.

"Mr. Villon—"

"Marcus," Ki corrected. "Mark'll do fine."

"Yes, well . . . perhaps we'll talk again." She paused then, and glanced past Ki. A dark-faced man in a white shirt and leather vaquero's trousers came out of the house and leaned intently over Brown's shoulder. After a moment, Brown's features twisted in concern. The messenger stood straight, and Brown's eyes flicked up to Ki.

"Mr. Villon—it seems we have a question that needs an answer."

"Yeah, what's that?" But Ki already knew. His gut went tight at the look in Brown's eyes.

"Where did you go last night, Marcus? Where did you go when you left your hotel?"

"Huh?" Ki's laugh feigned disinterest. "Now, if I did, how'd that be your business, mister? I haven't been working for you for more than two or three minutes."

Brown didn't blink. "Where, Marcus? I want the question answered."

Ki was certain no one had seen him leave the hotel. Which meant they'd talked to Juanita, given her money and asked if she'd learned anything of interest from the *gringo* customer named Villon. It was a natural thing to do. The

37

girl had undoubtedly said he'd left her and gone for a walk, seeing no harm in the answer.

"Shit," Ki growled, "it's none of your concern, but I went out for a spell."

"Where? We know that. You went out where?"

"Like I said—my business."

"No," Brown said coldly, "you're wrong. It is my business, *amigo*. Juan!"

The man in leather drew a short-barreled pistol out of his belt and leveled it at Ki. "Get a couple of men, Juan. Take Mr. Villon out and show him the countryside."

"Hey, just a goddamn minute," Ki protested. "What are you doing?"

"Terminating your employment, Marcus," Brown said tightly.

"Gaylord"—Ellie bit her lip—"do you *have* to do this?"

Brown gave her a withering look. "Do you think I intend to take a chance on this man? Good God, woman! Juan, get it done."

"Uh, look," said Ki. "Christ, mister, this isn't funny. If it's all that important—"

"It is not,"Brown said tightly. "I'm not interested anymore."

"Señor..." Juan motioned with the gun. "Get up, *por favor.*"

Ki stood. He glanced at Ellie Slate, but the girl turned quickly away. Two men came out of the house and stood beside Juan.

"Listen, this doesn't make any sense," said Ki. "We've got to talk some."

"Go with Juan," Brown told the two men. "You know what to do and how to do it."

One of the men, skinny and auburn-haired, stared intently at Ki and then grinned. "Well, you sure get around, don't you, hoss?"

Brown turned sharply on the man. "You know him? You've seen him before?"

"Don't know him. Seen him, though, Mr. Brown."

"Where? When was this?"

The man shrugged. "Last night. Over to that fancy whorehouse in El Paso. He come in right after I did."

"What?" Brown's mouth fell open. He stared incredulously at Ki. "You're certain? You're sure this was the man?"

"Yes sir. I saw him come in."

"Did you see him leave?"

The man flushed. "I uh—wasn't downstairs then, Mr. Brown."

Brown gazed at Ki in disbelief, then threw back his head and burst out laughing. "Jesus Christ, boy—you got up and left one whore and went looking for another?"

Ki looked down at his boots. "I, uh—had an itch for something different, I guess."

Laughter shook Brown again. "Damn, we've got a crazy man or a stud horse here, boys, I don't know which. Why the hell didn't you answer my question?"

"I tried to," Ki said dully. "You said you weren't interested anymore, remember?"

Brown cleared his throat and spread his hands on the table. "No one saw you leave the Alberto, Marcus. How did you get out?"

"Over the roof," Ki said honestly.

"Why in hell did you do that?"

Ki hesitated. "I wasn't figuring on coming back."

"You were dodging the hotel bill?"

"I guess."

"You weren't broke, were you?"

"No, goddamn it," Ki said irritably. "Just don't like to pay for a place to sleep. Figured on stopping at Lorna's in El Paso, then going on north, maybe, up to Sante Fe or somewhere."

"You didn't do that, though. You came back."

Ki colored. It seemed to come naturally, with Ellie Slate standing over his shoulder. "I got to thinking about that Mexican gal again," he said through his teeth. "Just kind of wandered back . . ."

Brown shook his head and grinned. "Get this fellow a room, Juan. I 'magine he needs the rest. Wouldn't you say so, Ellie?"

Ellie gave Ki a killing look, turned on her heel, and stalked off, the holstered Colt slapping her hip.

"Don't feel bad," Brown laughed. "You can't have 'em all, son. Don't think you'd really *want* that one, if you could get her."

# Chapter 6

No one had to tell him he was different, set apart from the others in Brown's house. Wherever he went on the grounds, people nodded and hurried about their business. No one asked for a match or stopped to pass the time of day.

Ki wasn't surprised; only Brown and maybe a couple of trusted subordinates would know about the cartel's school for killers. The hired hands and household staff would merely follow simple orders: there were people to talk to, and people to leave alone.

Brown's offer to bring his valise from Paso de Norte had set the pace. He was free to do what he liked—as long as he didn't leave. Until he and Ellie went wherever they were going, the high wall around the house was his border. It wasn't really a bad place to be. His quarters were first-rate, and so was the food. But getting in touch with Jessie presented a problem. Brown had been ready to kill him for leaving his room—before he even took the job. What would he do if Ki managed to sneak off, and Brown found out he'd been gone? He knew the answer without asking. The whorehouse trick wouldn't save him again. If he left, he couldn't return. It was as simple as that. He'd be safe across the border, but he'd never get close to the cartel's operation.

He worried about what Jessie might do when he didn't return, but tried to put that out of his head. He'd get out when he could. Jessie would know exactly what he'd done. She wouldn't like it, but she'd know.

During the day he thought a lot about the tall, regal beauty he'd met at breakfast. It was clear that Ellie Slate was someone special in Brown's organization. She was too much at home to be a "recruit" like himself. They'd be traveling together, Brown said. Where else could they be headed but the school? If Ellie was going along, she had a reason. He doubted it had much to do with him.

He didn't see her again until evening. He ate a good steak, fresh corn, and tomatoes in his room, then started on a walk around the grounds. He found her in the cottonwoods west of the house. She was leaning against a tree, arms folded under her breasts. She'd traded the riding clothes for old denims and a worn cotton shirt. She still wore the Colt, and Ki couldn't imagine her without it.

"Evening," he said. "Real nice night."

"I guess." She glanced in his direction but didn't smile.

"I'll move on if I'm disturbing you," said Ki. "Didn't mean to intrude."

"You're not."

"Well, then . . ."

Ellie pulled a thin cigarillo from the pocket of her shirt, dug in her denims for a match, found one and struck it on the heel of her boot, and lit the smoke. The flame etched the lovely planes of her face. Lighting up was a man's gesture, but Ellie gave it a graceful feminine touch.

"I want to thank you," said Ki. "For this morning."

"This morning? What for?"

"I was in a little hot water. You spoke up."

Ellie shook her head, a slight touch of irritation in her voice. "Don't be foolish, mister. Nothing I said made the slightest bit of difference. I'm sure you're aware of that."

"Well, you cared. That's something."

He couldn't see her features, but he sensed she was studying him again, as she had that morning with Brown. He could almost feel the intense, ice-blue eyes hunting for answers. "I don't like to see people die," she said plainly. "Even people I don't know."

A curious thing to say, thought Ki, for someone in Brown's employ.

"It's just as well we talked," said Ellie. "Gives me a chance to say something I need to say." Ki waited while she drew smoke from the cigarillo. "We'll be traveling together soon. We'll get along fine if you remember I'm not available for your entertainment."

"Hey, wait a minute," Ki protested. "That stuff this morning—"

41

"Don't get your back up, now." There was no anger at all in her voice. "I'm just trying to save us both some trouble. I'm not a prude, and I don't care if you need a dozen women a night, as long as I'm not one of them."

"Hell, I think you've got me all wrong."

"No. I *think* I've got you just *right*." There was a slight touch of amusement in her voice. Ki didn't like it at all, but he couldn't rightly blame her—or tell her he didn't really dash madly across the border to bed women.

"You've got nothing to worry about," he said coolly. "You're as safe as you can be."

"I don't mean any offense, Mr. Villon."

"Mark."

"All right—Mark. I just like to pick my own men. Some men have trouble understanding that."

"I don't."

"Good. I'm pleased to hear it."

"Yeah, well, it's sure been nice talking."

"Good night, then."

Ki nodded and walked off back to his quarters. Inside, he took off his clothes and eased back on the bed. He wasn't tired at all but there was nothing else to do. Moonlight angled and squared the tile floor. *At least I know I'm safe*, he thought dully. *Ellie Slate won't be breaking down the door to get at me . . .*

It seemed only minutes after he drifted off to sleep that an urgent knocking brought him awake. Ki moaned and padded across the floor.

"What is it?" he called through the door.

"*Buenos días, Señor.* It is I, Juan. Get dressed, please. You leave in half an hour."

"What? You mean now?" Ki shook his head in irritation. "It's the middle of the night!"

"It is three-thirty," Juan said softly. "You leave at four, Señor. I have your breakfast here."

Ki cursed under his breath and opened the door. Juan set his breakfast on the table and left. Ki slipped into his clothes in the dark, splashed cold water on his face, lit the kerosene lamp, and sat down to coffee, thick bacon, eggs, and freshly baked bread. Then he left the room and carried his leather valise down the hall and into the dark courtyard. Juan was waiting, and guided him back past the kitchen and outside, to a part of the house he hadn't seen. A flatbed wagon in obvious disrepair stood just outside the door. A swaybacked mule was in harness. Two young Mexicans sat on the springboard seat. Someone moved in shadow, and Ki saw the glow of Ellie Slate's cigarillo.

"Get in, please, Señor Villon," said Juan. "It is time to leave."

"In *that?*" Ki asked incredulously. "We're going in the wagon?"

"Just for a while. You will not be uncomfortable for long."

Ki gave him a look and climbed in. Juan put his valise in the wagon and placed Ellie's beside it. Ellie climbed in and scooted up next to Ki.

"Good morning," she said, her voice still husky from sleep. "I told you we'd be traveling soon."

"Yeah. You didn't say how, either." Ki noticed then that she was wearing a light cotton dress instead of trousers.

"Please to lie down," said Juan.

"What?"

"Go on, it's all right," Ellie assured him.

Ki did as he was told. Juan spread a light sheet of canvas over them both, secured it to the sides, and spoke to the driver in Spanish. The wagon started off, smoothly at first, then rode considerably rougher as it left Brown's estate and found rutted dirt roads. The ride brought Ellie Slate against him, pressing her body to his in a pleasant little jolt. The canvas was confining, and Ki enjoyed the sweet woman-scent so close at hand. That, combined with the touch of her body, was more than a little arousing—until it dawned on him that the pressure against his thigh wasn't the finely padded curve of her hips, but the Colt fitted snugly into its holster.

As near as he could guess, the ride lasted close to an hour. Enough to take them back to Paso del Norte, though Ki didn't believe that was where they'd gone. There were no sounds of people, there was no feel of cobbled streets. It was a good idea, he'd give Brown credit for that. Wagons

43

and rigs of all shapes and sizes entered and left his grounds all the time. Even if a man had the means and the reason to follow them all, they'd seldom lead anywhere of interest. Brown took all the precautions, likely a great many more than he really needed.

The flatbed wagon and the tarp answered another question for Ki. Unless Ellie Slate was playing a game, they were both in the same boat. She wasn't allowed to know the route either.

The wagon came to a halt and someone untied the tarp and tossed it aside. Ki sat up and climbed down to stretch his legs. They were inside a big barn. Three other men were there, besides the drivers of the wagon. The barn was empty, except for a much larger wagon hitched to six strong mules. It was a high-sided rig, its slat-wood walls stretching a good six feet or more above the axles. The wagon was fully loaded with crates and kegs. He could see the top of the cargo above the sides.

"Well, now what?" he asked. "Is this what all the sneaky business was about? To get us to a barn?"

One of the Mexicans laughed. "Just the start, I'm afraid," Ellie sighed. "Come on, no use standing around here."

Before Ki could ask another question, one of the men stepped up to the big wagon and slid his hands along the boards. Ki stared as the whole back end opened up like a door.

"Well, I'll be damned," he muttered. A few kegs and boxes were wired to a false roof atop the wagon. Otherwise, the wagon held no cargo at all. The inside had been rigged as living quarters—cots bolted to the floor, a firmly anchored table, lanterns affixed to the walls. Storage boxes for water and provisions were nailed to the rear wall.

"Are you serious?" said Ki. "We've got to ride in *that?*"

"You'll get used to it," said Ellie.

"It's a sweatbox. We'll suffocate in there."

"You won't," Ellie told him. "You'll think you will, but you won't."

Two hours after sunrise, Ki was dead sure she was wrong. The heat inside the wagon was stifling. He didn't imagine it could get a lot worse, but he was next to certain it could.

Midday would be pure hell, and the afternoon something awful. The drivers opened vents up above, but these only managed to churn hot air from one side of the wagon to the other.

"I take it you've been on this trip before," he asked the girl.

"Couple of times. It's not any fun."

"That's one way of putting it," Ki grumbled. "Some windows in the sides wouldn't hurt. Anyone ever think of that?"

Ellie gave him a curious frown. "Why do you bother to ask a question like that? You already know the answer. If they wanted us to know where we were going, why bother with the wagon at all?"

"*They* know where we're going," Ki pointed out. "The drivers. How come he trusts them and not us?"

"I expect he has his reasons," said Ellie. Something in her voice told him this was more than a guess. Ki didn't pursue it any further.

"I suppose we could travel at night," Ki said, half to himself. "But that wouldn't look normal, right? A real freighter wouldn't do it."

"That's right."

"We *do* stop at night? We don't just keep on going?"

"We stop. You can sleep outside the wagon and cool off."

"That's something to look forward to. If I make it that long. How many days are we going to be in this thing?" Ellie hesitated, and Ki gave her a weary smile. "Lady, I'm a little smarter than I look. I can *count* how many days. It isn't going to be a big secret."

Ellie shrugged. "About three days."

Ki groaned.

"You asked, right?"

"Yeah, I asked." It told him something, but not much. They'd make thirty or thirty-five miles a day, tops. Maybe more, since the mules weren't really carrying a load. Still, in the dead heat of summer you couldn't drive an animal too hard whether it was hauling weight or not. So that meant what? Over a hundred miles, maybe. Which way, though? South, deeper into Mexico? Southeast, into the bend of the

Rio Grande? If the nights were clear, he could get some idea from the stars. That, and which side of the wagon got the sun.

"Trying to figure where we're going?" Ellie asked abruptly.

"Yeah, I'm kind of curious," Ki admitted. "Where we're going and what for."

"Don't," Ellie said flatly. She sat up straight and looked right at him. "That's a friendly warning, Marcus Villon. Don't *ever* ask questions of anyone you meet where we're going. *No* one. Don't even look like you're thinking too hard."

Ki nodded and said, "Thanks for the advice." Just for an instant, the ice-blue eyes had softened. It was the first time since they'd met that she'd revealed a part of herself. It was gone almost at once, but it was there. And what he saw was a touch of fear, something buried deeply and hiding, the hint of a woman not nearly so sure of herself as the face she showed to the world.

Ki leaned back on his cot and closed his eyes. The still air and the swaying of the wagon made him drowsy, but the oppressive heat kept him awake. He drifted in and out of uneasy sleep, fighting off one frightening dream after another.

Finally he groaned, sat up, shook his head, and wiped sweat off his face. He glanced at Ellie Slate, looked away, then blinked to make certain he was awake. She'd pinned her pale hair atop her head, and was undoing the bodice of her dress and the hooks at her waist. Bracing herself on the cot, she pulled the dress over her shoulders and tossed it aside. She wore only a thin chemise that covered the swell of her breasts and reached to the tops of her knees. Her shoulders were sweet and tender, her bare legs incredibly long. Ki's throat went dry at the sight. In a way she was more exciting, more wanton like this than if he'd suddenly seen her naked. The garment clung moistly to her flesh, revealing every curve and hollow. Her nipples were dimpled shadow, the darkness between her thighs a secret that teased his eyes.

Ellie looked up without expression. "I'd suggest you take off your shirt," she told him. "There's a barrel of water over there, and a sponge. It helps. And Mr. Villon"—the smile was a cold challenge, no hint of an invitation—"going nearly naked is the only way to keep comfortable on this trip. That's one reason I tried to make myself clear last night. I can't stop you from looking, but I suggest that's *all* you do."

Ki sighed and stripped of his wet shirt. Clearly, the trip was going to be more trying than he'd figured.

# Chapter 7

It was half past five in the evening when Jessie drove the rig over the border to Paso del Norte. A heavy summer storm, a rare and pleasant surprise in that part of the country, had swept past the Hueco Mountains and washed the town clean. The rain had moved on but left pearl-colored clouds overhead and a lingering smell of freshness in the air.

A few people glanced up idly as she passed, women carrying goods home from market, men gathered in the plaza, sharing talk and tobacco. Lorna had loaned her the rig and the horse, and the girls in the house had delighted in fixing her up in the dark, lacy gown, piling her hair atop her head and covering her face with the heavy veil.

"They're ol' lady clothes, Miss Jessie," a pert little brunette told her, "but we goin' to have to give you some help. Lord knows, you ain't got a ol' lady figure!"

Then they crowded around her and laughed, vying to see who could make the best folds of fat out of batting, the finest matronly bosom. Jessie finally had to bring the proceedings to a halt.

"Dumpy's all right," she warned them, "but I don't want to look like I ran away from the circus."

Lorna herself stood back and offered a final, stern inspection. "Don't let 'em see your legs," she said darkly. "Fat lady or not, some bastard'll have you on your back in a minute. By God, it isn't easy to hide what you got, Jessie. I could make us both rich in a month, no offense intended."

She'd promised Ki she'd wait, stay in El Paso, and not do something foolish. Only that was three days back, time enough unless he'd bitten off more than he could chew. She

48

half blamed herself for letting him go, but that didn't count for much now.

Finding the Hotel Alberto was no problem. She sent a small boy inside. He was to pick up an envelope from Señor Marcus Villon, who owed the boy's employer a gaming debt. The desk clerk laughed and told the boy his employer was out of luck. Señor Villon was gone and had left no message of any sort.

Jessie's heart sank. She'd expected no more, but that didn't help a great deal. Next she rode through town and left the rig in the hands of another youth, giving him half an American dollar and showing him the money he'd get if he watched the rig with care. Bending her back and walking slowly, she made a few purchases at a *tienda* across from the Azteca cantina. Going in, of course, was out of the question. Respectable ladies, young or old, wouldn't dream of going near such a place.

She watched for a half hour, on the off-chance that Ki was still around. She'd hoped for a little luck, maybe a glance at Brown himself. She realized it was a waste of precious time. Standing in front of saloons wouldn't get her any closer to Ki.

Waddling back to the rig, she faced the young boy. He was eager for the chance to increase his fee, and understood English well enough. Jessie explained in a cracked voice that she was a widow lady from El Paso who worked with the Good Sisters of Mercy, who ran an orphanage for Mexican children. She had the names of wealthy men in Paso del Norte, men who might give generously to further the Sisters' work. She had the addresses of all but three. The Señores Carlos Mendoza, Luís Alvarez, and Gaylord Brown. She would be glad to give the boy a few more coins if he would help.

"You wait," he said quickly. "I be back in *uno momento*."

"What? Hey!" Jessie called out.

The boy vanished, and returned minutes later with two older boys in tow. *"Mi hermanos,"* he said proudly. "My brothers. They help you, Señora."

Jessie didn't like their looks at all. They were barely in their twenties, with dark eyes entirely too knowing for their

49

age. She was almost certain they weren't the boy's brothers.

"How may we help you, Señora?" the first asked politely. "I am Hernando and this is Julio Vicente."

Too late now, Jessie decided. She'd have to give it a try. She repeated her story, and the two nodded understanding.

"We can surely help," Hernando said solemnly. "The Señores Mendoza and Alvarez are only minutes away, near the center of town."

Jessie already knew that from Lorna. Both gentlemen were favored customers at her establishment. She'd heard of Brown, but just barely, and couldn't help.

"And the other," Jessie asked, "Señor Brown?"

"How much money you give us?" Julio blurted. "You don' ever say."

"What is the matter with you?" Hernando lashed out in anger. "Is for the church, the *iglesia*. You take money from the Señora, it is a sin!"

"Oh no," Jessie assured him, "really..."

"Sure, we help. For nothing," Hernando insisted. The pair hopped onto the sides of the buggy and held on, waving their younger "brother" away.

Jessie gritted her teeth and drove, not caring at all for the new arrangement. First the brothers pointed out the home of Mendoza, and then the equally imposing dwelling of Alvarez.

"That way," Hernando said, pointing. "We follow this street, yes?"

"You can just tell me," said Jessie. "I don't want to take up your time."

Hernando grinned. "Is no trouble at all. This way, Señora."

Evening was closing in fast. Sooner than Jessie had hoped, they left the last houses of Paso del Norte behind. Five minutes later, Hernando signaled her to stop.

"A moment, Señora, *por favor*."

"Why? What are we stopping for?"

"I think we talk," said Julio. "I think the Señora let us take a good look at her purse."

"Why, I'll do no such thing!" cried Jessie.

"*Sí*. You will. The purse. Please, Señora. No trouble."

50

Hernando brought a short-bladed knife from his pocket and held it an inch from her face.

"Get off this rig," Jessie warned him. "Get off and get that thing out of my face."

Hernando grinned and playfully hooked the edge of her veil. "Let's see how ugly you are, *sí?*"

The derringer nestled in the folds of Jessie's dress suddenly exploded. Hernando cried out, fell to the ground, and writhed in pain. The knife was still in his fist, half of the ruined veil caught in the blade. To Jessie's left, Julio froze an instant too long, staring at the suddenly young old lady. Jessie lashed out and kicked him hard in the belly. Julio staggered, caught himself, and came at her, his dark eyes narrow with anger. Jessie fired the second barrel. Burning gunpowder streaked Julio's cheek and lead tore away the lobe of his ear. He howled, clawed at his face, and slapped Jessie hard. Jessie fell back and he came at her, tearing at her face with a vengeance. His eyes widened with pleasure as he loosed a fiery tumble of amber hair, saw the green eyes and honeyed flesh.

"*Dios,* Hernando—we got us some *viejota* here. *Ai!*" He hauled Jessie roughly off the rig and threw her to the ground. Thrusting one hand in the vee of her breasts, he ripped the dress to her waist. Lumps of cotton batting fell away, revealing the slender figure beneath. Jessie backed off over the ground, one hand clutching the shreds of her gown. Hernando struggled to his feet, his face drawn with pain and anger. He stared down at Jessie, one hand clamped to his shoulder.

"You shoot me," he said hoarsely. "You shoot me with that thing!"

"Damn right I did," Jessie snapped. "You asked for it, *amigo!*"

"You goin' to pay, too, yes?" Hernando's face split in a grin. "You going to pay good, lady!" The smile suddenly faded. He looked at her thoughtfully and bit his lip. "Why you dress like that an' change your voice? Why you do this?"

Jessie held his eyes and didn't answer. Hernando glanced over his shoulder at Julio, ordering him in rapid-fire Spanish, "Get this buggy off the road before someone sees it.

51

In the trees, over there." He kicked out at Jessie and she scooted away. "Get up, *viejota*. Go with him." He licked his lips in pleasure. "Hernando goin' to show you a real good time."

"Hernando's going to bleed to death," Jessie told him, "unless he gets someone to look at that shoulder."

The boy showed his teeth. "You don' worry 'bout me, pretty lady. You goin' to be dead a long time before Hernando." He flashed the knife in her face and Jessie scrambled to her feet. She didn't think he could catch her if she ran, but Julio wasn't hurt badly and he could stop her before she got ten yards. Hernando read her thoughts, grabbed her, and tossed her savagely toward the trees.

"No time for that," he said almost gently. "No time for that now, *bonita*." He wasn't bleeding as badly now, but his breath was coming faster as shock and pain took hold of his body. Julio came back from moving the buggy, helped his brother to the trees, and eased him down to look at the wound, keeping one eye on Jessie. Jessie saw him tear Hernando's shirt and bind it tightly over the wound. Hernando ground his teeth and cursed in Spanish. Julio left him, turned, and threw Jessie roughly to the ground. Pinning her to a wheel of the buggy, he bound her hands above her head with a strip of leather.

"He's going to die," Julio said harshly. "You kill him!"

"He's hurt, but he won't die. Not if you get him some help. Look, just leave me here and take him back to town in the rig. He'll be—"

Julio hit her hard, a blow that snapped her head to one side and set her ears ringing. His hands ripped her shredded gown aside, found the chemise, and tore it away. He buried his face hungrily in her breasts, his hand grasping eagerly under her skirts.

Jessie lashed out with both feet. He was small-boned, almost fragile in appearance, but his frame was corded with muscle as tough as rope. He held her legs apart painfully with his knees, hands groping past her thigh. When he found her, an astonished cry of pleasure escaped his throat.

"Goddamn you!" Jessie kicked out with all the strength she could muster. "Your brother's hurt!" she shouted in his ear. "He's going to die if you do this, you bastard!"

Julio didn't hear. He took her breasts roughly in his

52

mouth and ripped the dress to her thighs, scrambling to hold her and loosen his trousers. Jessie jerked one hand free of her bonds and tore at his eyes. Julio bellowed and hit her again. Jessie cried out and went limp. His breath was hot against her flesh. He spread her legs roughly and tugged at his pants. Jessie stared up in horror and tried to move. Nothing seemed to work. Her head felt hollow and her arms were as heavy as rocks. Julio clutched her hips and pulled her to him. Jessie saw his eyes go wide with pleasure and then surprise. His tongue shot out of his mouth like a lizard's and he rose straight up in the air, trailing a terrified scream in his wake.

Jessie blinked and struggled to shake cobwebs out of her head. Somewhere to her left, Julio seemed to slam himself hard against a tree again and again, sobbing with pain and fear at every strike. Finally he slid to the ground and sat still.

Someone bent close to her face. "You all right? You hurt any?"

"No, no." Jessie drew in a breath. "I'm . . . all right."

A blade reached up and snipped her hands free. "Here, take this. I'll be back." The voice left, leaving a canteen in her grip. Jessie held it up shakily and drank. Pulling herself erect, she gathered her garments about her as best she could. A match flared, caught a wisp of grass, and flickered into a fire. The man added a few dry sticks. She caught his features in the flickering light—olive skin, deepset eyes under straight, heavy brows, a hawklike nose broken and never set right. The flames caught lines etched as deep as scars from his cheeks to the corners of his mouth. He glanced at her once, looked at Julio's still form, and turned back to the fire.

Hernando watched him with open fear. The man flicked the blade of a long knife in the flames.

"No, *Cristo!*" Hernando cried hoarsely.

The man clipped him with a short, quick blow to the jaw. Hernando's head rolled on his shoulder. The man squatted over him and went to work. Jessie winced as the knife twisted deftly into flesh. He pulled the lead slug out of the wound, looked at it, and tossed it away.

"Bring me that canteen, will you?" he called over his shoulder. Jessie took it to him. He reached for it without looking, washed the wound, and bound it with a wide strip cut from Hernando's shirt.

"He going to make it?" asked Jessie.

"Oh yeah, he'll make it. You shoot him?"

"Yes."

"Should've aimed a little lower."

"Killed him, you mean."

"Uh-huh. The other bastard too."

"What's the point of that?" Jessie said sharply. "Killing two men?"

"Don't know. What's the point of them cutting your throat? After he got around to it, I mean."

Jessie couldn't think of a good answer. The man took another quick look at Hernando, and sat back on his heels.

"There. Guess that'll do."

"Why?"

"Why what?"

"What's the point of patching him up? Why don't *you* let him die?"

The man grinned. "Beats the pure hell out of me." His glance took in her bare shoulder, her features half covered with tousled hair.

"Look, I owe you a lot. I'm very grateful for what you did. My name's Jessie. Jessie Starbuck." She blurted out her name without thinking, gratitude overcoming caution.

"I'm Jeff. Jeffrey Diego Escobar, if you want it all." He caught the quick touch of surprise in her eyes. "I have a *gringa* grandmother," he said soberly. "No family's perfect, you know. We try to keep it quiet."

Jessie laughed. "That's sure an awful thing to live down."

"She's a grand old lady, if you want to know the truth. The 'Jeffrey' comes from her. Maiden name."

"It isn't the 'Jeffrey' that surprised me," said Jessie, "it's the 'Diego Escobar' part. The Spanish is in your face, but I figured I was wrong when you opened your mouth."

"Grew up speaking two languages at once. Another thing Grandma Jeffrey insisted on. She insisted on a lot." He paused and raised a brow in thought. "Mind if I ask *you* a question in turn? I'm just a might curious, lady."

"I wouldn't be surprised."

"Uh-huh. So what in hell happened out here? All I know is I hear this shooting and screaming, and I find one of these jaspers out of action and the other going after a fat old lady—who isn't all that fat and old either, if you don't mind me saying."

"It's a very long story, Señor."

"Señorita, I don't doubt it a minute." He looked at her, then nodded off to the side. "Hold on, I got something needs doing." He left and walked over to Julio, who was groaning and shaking his head. Jeffrey Diego Escobar lifted him up by the collar and hauled him, kicking air, to his brother.

"You're about through sleepin', I'd guess," Jeff muttered. He kicked Hernando in the thigh, and he howled and opened his eyes. "Figured you were awake. Get up."

"Señor, I—"

"Get up, *tulipán!*" Jeff drew back his boot for another blow. Hernando lurched to his feet looking sick. He held his shoulder and staggered against a tree. Jeff sent Julio sprawling at his feet. He pulled himself up and helped his brother.

"Now," Jeff said darkly, "you two listen to me carefully, *sí?* Very carefully indeed." He looked at Hernando. "You know me, don't you? You know my name."

"No, no." Hernando went pale. "I never saw you before, Señor!"

"Don't lie," Jeff said softly. "I can see the lie in your eyes. Now. I ask you again. Who am I?"

Hernando glanced fearfully at his brother. "You are . . . *El Rosario*, Señor."

"Ah, very good. *Bueno.* Now—" He came very close to the two. "Here's what I'm telling you. You don't know this lady and you don't know me. You've never seen me before. *Comprende, gatito?*"

"*Sí. Comprendo, Señor!*" Hernando shook his head eagerly.

"Leave this place right now. Go. If I see you again, ever, you are *carne, chuleta de puerco!*"

Juan wrapped his brother's good arm over his shoulder and vanished quickly back through the trees toward the road. Jeff watched them go.

"I hope he doesn't bleed to death," said Jessie. "It's a long way back."

"*Dios!*" Jeff turned on her with sudden anger. "You can say that? I don't understand you at all, lady. *Loca!*"

55

"I'm likely crazy, all right. You're not the first to notice."

Jeff shook his head. "I'm sorry. That just came out."

*"De nada."* Jessie nodded toward the road. "What was that they called you? *El Rosario?"*

Jeff gave her an irritated look. *"Sí.* The Rosary."

"What for? Where'd you get a name like that?"

"Forget it. All right?"

"No." Jessie grinned. "I want to know."

Jeff frowned. "It's a damn fool thing, is all it is. I've got kind of a . . . reputation, I guess."

"And?"

"People hear about Diego Escobar, they're supposed to pray or something," he said under his breath. "Make the sign. There's nothing to it, though."

"They *pray?* What are you, a saint? I'd sure never have guessed."

Jeff looked her in the eye. "Then you'd be right, Señorita. I am not a saint. I rob people. Steal things."

"You *what?"*

Jeff laughed at her expression. "I lied. I'm the black sheep of the family, not my *gringa* grandmother."

# Chapter 8

*My God,* thought Jessie, *what have I gotten myself into now!* "Looks like this just isn't my day," she said aloud. "Out of the old frying pan into the fire."

"I don't steal from women," Jeff said stiffly. "No one ever accused me of that."

"Oh, I see."

"You see what? What's that supposed to mean?"

Jessie swept back her hair and straightened her dress. "Let me guess. You rob from the rich and give to the poor."

"Nope. Mostly I keep it myself. Look, lady—if you'd feel any better, I'll steal your purse and tie you to a tree."

Jessie saw the anger, the stubborn defiance in his eyes, and burst out laughing. Jeff looked startled, then turned away and grinned.

"I'm sorry," Jessie told him. "That wasn't called for at all. I'm not acting real grateful, am I?"

"Not a lot, no."

"Señor Escobar, it's been one hell of a night. That's my only excuse for bad manners. I apologize."

"Accepted," said Jeff. "No one ever said El Rosario wasn't gracious to old ladies." He searched the ground and found his flat-crowned Stetson, then used the side of his boot to kick dirt over the fire. "I've got a suggestion, if it's all right with you. I could use a drink and I figure you'd like to do some fixin' up. If you'll take your rig and follow, it isn't far."

"Fine. And just what is it that isn't far?"

"A real robber's den. Ask me real nice and I'll show you my loot."

Jessie laughed. "I don't guess I can pass up anything as exciting as that!"

She found where Julio had tossed her valise, then searched the side of the road until moonlight caught the ivory-handled derringer. Jeff's horse appeared out of the trees, and Jessie followed, riding no more than two miles back up the road. Jeffrey Diego Escobar's "den" was a small, three-room adobe set well off by itself. The front yard was a forest of cholla cactus ten feet high, and thorny ocotillo. The back sheltered a small corral and outbuildings. The inside of the adobe was clean and well kept, furnished with stout wooden furniture, Mexican reed rugs, and a shelf of books and ancient Indian pottery. Jessie retired to the bedroom, took a standup bath in cold water, and put on a pair of denims and a blue cotton shirt from her valise. When she joined Jeff again, he had a pot of coffee going, and glasses and a bottle of brandy stood on the table. He turned as she entered, looking her over with honest appraisal.

"I knew you were a real pretty lady," he said solemnly. "But by God, that doesn't cover it at all."

"Well, thank you, sir," Jessie replied with a smile. "You're not a bad-looking man—For a *bandido*, I mean."

Jeff toasted that with a drink. Jessie poured herself a cup of Mexican coffee and sat back in a cane-bottomed chair. "I kind of decided something," she said plainly, "when I was in the other room. I decided I want to trust you."

"You sure?"

"Yes. I'm sure." She raised her head and caught his eye. "I made one bad mistake tonight. I don't think you're another."

"*Gracias,*" Jeff said politely.

"No. I mean that. I need help, Jeff. I think you'll give me honest answers if you can." She paused, then went on to tell him most of the story, all she figured he needed to know. A friend had come to Paso del Norte to gather information about a man. The man belonged to a group who'd kill her if they could. Her friend had learned a great deal, and returned to Paso del Norte. She hadn't seen him since. She'd borrowed the rig and the disguise, and Jeff could guess the rest. Hernando and Julio had given her more "help" than she could handle.

Jeff scratched his chin in thought. "This, uh, friend of yours. What do you think happened to him?"

"I think he found a way into the man's operation. The one who wants to kill me."

"You want to tell me the man's name?"

Jessie let out a breath. If she misjudged Jeffrey Escobar, she figured, this would reveal her error. "His name's Brown. Gaylord Brown."

Jeff stared and set down his glass. *"Dios!* You don't mess around with small-timers, do you?"

"You know him, then."

"I know who he is. Haven't met him, and don't think I want to, either."

"And why's that? I've got my own reasons. I'd like to hear yours."

Jeff made a face. "Señor Brown bought the old Rodriguez spread a year or so back. Supposed to have big money in mining and cattle. Maybe he does. Word is, though, he's got something going besides that."

"Any idea what?"

"Word *also* has it," he added dryly, "that is isn't healthy to ask."

"I see." She wondered what he'd say if she told him how right he was.

"You're working up to something," said Jeff. "Why don't you go ahead and get it done?"

Jessie folded her arms under her breasts. "He's got an operation of some kind, Jeff. I don't know where. North, maybe, back over the river. Or south, farther into Mexico. I've *got* to know where it is. I don't know where to look, but I'm guessing he supplies it from right here. Goods of all kinds, the things a large group of people would need day to day."

"Doesn't have to be sending stuff from here," Jeff reminded her.

"I know that." She leaned toward him intently. "But I'm willing to bet he *does*. This isn't something he'd trust to someone else."

"You might be right," Jeff said thoughtfully. "I'm inclined to think you are. 'Bout the same way I've been figuring it, for a fact."

"What?" Jessie came suddenly alert, grasping the arms of her chair.

"Hey, take it easy," he said quickly. "It's not what you're

59

thinking. You going to trust me or not?"

"I . . . all right, let's hear it."

Jeff showed her a sheepish grin. "I've been sort of . . . laying low here three or four months, *comprende?* Some gentlemen with the railroad down at León and thereabouts were starting to paper trees and outhouses with my picture."

"Looks to me like you haven't been laying low enough."

"Huh? Oh, Hernando and Julio? You're right, and I don't figure they're the only ones who've recognized me, either. Been meaning to move on, just too lazy to get to it. Anyway"—he waved the problem aside—"I've been spending a little time keeping an eye on Mr. Brown's business. Figuring as how we were both in the same line of work, you might say. And you're right, lady. He *does* do an awful lot of hauling here and there. Goes to a hell of a lot of trouble to make it look like *nothing* belongs to him."

"And you figured if he was going to all that trouble, he might be hauling something worth stealing."

Jeff looked pained. "Sounds awful when you come right out and say it."

"Uh-huh. You're the most sensitive outlaw I ever met, Diego Escobar. You know that?"

"A man has feelings," Jeff said humbly.

"Jeff . . ." Jessie leaned toward him again. "I'm dead serious, now. How offended would you be if I offered you money—a job? Helping me find where those wagons of Brown's are going?"

Jeff raised a brow. "You're a *rich* fat lady too, are you?"

"Just give me an answer, okay?"

"More than likely wouldn't offend me too much. You didn't ask if I'd help you for nothing."

"And would you?"

"Probably. But I'd rather have the pay."

"How would you feel about, say, two thousand dollars?"

"How about three?"

"Two and a half, and that's it."

"Done," said Jeff. He grinned and stuck out his hand. Jessie took it, and Jeff poured them both a brandy.

"You *got* that kind of money, I suppose," he asked warily.

"Uh-huh. I'm a rich, elderly fat lady, remember? I told you my name was Starbuck, Jeff. Jessica Starbuck."

Jeff raised the glass to his lips, then brought it down slowly. "Jesus Christ! It didn't even stick when you told me back on the road. *That* Starbuck, huh?"

"That's the one."

He ran a finger up the side of his broken nose. "Hell, guess I could get four or five times that, just holding you for ransom."

"At least," said Jessie.

Jeff shook his head in regret. "Naw, wouldn't be proper. We already shook on it."

Jessie threw back her head and laughed. "Escobar, you are the *loco* here, not me."

"I guess." He studied her from under a shaggy brow. "Really ought to charge you more, considering."

"Considering what?"

"That I already know where Brown sends his wagons. At least the right direction."

Jessie was so surprised she spilled brandy down her shirt. "My God, how do you know that?"

"Told you I haven't had anything to do. I just took a little time and figured it out. He lays a lot of decoys and false trails. Switching wagons and sending one this way and one the other. But where they're going is southeast, just over the border. Down the Rio Grande, past Socorro toward the Quitman Mountains."

"Well, I'll be a son of a bitch," breathed Jessie.

"No, I expect that'd be me, Señorita." He stood and set down his glass. "You can take the bed—it's soft and the sheets are clean. We'll have us some breakfast and get off early, if that's all right with you." He gave her a crooked grin. "Maybe when we get to know each other better, you'll tell me what you were doing in Miss Lorna's buggy. Reckon that's quite a story."

"Uh-what?" Jessie felt the color rise to her face.

"I recognized the rig and the fancy tassels. Seen it before a couple of times. By God, you are full of surprises, *chiquita*."

They crossed the river after dawn, a sandy stretch of brown water between Socorro and San Elizario. The country was dry, the only colors shades of tan and dusty rose. After the crossing, they followed the road south. The highlands on

61

the horizon seemed hazy and indistinct, a thousand miles away.

Jessie studied the man riding beside her. She'd put her trust in Jeffrey Diego Escobar, knowing full well what he was. She didn't approve of living outside the law, whatever reason a man might give. Still, she'd known a few badmen in her time, and barring the few with killing fever in their heads, she'd found them no better or worse than merchants and bankers. Men in stiff collars and clean suits stole too, and called it "business." An outlaw robbed a train and earned a poster and maybe a noose, while the president of the line slipped twice as much in his pocket. One was a thief, the other a clever rascal. It wasn't honesty, then, that she'd seen in Escobar. Honesty wasn't the same as honor, and she didn't think she could fault him on the latter.

"It's none of your business," she said when they stopped by the river at noon, "but I had a very good reason for borrowing Lorna's buggy."

"Oh, I'm real sure of that," said Jeff.

Jessie didn't care for the tone of his voice. "She's a fine lady and a friend. I've met a lot of 'respectable' women I trust a whole lot less. And that goes for her girls, too."

"I'm not about to argue."

"Meaning exactly what?"

"Meaning Miss Lorna's a fine woman, like you say."

"And?"

"And nothing at all. Except you're right about those girls," he said soberly. "I never met finer, friendlier folks outside of church."

Jessie laughed aloud. "I've got an idea you're a man who makes friends real easy."

"A man does the best he can," Jeff told her.

They rode on in silence, keeping to the road north of the flat and brassy river. The traffic was fairly light: farmers and traders taking wagons up to El Paso or coming back. The afternoon sun baked the land; the only sound was the weary drone of locusts in the trees.

"I expect it's time I asked," Jessie said finally. "I'm sure you've got a good answer—just haven't found the time to pass it along."

"Got an answer to what?"

"Exactly how we're going to get on the trail of Brown's wagons. I know you say they came this way. But you never followed one farther than a few miles north of the border."

"Nope. Never did." Jeff raised his hat and wiped a bandanna across his brow. "Got a better idea than following wagons. Appears to me it's some easier to figure just what those wagons have got to do."

"All right. I'm listening."

"They have to stop, Jessie, especially in this kind of heat. They've got to get water and rest the horses and, somewhere along the way, trade off for fresh teams."

"Makes sense," Jessie agreed. "And we're going to check the way stations?"

Jeff shook his head. "Maybe we can do better than that. If you were a man like Brown, playing every hand close to your chest, would you trust another fella's station to rest up and get your mounts? There's all kinds of folks stop at a place like that, for horses, a meal, or a drink of whiskey. Or just to pass the time of day. And that's the part Brown'd want to avoid. *Talk's* what gets a man in trouble. Hell, I guess I ought to know."

"Why, of course!" Jessie exclaimed. "You're right, Jeff. He'll have his own stations. Points along the way where no one asks questions—or gets used to seeing familiar wagons and drivers."

"Seems to me it's the smart thing to do."

"And you think we can find them?"

"I don't know where the first station is, but I know where it *ought* to be. A day's wagon ride from Paso del Norte. Might be closer, but it won't be farther. We'll have to do some hunting. But it'll be there, sure."

"Maybe we can narrow that down," Jessie said thoughtfully. She squinted against the sun and caught his eye. "A private station would cause talk, too. Folks wondering who it belonged to and all."

"That's a point," Jeff said. "What are you getting at?"

"Just that maybe what we're looking for doesn't appear to be what it is. Does that make any sense?"

Jeff showed her a crooked smile. "By God, it does. I'm glad I didn't steal that purse of yours, you know? Don't think I'd want you tracking me down."

"That's a compliment, I guess," Jessie said dryly. "Comin'

from El Rosario himself."

"Wish to hell you'd never heard about that El Rosario business," Jeff muttered.

"Mister, you're stuck with it now."

Jeff shook his head and kicked his horse into a run. Jessie grinned to herself and leaned into the saddle to catch up.

# Chapter 9

An hour after dark the wagon turned abruptly left, climbed rocky terrain a few miles, and came to a halt. A new team of mules took over and the wagon lurched off again.

Ki glanced drearily at Ellie Slate. "I thought we stopped at night. What's happening now?"

"We do," said Ellie. "Won't be long. It's always right after when we get a fresh team."

Ki nodded, thinking he should have figured that out for himself. People in the wagon would never see a station— a building, corrals, people, a setting they might remember.

Half an hour later the wagon stopped again. Someone walked around the sides and opened the trick door in the back. Ki and Ellie stepped out and gratefully breathed fresh air. The night was anything but cool, but after a day in the stuffy wagon, neither of them complained. Ki noted at once that the drivers weren't the pair they'd started with in the morning. One was a Mexican, the other a *norteamericano*. Both looked as if they could handle the weapons on their hips.

"I think this'd be a good time to tell you the rules," Ellie said quietly. "They handle the cooking and cleaning up. *Don't* talk to 'em. They won't talk to you. If you have to . . . go back into the bushes or anything, fine. Just don't wander off."

"I don't know where the hell I'd go."

"I'm just *telling* you, Mark."

"Yeah, I know." He gave her his best smile. "Sorry. This business makes me kind of itchy."

"I know. It's all right." She nodded toward the wagon. "I'm going to wash up and change clothes before supper. Makes you sleep better, too."

"I'll take the suggestion," said Ki. Ellie turned back to the wagon and pulled the door shut behind her. Ki walked over and watched the men. One was unhitching the mules, while the other started a fire. The camp was set in a shallow depression, ringed on every side by a rocky ridge. The stars told him a little, confirming what he'd guessed inside the wagon. They'd traveled east and maybe south from Paso del Norte. Then north for a few miles after they got the new team. Not much to go on, but maybe that would change.

Ellie came out of the wagon looking fresh and clean and luscious as a peach in denims and a worn cotton shirt. Her boots were gone and her feet were bare. The ever-present Colt clung to her hip. Ki took a breath and let it out. A day of watching the thin chemise cling to her body had left him wound up as tight as a cheap watch.

Inside the wagon, he moved to the rear wall and went quickly through her valise. There was nothing there but clothes, and a cabinet card photograph wrapped in stiff paper. The girl in the picture was maybe ten, the boy a few years younger. The photographer's stamp told him the picture had been made in St. Louis. He studied it a moment, then carefully put it away. The girl could be Ellie, or one of a thousand other girls. He stripped off his trousers and washed off the grime and dust of the day. Ellie was right—fresh clothes helped. He left his boots in the wagon, grateful for an excuse to set them aside. Most men wore the damned things all their lives and didn't mind. To Ki, it was as unnatural as lacing up your head in a sa

Outside, he filled his plate with smoked ham and beans. The food was good, and there were airtights of peaches for dessert. He sat beside Ellie on a rock; the drivers kept to themselves away from the fire.

"What I'd like to do," he said darkly, "is ride Mr. Brown around in that wagon for about a week. Make him wear a big fur coat and give him half a bottle of water."

"You'll have to get in line." Ellie threw back her head and laughed. "Lord, I've dreamed about it a couple of hundred times!"

He'd never seen her in such spirits and found it delightful. Maybe getting out of the wagon had lightened her mood— or getting away from Brown. Whatever the reason, she was a different woman altogether. The ice-blue eyes turned warm and friendly. The planes of her cheeks, the firm angle of her chin seemed to soften, lending her a different kind of beauty. Ki finished off his plate and set it aside, aware that she was studying him as well. He guessed it was something she couldn't help, looking into people and trying to figure what made them tick.

"I'm wondering," she said, a hint of mischief in her voice, "just what kind of face is hiding behind that beard."

"Just a face. Afraid it's nothing special."

"Oh, I doubt that, now."

"You do, huh?"

"Yes, yes I do." She cocked her head, letting a veil of silver-blond hair fall over one eye. "There is something real interesting there. The eyes—especially the eyes."

"French Canadian, Roosian, a little Cree Indian somewhere back. Take your pick. Kind of a mixed pup, I reckon."

Ellie answered his smile. "The combination goes together well. Except for the beard." She shook her head in mock disapproval. "I *don't* see you with the beard. I don't think that's what you are."

"Good." Ki fingered his hairy cheeks. "Maybe a couple of sheriffs don't either."

"Yes, well . . ." The easy smile faded. "That's certainly a sound reason." In an instant she was the old Ellie Slate once more—the eyes cool and distant, shutting him out. What was it? Ki wondered. The reminder of what he was—or what she thought he'd likely be? And so what? Wasn't she in the killing business too? They talked a while longer, but it wasn't the same now. Before long she muttered some excuse and pulled her bedroll out of the wagon and found a spot far from the fire. Ki stayed awake for a while, then made his own bed and settled down. There wasn't much question of wandering off, climbing the ridge to see what lay on the other side. While one driver slept, the other stood guard. Ki awoke in the middle of the night and saw the second take over from the first.

Dawn came sooner than he liked. Ellie gave him a quick half-smile over breakfast and nothing more. She looked better than ever, eyes lazy with sleep and hair tousled like a web about her face. Lord, there wasn't anything prettier than a good-looking woman waking up. He caught himself almost looking forward to another awful siege in the wagon, and decided he was acting like a fool. Eyeing Ellie Slate nearly naked another day wouldn't ease the growing ache below his belly.

The second day's journey was more of the same. The third was pure hell. The wagon took them over country where wagons weren't meant to go. There were no fresh teams now to meet them. Ki stumbled, sore and exhausted, out of the wagon. They were camped in a deep arroyo, sheer canyon walls rising up on every side. If there was anything more than dry brush growing about, Ki couldn't find it. Picking up a handful of soil, he felt it crumble like sand between his fingers.

"I was wondering why the pay was so good," he said sourly. "Now I know. It isn't the job at all, it's getting there."

Ellie gave him a hollow-eyed look. "Wait till you see tomorrow."

Ki didn't believe her, but she was right. They broke camp at two in the morning and Ki soon learned the reason why. The canyon country dipped into desert, and the drivers wanted to cross all they could in the dark. When the sun finally rose, the wagon became a furnace. Hot, burning air seared his lungs. Dust coated his mouth and clogged his nostrils. And with the dust there was the smell and taste of something else. *Salt,* thought Ki. *We're on salt flats or a dry salt lake*.

"We crossed the worst of it during the dark," said Ellie. "It won't last much longer."

"It better not, because *I* won't," Ki said dully. He looked at Ellie's red-rimmed eyes, skin flushed the color of raw meat. "You going to be all right?"

Ellie forced smile. "I've done this before, remember?"

"I'm trying to keep that in mind. I just hope to hell I never do it again."

"We'll get where we're going late tonight. It'll cool off some before then."

Ki soaked the sponge in the barrel and dripped it over his head. "What kind of country is it?"

"Mountains. Pretty high up."

"Uh-huh."

*"Don't,"* she said sharply. "It's not a good idea. I told you that before."

"Don't what?"

"You're thinking where we are and the way we came."

"Come on," Ki chided, "that's plain natural, Ellie. Don't tell me you haven't wondered."

"No. I haven't. I *know* better."

Ki didn't pursue it any further. He was good at reading faces, but Ellie was a master at hiding her feelings from the world.

Late in the afternoon, men met them with a fresh team of mules. The drivers opened the door and let Ki and Elli get some air. They weren't allowed outside, but it was better than nothing at all. Ki saw a high rocky wall stained pink and white. The drivers gave them a barrel of fresh water and closed the door.

Well before sundown, the wagon started climbing. Ki heard a bird's song, smelled pine and fresh water. The road got rougher after dark, but it was bearable inside. He drifted into restless sleep, then woke up abruptly as the wagon came to a halt. The rear door opened. Ellie had slipped on her dress while he slept.

"This is it," she said wearily. "We're here."

Ki gave a deep sigh of relief. He stretched, put on his shirt and boots, and found his valise. Outside, junipers closed in on the narrow road. Beyond, limestone cliffs loomed against the night sky. Three men came out of the dark. Two carried rifles and stayed behind. The third was tall and broad-shouldered. A high-crowned Stetson covered his features. He grinned.

"Evening, Ellie. Have a nice trip, I reckon."

"Sure, Dan. A pure delight," Ellie said dryly.

Dan laughed, then turned to look at Ki. "I don't guess I know you, do I?"

"Dan Cooper, Marcus Villon—calls himself Mark," Ellie said without expression. She drew a thick envelope from her dress. "This is from Brown." She nodded at Ki, and he knew the papers concerned him. He wished to hell he had a peek at what they said.

"Pleased to have you with us, Mark." Dan stuck out his

hand and Ki took it. "Got any idea where you are?"

"Yeah," Ki said darkly. "Outside of that goddamn wagon."

Dan grinned. "Good answer. You'll do just fine. Come on, we'll find you some food and get you settled. You've got your usual cabin, Ellie." He paused and leaned closer in the dark. "I'll send someone with supper. I could drop by later if you like."

"Now, Dan," Ellie said sweetly, "you know I shoot just as good at night as I do in the day."

"Right, right. No harm in asking, is there?" Dan laughed her off, but Ki caught the edge of irritation in his voice.

Windows of yellow light peeked through the trees. Ellie bade Ki good night and disappeared down a path to the right. Ki followed Cooper, the two men with Winchesters trailing behind. Cooper stopped before a small, darkened cabin.

"Everything you need's inside," he told Ki. "Lamp's on the table, should be matches close by. I'll send a man with supper. You can start eating with the others in the morning. Any questions? Anything you want?"

"Any chance of washing off the day?"

"Sorry. Too late to go down to the river. You'll have to stink tonight." Cooper gave him a broad wink. "Doesn't matter. Won't be anyone in there but you. There's a basin inside and a barrel."

"That'll have to do."

"Oh, one more thing." Cooper looked him straight in the eye. "Stay inside. You got to pee or anything, use the pot. That's the rules. Period."

"I got it."

"Good. See you in the morning. Supper'll be along." Cooper and his men disappeared. Ki watched them go, took his satchel inside, and lit the lamp. The cabin was clean and simply furnished: a bed, two straight-backed chairs, and a table; hooks for clothes on the wall; a fireplace with a pile of worn half-dime novels on the mantel.

"Well," he muttered under his breath, "I'm in. Now all I've got to do is get out."

He peered into the mirror over the basin. His eyes were full of grit, his face red with dust. He was moving for the basin when someone stepped lightly on the porch outside.

"Got your supper," the gruff voice spoke behind him. "I'll put it on the table."

"Thanks," said Ki. He started to turn, then froze. He saw the man's face in the mirror—square jaw, heavy brows, and broken nose. The man waited, but Ki pretended to find something in his eye. Finally the man shrugged and walked out the door.

Ki let out a breath. He'd recognized the man at once. They'd fought on the deck of a sternwheeler going up the Red River to Jefferson, Texas. Ki had broken his arm and a couple of ribs and cut his face up badly. The man had every reason to remember him, bearded face or not.

Ki muttered darkly, "What a way to start my first day at school."

# Chapter 10

After his trip in the closed wagon, Ki was more than ready for a good night's sleep. The air was clean and cool, heavy with the scent of juniper and pine. He stripped off his clothes and fell into bed, dozing off almost at once.

Well before dawn he was awake and dressed again. Another two hours would have suited him fine, but this wasn't the day for that. Someone would come for him soon—maybe the man who'd brought him supper. It was a rotten piece of luck, meeting a man he'd tangled with before. He didn't need any extra problems now.

But the man who came was a stranger, a dark-haired fellow with sleep in his eyes. Ki breathed a silent sigh of relief.

"Up and dressed, are you?" The man yawned and scratched his crotch. "Good. Let's get going."

"And where is it we're going?" asked Ki.

"He wants to see you. Mr. Kahr."

"Someplace I can wash up first and get breakfast?"

The man looked at Ki with disbelief and laughed. "I said Mr. *Kahr* wants to see you. Shit, you deaf or something, friend?" He shook his head and ambled down the path, not bothering to check whether Ki was there.

His first real view of the camp told Ki the cartel had picked a perfect spot for its operation. From the thickly wooded floor of the canyon, eroded limestone walls rose five hundred feet toward the crisp morning sky. The sheer palisades were the color of bone, topped with rocky spires and weathered sentinels of pine. No one was going to climb those walls, nor anything bigger than a lizard. Ki guessed each end of the canyon narrowed to little more than a wagon trail. Two or three men on either side could make certain no one entered or left.

The path led down past tall columns of ponderosa pine, through stands of oak and ash and bigtooth maple. Other cabins like his own were nestled in the trees. Through a break in the foliage, he saw three men and a woman in a clearing. Another man stood apart, and Ki guessed he was the instructor. Three students were tossing hand axes at a target. Another was practicing fighting stances with a knife. Moments later he saw a sight that caught his attention and held it. Six men were practicing hand-to-hand combat—poorly, Ki thought, but the style was clearly Japanese. He muttered an oath under his breath. Miguel Vargas, dying in Sweetwater, Texas, had told them there was a Japanese member of the staff. Ki hadn't forgotten; he'd merely hoped that Vargas was wrong. Damn, that was all he needed! A man he'd beaten in a fight, and another who'd know his style of fighting in an instant. He lingered a moment, hoping to get a look at the instructor. If he was there, Ki didn't spot him.

His guide stopped on the path and turned back. "Come on," he said sharply. "That's none of your business, mister."

"Just looking," said Ki.

"Well, *don't*. Lookin' ain't a good idea around here."

Ki kept his silence and followed. The woods gave way to a narrow stream and a series of limestone pools. Salt cedar and cottonwood lined the banks. Water trickled into a pond from the boulders above. Ki's guide crossed the creek and led him along the far side for a hundred yards. A cabin, larger than the others, was nearly hidden under the pines. A man cradling a shotgun in his arms sat in a chair tilted back on the porch.

"Wait here," Ki's guide called back. The man walked up to the guard and exchanged a few words with him. The guard stood and went inside, then came back again and nodded.

"Go on in," he told Ki.

Ki mounted the steps and went in, ignoring the guard's curious glance. The room's plain furnishings were a surprise. The straight-backed chairs and wooden table were no fancier than his own. If the cartel's man liked carpeting and plush sofas, he kept them in another part of the cabin.

A door opened behind him and Ki turned. At once his trained senses came alert. Hairs bristled on his neck in an instinct as old as life—one dangerous animal meeting another in the dark.

"Marcus Villon? I am Wilhelm Kahr. Welcome to our camp." He offered his hand and a wolfish smile. His grip was corded steel under flesh. Ki glanced at the gold ring and saw the stylized crown, symbol of the cartel's power. "I will not ask if you had a good trip," Kahr said. "No one ever does."

"I've sure had better." Ki risked a smile, and got no response at all. Kahr was tall and broad-shouldered, his body slim and hard, with masses of well-toned muscle. Ki was sure the man wouldn't tolerate an ounce of useless fat. His face was lean and harsh, features sharp and pronounced, gray-blond hair trimmed nearly to his scalp. It was the man's eyes, though, that caught Ki's attention. They were the color of pale jade, and just as devoid of life.

"I will not keep you," Kahr said shortly. He stood straight, hands locked behind his back. He was clearly of Prussian stock, his English clipped and precise, lacking any emotion. "You are here to do a job—a job for which you will be extremely well paid. Follow our rules and we shall get along fine."

"All right with me," said Ki. "I'm anxious to get—"

"Wait. Please." Kahr showed him a mechanical smile. "Our rules are very simple. Do as you are told. Watch. Listen. Learn what you are taught. You have a question?"

"Just one. What is it I'm supposed to learn? I don't recall anyone ever saying."

Kahr raised his chin. "Killing, Mr. Villon. Group and individual techniques. Quick and effective methods of putting a man out of action." The cold eyes blinked once. "This doesn't surprise you, does it? I imagine you guessed why you were hired."

"I figured your outfit needed men who could handle themselves. No one said anything about *learning* how to fight."

"Ah, of course." Kahr rocked back on his heels. "And you do not imagine that you *need* such instruction."

Ki met his glance and didn't waver. "Mister, I know how to do what I do," he said evenly. "I'm not bad at it, either, I don't mind saying. I figure there's things another man can do better."

His last remark seemed to please Kahr. "A good answer, Marcus." He raised a slender finger. "A man must have confidence in himself, but he is a fool if he imagines there's not a man somewhere who can beat him. I have no tolerance for fools. Not in this place." He paused and squinted thoughtfully at the wall. "Gaylord wrote me about your past, your family. You have an interesting face. Brown also says you are good with your hands and with a knife."

"I can hold my own."

"Well. We shall see, won't we? That's all, Villon. We'll talk again." Kahr turned abruptly and walked out, leaving Ki watching his back.

Outside, he found his guard waiting. "I'll take you back," he said. "You can get cleaned up and hang around your cabin till dinner."

"Dinner?" Ki gave him a piercing look. "Hell, I haven't even had breakfast."

"Uh-huh." The man gave him a nasty grin. "You *missed* breakfast, fella. Talkin' to Mr. Kahr. Now you gotta wait."

"One of the rules, I'll bet. Right?"

"You got it."

"Then I'll wait."

"That's what I'd do, if I was you." He turned and led Ki away from the house and back to the creek.

Dan Cooper came for him around noon. Ki saw his features clearly for the first time. He had a broad, cheerful face, dark and lively eyes, and a disarming grin. Cooper's easy, friendly manner put Ki instantly on the alert. He looked like a man you could trust, a man who'd stop and listen to your troubles. Ki was certain Wilhelm Kahr would have nothing to do with such a man—which meant Dan Cooper wasn't all he seemed to be.

"You get a good night's rest, I hope?" Cooper smiled and offered his hand. "That damn wagon's pure awful, isn't it? God, I hate the thing. Glad I'm stuck out here most of the time."

"It's nice country," Ki agreed, knowing Cooper had likely never seen the inside of the wagon.

"Probably real curious about where we are."

Ki wondered if Cooper remembered he'd asked the same question the night before. "Sure," said Ki. "I imagine everybody is."

"Nothing wrong with a little healthy curiosity." Cooper let the subject drop and led Ki through the trees, turning north just before they reached the creek. Ki saw a long, narrow cabin he hadn't seen before.

"That's the lodge," Cooper explained. "Kind of a general meetin' place and where everybody eats." He stopped and took off his hat to scratch his head. "Couple of things you need to know 'fore we go in, Mark. You'll sit at the same table every meal. The people there belong to your group. You'll be joining Group Three. There's other groups you'll see, but you just stick with your own. This is kind of important, so I want you to remember." He offered a shy, almost apologetic grin, as if it pained him to waste Ki's time. "Damn rules, you know? Things we just gotta put up with here. You'll train with your group, eat with 'em, spend your off-duty time with them. *Don't* talk to the people outside your group. If you meet them on a path, in one of the training areas, or anywhere else, just pass 'em on by. They'll do the same with you. Instructors and staff all know who you are. You'll be wearing this. Here." He pulled a green bandanna from his pocket and wrapped it around Ki's arm. "That says you're Group Three. Every group's got a color. You got any questions about this?"

Ki shrugged. "All right by me. You folks are paying. You got a right to run the show however you like."

"Good. I like your attitude, Mark. I really do." He gave Ki a friendly pat on the shoulder. "You'll do just fine, by God."

Ki followed him up the hill to the lodge. Inside, there were nine long tables—six for "students" and three for instructors and staff. There were five or six people at each table, and Ki was struck at once by the fact that fully a third of them were women.

Every face in the room glanced up to look him over. Ki ignored them and let his eyes sweep the three staff tables. To his relief, the man who'd brought him supper wasn't there.

Cooper quickly introduced him to Group Three, left him on his own, and joined Wilhelm Kahr and the others. Ki

76

was pleasantly surprised to find that Ellie was part of the group. The others were Wolf Voegler, Kurt Strasser, Peter LaGrange, and a girl named Cindy Dunne. Cindy was a small, slender brunette with dark eyes and a pouty mouth. LaGrange was sandy-haired, nondescript, and skinny as a reed. Ki thought he looked more like a storekeeper than a killer.

"You sleep good?" Ellie smiled. "Lord, I didn't want to *ever* get up."

"About two more days would have suited me just fine," Ki agreed. He attacked his steak hungrily, devoured a hot biscuit, and buttered another.

"A man who has missed his breakfast," Kurt Strasser observed. He offered Ki a thin smile. "It is one of the rules, I think. The new one gets no breakfast."

"Sure isn't one of the rules that suits me," said Ki. Strasser was blond and well built, clearly German, a slightly younger version of Wilhelm Kahr.

"You're taking the pay," Wolf Voegler said bluntly. "I wouldn't complain about the rules."

Ki looked up from his steak. There was no mistaking the challenge in Voegler's face. He'd seen it there the moment he joined the table. He was a lean, hollow-cheeked man with deepset eyes under brows that grew together like a bush. Coal-black hair was slicked back over his skull. The dark hair and brows formed a startling contrast to the unhealthy pallor of his skin.

"Ah, but I would guess you are a man who doesn't care too much for the rules, *ja?*"

"I can live with them," Ki said without looking up.

"But you would rather not, I think."

"Wolf, stop it," Ellie said coolly.

"Am I correct, Herr Villon?" Voegler refused to let it go. "What kind of a man might you be?"

Ki looked up at last. "You're pushing hard, friend. I never saw you before, so there's got to be a reason other than that. You want to tell me what it is?"

"Wolf's a sorehead," Cindy Dunne said flatly. "There's your reason, mister."

Voegler ignored the remark. "You haff not answered my question," he said sharply. "What kind of a *man* are you, Villon?"

Ki set down his fork and glanced at Strasser and La-Grange. "Boys, I'm new here," he said. "What do you figure I ought to do?"

Strasser frowned and LaGrange shook his head. "I don't get your question, mister."

"It isn't too hard," Ki explained. "This fellow's looking for trouble and I'm not. What I'm thinking is that Mr. Kahr doesn't take real kindly to fighting at dinner. I've got an idea Mr. Voegler here knows that too." His eyes shifted across the table. "Am I close enough, friend?"

Voegler sat up straight and glared.

"You start anything in here, that's it," Ellie said shortly.

"Doesn't matter if *he* pushed it, either," Ki finished.

"No. It doesn't matter at all."

Ki gave Voegler a broad grin. "Mister, you're a tricky son of a bitch. So how do you settle arguments around here?"

"You don't, Herr Villon." Voegler offered Ki a bloodless smile. "There iss no fighting at all. We are a team, *ja?* We are trained to work closely together."

"But you just had to try."

"One likes to know with whom he is working. A joke, nothing more."

"Christ!" Cindy Dunne made a noise in her throat. "You tried to get the man shot and you know it." Her small mouth curved into a grin. "Figure maybe he got what you couldn't on the trip up, Wolf?"

Ellie gasped. "You damn little whore!"

"Wrong, darlin'." Cindy laughed, her dark eyes flashing with pleasure. "If I want a man, it doesn't cost him a thing."

"Not exactly true," Strasser said dryly.

Cindy winked at Ki. "Our Kurt is such a refined little German. Aren't you, Kurt?"

Strasser looked at his plate. Voegler sat back in his chair and smiled. "You see? We haff a friendly little group, *ja?*"

Ki didn't answer. His fork stopped halfway to his mouth as a man stalked heavily across the room to the first staff table and pulled out a chair. His features were smeared carelessly across his face, his dark hair tied in a knot atop his head. He was big, built like a bear, and all his weight was clearly bone and muscle.

Strasser caught Ki's expression. "His name is Matsuo

Tanaka. You will get a chance to meet him this afternoon."

Cindy gave a quick little laugh.

"What's so damn funny?" Ki asked.

"One of Tanaka's little pleasures," LaGrange said quietly. "He likes to welcome new students himself."

"So?"

"So he'll do his best to break your damn skull," Cindy said flatly.

# Chapter 11

After the noonday meal, Ki's group walked half a mile down the canyon to a clearing set up as a firing range. A man in his forties named Wagner was the instructor. He was a softspoken man who knew all there was to know about weapons—from taking them apart to hitting a target dead center. Wagner was short and heavyset, awkward and ungainly until his hands touched a pistol or a rifle. Then he moved as gracefully as a gambler with his favorite deck of cards. Ellie served as his assistant, and Ki noted that she watched the man with awe.

"He's good," said Ki. "I don't believe I've seen better."

"He's good like a hawk's good at flying," Ellie corrected. "Good doesn't even come close."

"And what about you?"

She smiled. "Now *I'm* good. About twenty or thirty notches under him."

Ki watched, and figured she was better than that. Peter LaGrange didn't seem to know one end of a rifle from the other, and Ellie gave him extra help—showing him how to let the weapon rest lightly in his arms, how to squeeze off a shot. Several rifles lay on a table, but Ellie had brought her own. It was a Model 1873 Winchester .44-40 that she kept in a buckskin scabbard. The stock was of polished ash, made to fit her shoulder.

"Not a one of you's ever going to shoot like Ellie," Wagner said plainly. "But it won't hurt you to see how it's done."

Ellie Slate wasted no time at all sighting a target or taking a breath. The rifle came up to her shoulder in a blur, one hand working the lever in an almost continuous motion. The sharp reports rolled off the canyon walls, the sound more like that of a Gatling gun than a rifle. Five pebbles lined up on a log disappeared. The targets were close to eighty yards away.

"Ah, well," Kurt Strasser said with a yawn, "the rocks, they were sitting still, *ja?*"

The others laughed and Ellie grinned. Her eyes searched the canyon for a moment, then she brought the weapon up fast and squeezed off a single shot. A small bird exploded in midair.

Ellie lowered her weapon. "You run down and hold a feather in your teeth," she said dryly. "A double eagle says I hit it."

Strasser snapped his heels together and bowed humbly. *Fräulein,* I do not doubt it for a moment."

Ki walked with Ellie back to the creek. The others were ahead, Cindy teasing LaGrange, Voegler talking earnestly with Strasser.

"That was some shooting," said Ki. "Are you as good as that with a pistol?"

"No one's as good with a hand weapon," she said seriously. "But I'm good, yes. Very good." She gave Ki an approving nod. "You're not bad yourself. I was watching."

"I don't care much for guns. Never have. But I can get by."

"No. You're better than that."

Ki laughed under his breath. "You and Wagner can work all summer and into spring, but you aren't going to teach Peter LaGrange how to shoot."

"No, I don't guess we will," she said absently.

"I hope he's got a talent better than shooting. If he doesn't—"

Ki caught her expression, the sudden tightness about her mouth. "Did I say something wrong?"

"No, nothing," she answered too quickly.

"Uh-huh, all right."

"Mark—" She stopped him with a hand on his arm. "Mark, be careful with Wolf Voegler. And don't trust Kurt. He's nice enough when he wants to be, but he's very tight with Wolf."

"I appreciate the advice."

The blue eyes softened for an instant. She opened her

mouth to speak, then shut her lips tight.

"Is something troubling you, Ellie? If it is—"

"No, damn you, there isn't!" Her lovely features twisted in a sudden flash of anger. "Stay away from me, please. You want company, try Cindy Dunne. You'll get all you can handle and more!"

She quickened her steps and left him, going ahead to catch up with the others. Ki stared after her and shook his head. Now what the hell was *that* all about? She'd turned on him for no reason at all. Something he'd said about LaGrange had got her going, but there was more to it than that. He walked down the path and came out of the trees, catching sight of Strasser's wheat-colored head and the darker pate of Wolf Voegler, slick and black as a raven's.

He swore under his breath. Voegler and Strasser and LaGrange. Ellie Slate and Cindy Dunne. Ki was almost certain he couldn't gather a more peculiar bunch if he tried. Was this Kahr's idea of a group—a fighting team trained to function together? Maybe, if they didn't all kill each other first . . .

His first look at Matsuo Tanaka had told him a lot. He didn't have to see the man fight; watching him stride through the tables at noon said enough. He carried his heavy frame like a man of half his size and years. He had the power of a bull, the cunning and quickness of a snake.

Now, watching him finish up with Group Two, Ki knew a great deal more about the man. He was good, likely not the fighting master he claimed to be, but damn good—good enough to unmask Ki for what he was, unless he handled himself with care. One slip, a too-familiar move, would alert Tanaka at once.

"Watch yourself, my friend," Kurt Strasser spoke beside him. "It is true. He likes to show the newcomers what he can do."

"What the hell for?" Ki said irritably. "I didn't come here to get crippled. I'm not going to earn any pay on a crutch."

Strasser swept back his thick blond hair and grinned. "He will not break anything. He iss very careful. A few bruises, a cracked rib, *nein?*"

"That makes me feel a lot better," Ki growled. He glanced

past Strasser to the others. "I'm going to ask you something, Strasser. Answer it if you like."

"Yes?"

"What's your friend's big problem? Is he mad at everyone, or just at me?"

"Wolf worries you, does he?"

"Is that what you think?"

"What I think," Strasser said soberly, "iss that Wolf will tell you himself. When Wolf iss ready."

"That's not much of an answer. Your privilege, I reckon."

"Yes. This is so." Strasser looked amused.

Ki figured that about said it. Whatever happened between Voegler and himself, Strasser would stand back and enjoy the action.


Matsuo Tanaka grinned broadly at Ki. He was bare to the waist, his thick arms folded over his chest. He wore loose black trousers and a wide red sash. Stuck in the sash were the two blades of the samurai: the longer, slightly curved *katana* for fighting, the shorter *ko-dachi* for *seppuku,* the act of ritual suicide. Ki wondered if he'd really earned the blades. *Bushido,* the way of the samurai, was a great deal more than swinging a sword. It was a code, a way of living your life. He wouldn't dare wear the *katana* in the Japans unless he truly had the right. Here, of course, he could call himself whatever he liked and no one would be the wiser.

"I am told you are good with your hands," said Tanaka. "And with the knife as well. Perhaps you will show me what you can do."

"Fine," said Ki. "Who do you want me to fight?" But he knew damn well exactly what the man had in mind.

Tanaka threw back his head and laughed. "Me. You will fight me." He jabbed a big thumb at his chest. "Show me what you are." He strolled about the clearing, touching the ground heavily with sandaled feet, as if he were testing the earth to see if it would hold his great weight. He paused under a tree, slipped the two blades from his sash, and dropped them to the ground.

Ki swallowed his anger at the gesture. He didn't know what Matsuo Tanaka might be, but he knew in that instant what he wasn't. No true samurai would show disrespect for the *katana*. He would never toss it casually aside.

"Come," Tanaka urged. "Come. Fight me now."

*Hell,* thought Ki, *it isn't going to get any easier.* He unbuckled his gunbelt and laid it on his vest, wishing he could shed the awkward boots as well. He'd only watched Tanaka for a moment. There'd been no chance to really see what he could do, what kind of moves he made.

He caught himself then, and shook the dangerous thoughts aside. What difference did it make? He wasn't about to try to *beat* the big ox. All he could do was lose—without giving himself away or going home with a broken neck.

Ki came in low, taking the same back-alley stance he'd used against Brown's man at the Azteca. Tanaka grinned, holding his open hands slightly bent, moving them slowly back and forth. Ki knew exactly what would happen to him next, and didn't dare do a thing to try to stop it. He circled past Tanaka, feinted with his left, and drove in hard with his right. Tanaka moved as if his opponent were standing still. One hand caught Ki like an ax across his chest, the other struck hard between his shoulder and his neck, numbing his arm clear to the fingers. Ki staggered back and cried out. Tanaka came in to finish him off, his big fist bent in a closed claw. He was careless now, knowing he had his man and taking pleasure in the finish. Ki could have twisted on his feet, kicked him in the crotch, and dropped him writhing to the ground. Instead he ducked under the blow and pounded uselessly on the big man's chest. Tanaka tossed him aside, slapping him savagely across the face with one hand and then the other. Ki spit blood, staggered and fell on his belly, and lay still. There was no use taking any more. The longer he stayed on his feet, the more bruises he'd have in the morning.

He sat up slowly, wiping blood off his face with his sleeve. Tanaka stood above him, shaking his head in disdain. "You think you are a fighter? Ha! You are not a fighter at all."

Ki forced a grin. "I have to hand it to you. I never saw any moves like that."

Tanaka grunted and turned away. "You, Mr. Voegler, and—ah, Mr. LaGrange. You will fight each other now. Show our new friend what you have learned."

LaGrange looked appalled. "Hey, look, I'm not any good at this."

"That is true," Tanaka said soberly. "If you were good, you would not need to learn. Do it. *Now*, please."

"Take it easy," said Voegler. He gave LaGrange a crooked grin. "I'll go soft on you, Pete."

"Yeah, sure." His eyes showed how much he believed that.

Wolf stripped off his shirt and threw it aside. Ki eyed the tight cords of muscle across his shoulders and down his arms. LaGrange didn't bother with his shirt. He stood, shoulders slightly stooped, arms hanging awkwardly at his sides. There was strength in his arms, and in the hands too big for the rest of his body, but that wouldn't help him against Voegler. LaGrange's skinny frame wasn't made for fighting. Wolf would destroy him. Both men knew it, and so did Matsuo Tanaka. He made no effort to hide his anticipation of the slaughter.

Ki glanced at the others. Strasser displayed his usual uncaring grin. Ellie ran a nervous hand over her cheek. Cindy held her lips pressed firmly together, her eyes as dark and brittle as glass.

Voegler moved lazily to the right, putting his opponent's eyes in the sun. LaGrange didn't even seem to notice. Voegler raised his hands, fingers up, the edges of his palms toward his foe, as Tanaka had taught him. His stance wasn't bad, Ki noticed. It wasn't his natural style, but he'd watched Tanaka and practiced. His moves were still stiff, but it didn't much matter with LaGrange. He could use the few tricks he'd picked up, put LaGrange away, and pretend he'd mastered whatever Tanaka had taught him.

Voegler struck without warning, lashing out with his left. LaGrange ducked, caught a glancing right on his arm, and moved agilely out of range. Voegler looked surprised. He came at LaGrange again, shifting from side to side. Again he struck with his left. LaGrange jerked back, showing more speed than Ki had expected. All the color was gone from his face; his flesh was shiny with sweat. He was scared to death of Voegler, forcing himself to hold his ground when he wanted to turn and run.

A tight, ugly grin stretched Voegler's lips. He read the man's fear and knew that a few quick moves couldn't save him forever. He came straight at LaGrange, fingers bent at the knuckles. LaGrange backed off. Voegler dug in his heels and brought his right up hard. LaGrange moved again and Voegler's left snaked out, caught his opponent full in the mouth, and sent him staggering on his heels. LaGrange cried out, shut his eyes, and threw his hands up over his face. Blood flowed from his nose and down his chest. Voegler hit him in the mouth, danced in, and slapped his hand across one cheek and then the other. LaGrange stumbled drunkenly in a circle, staring blankly at the sky. Voegler's eyes flashed. He stalked leisurely around LaGrange, slapping him cruelly about the eyes, landing short blows to his mouth and nose. LaGrange refused to fall. He stood up and took the blows, arms hanging limply at his sides. One eye was shut and his cheek was an open wound. Blood formed a beard down his chin.

Ki glanced at Tanaka. His eyes told him what he already knew. Tanaka wouldn't stop the brutal display. Voegler could cut his man to stew meat and Tanaka wouldn't move. Ki cursed under his breath, took three long strides, and grabbed Voegler's arm. He turned him roughly around and threw him aside.

"No!" Matsuo Tanaka's face purpled in rage. "You do not fight. I *tell* you when to fight!"

"Then you damn sure better start tellin'," muttered Ki. He turned and saw Voegler coming at him, brought his right up from the waist, and hit Voegler savagely across the mouth.

Voegler went down, stunned and surprised at the fury of Ki's attack. Ki gave him no chance to recover. Voegler was shaking his head, bringing himself to his knees, when Ki kicked him solidly in the ribs. The blow lifted him off the ground and sent him sprawling. Voegler howled and rolled up in a ball. Ki loomed above him, legs spread wide, hauled the man up by his chin, and hit him once across the face. Voegler went limp and Ki tossed him roughly away.

He heard Matsuo Tanaka before he saw him. The man came at him like a bull, with a deep growl in his throat. Ki leaped desperately aside. A chopping blow caught the small of his back. He gasped against the pain and rolled free. Tanaka turned on his heel and came at him again. Ki scrambled to his feet, ran for the holstered gun where he'd left it, jerked the weapon out, and turned in a crouch.

86

"Hold it," he snapped. "I'll blow your goddamn head off, mister!"

Tanaka stopped, stared at Ki in disbelief, and clenched his fists in anger. "Give me the gun," he said sharply. "Now! Give it to me!" He thrust out his hand, sliding his left foot swiftly forward. Ki backed off, sensing his move before it began.

"Go on," Ki said softly, "try it. See if those fancy moves are faster than lead."

"Marcus. Put the gun away."

Ki stepped to one side, glanced over his shoulder, and saw Dan Cooper, the Colt in his fist aimed casually at his back.

"Get him off me," said Ki. "Tell him to get across the clearing and stay there."

"Go on, Tanaka," said Cooper. "I'd back off, I think."

Tanaka glared his defiance, cursed Ki under his breath, and stepped away. Ki waited, knowing how fast the man could move, what he could do himself from such a distance. Finally he turned to face Cooper, one eye still on Tanaka. He held the pistol loosely at his side.

"All right. Now what?"

Cooper grinned. "Talking, that's all. All right?"

Ki didn't believe him for a minute. They couldn't let him walk away from pulling a gun on Tanaka. Still, he didn't have much choice. Go easy, or start shooting everyone in sight and try to make it out of the canyon. He eased down the hammer of the pistol and tossed it to the ground.

"Keep it," said Cooper. "I don't need it." Turning his back on Ki, he stuck his Colt in his belt and started off through the trees. Ki retrieved his own weapon, picked up his belt and vest, and followed Cooper. Looking back, he glanced once at the others. Voegler was still out cold. LaGrange, Strasser, and the two women stood perfectly still, as if they weren't exactly sure what to do. Tanaka watched Ki, and there was no mistaking the fury in his eyes.

"That was a damn fool thing to do," Cooper said flatly. "Not smart at all, Mark."

"You saw it? You know what happened?"

"I saw it."

"Then you tell *me* what the hell's going on here," Ki

said bluntly. "He was going to let Wolf Voegler beat that man to death. Is that part of your training program?"

"You don't know that he'd let it go that far."

"Come on. I'm not a fool, mister."

Cooper's easy smile vanished. "You *work* here, fella," he flared. "You are not running the show. That's our job, not yours!"

"Fine," said Ki. "You're right and I'm wrong. If I see a member of my group getting killed, it's all right, as long as there's an instructor in charge."

"I didn't say that, damn it." He bit his lip and glared straight ahead. "It's a hell of a time for somethin' like this to happen," he muttered. "One hell of a time."

"Yeah? Why's that?"

"What?" Cooper looked blank, as if he'd forgotten Ki was there. "Nothing," he said shortly. "Forget it."

Ki looked curiously at Cooper. He was certain the man had spoken before he thought. His fight with Tanaka and Wolf Voegler couldn't be all that important, unless it had some bearing on something bigger—something that Dan Cooper knew and he didn't.

Cooper stalked off, leaving Ki behind. Kahr's big cabin was just ahead through the trees. Cooper stopped abruptly, cursed under his breath, and turned to Ki.

"Go on," he said shortly. "Go back to your cabin and stay. I'll talk to Kahr and see you later."

"All right. What's the problem?"

"Go on," Cooper said, the tight smile hiding his irritation. "Get back over the creek, Mark."

Ki shrugged, turned, and walked through the trees. When he was well out of sight he moved back quietly and peered through the foliage at the cabin. Cooper had quickened his pace, almost breaking into a run. Whatever it was, Ki knew it had nothing to do with him. Cooper had changed his mind the moment he spotted the two horses at Kahr's cabin. The mounts were covered with lather, nearly run to death. Whoever had ridden in, they'd been in a hell of a hurry to see Kahr.

Ki waited another moment, then made his way back down the path. Maybe Kahr's being busy was a piece of luck he shouldn't ignore. What he'd done was enough to get him shot. All Kahr had to do was tell Cooper, and that would be that. He stopped by the creek, thinking about his prospects for a possible escape. Find the end of the canyon and try to make it past the guards. It was better than sitting still and letting someone come to the cabin and put a bullet through his head. Just going back and waiting like a—

The branch snapped behind him and Ki jerked around fast. The man stepped from behind a boulder, the Winchester cradled in his arms.

"You got business over here, mister?"

Ki sucked in a breath. Christ, it was *him* again—of all the damn luck!

"Just going," Ki muttered, scratching his cheek and lowering his head to hide his face. "Heading back to my cabin."

"Yeah? Well, get on and do it. Don't be hangin' around here."

Ki nodded and turned away.

"Hey—*hold it!*"

Ki half turned, his fingers inching casually toward his Colt.

"Don't I know you?" the man said narrowly. "I seen you somewhere before."

"Sure you have," said Ki. "You brought me my supper last night."

"I don't mean that. I mean before. Somewhere else."

"Beats me. I don't remember you."

"Uh-huh." The dark eyes studied him intently. "All right," he muttered, "go on. It'll come to me."

Ki let out a breath and walked off. He could feel the cold muzzle of the rifle, itching a hole in his back.

Cooper came just before supper. He was alone, and Ki figured that was a good sign. "Kahr's going to forget what happened," he said absently. "It wasn't exactly all your fault. That doesn't mean you're off the hook, Mark. We don't want any more trouble. I've talked to Tanaka and Voegler. They're not going to push it any further, and neither are you."

"Fine with me," said Ki. Cooper nodded, the subject clearly closed. They walked together to the lodge. Dan Cooper was his smiling, easygoing self once more. He told Ki a funny story about something that had happened to a girl in Group Five. Ki half listened, smiling in all the right places. He didn't believe Cooper for a minute. Kahr was a stiff-necked Prussian, a stickler for his rules. If he was breaking those rules, he had a reason. Damn it, he'd torn up Voegler and pulled a gun on an instructor, and they weren't even slapping his wrist! Ki was more anxious than relieved. The other boot was bound to fall, and he didn't want it falling on him.

Supper with Group Three passed in silence. There was a moment of surprise when he appeared, as if they hadn't expected to see him again alive. LaGrange wasn't there. Voegler sported a red, ugly bruise on his face. He gave Ki a killing look and bent to his plate. Cindy and Kurt Strasser ignored him completely. Only Ellie Slate showed any emotion. She stared openly at Ki, the flesh drawn tight across her cheeks. He wide-set eyes were bright with fear, like those of a rabbit ready to jump. Finally she dropped her cup with a clatter, then rose and fled quickly from the lodge. Ki hurried after her, caught her a short distance down the path, and grabbed her arm. Ellie gasped and jerked away.

"Mark, please!" she said hoarsely. "Not now. I—I don't want to talk!"

"Fine," he told her. "Just tell me what's wrong. You ran out of there like a—"

"What's *wrong?*" She gave him a nervous little laugh. "My God, how can you ask that, after what happened this afternoon? I thought—I didn't know what they'd do to you!"

"I appreciate the thought, Ellie, but that's not it. If you're so relieved to see me, what's the hurry? Come on, Ellie, it's something else. I'd just like to hear what it is."

She laughed again. "I don't know what you're talking about."

"Ellie—"

"Mark, I *can't!*"

She started off and he held her. "I need to talk to you now. There are some things I need to know. It doesn't figure, Kahr just letting me off like that."

"I wouldn't complain if I were you," she said shortly. "People sometimes just . . . disappear in this place."

"I don't doubt that. And that's what's got me thinking. That and the way Dan Cooper acted, when he took me up to Kahr's. There were some horses there, run half to death.

Till Dan Cooper saw them, he was hauling me up on the carpet."

Ellie backed off. "Mark, I don't want to hear any of this."

"Well, you're going to, damn it," he said crossly. "I can't trust anyone else."

"You can't trust *me*, either," she said quickly. "And I can't trust you. We're all on our own here. Don't you know that yet?"

"We don't have to be, Ellie. Not you and me."

Ellie blinked. "Oh yes. *Especially* you and me." She jerked out of his grasp and vanished through the trees. Ki watched, then let her go. She knew something, he was dead certain of that. The instant he'd seen her at the table, he was sure. And whatever it was, it had scared her out of her wits. When he'd mentioned Dan Cooper and the horses at Kahr's cabin...

Whatever it was, he wouldn't find out from Ellie Slate. Or anyone else in the damn camp. As Jessie was fond of saying, he'd chewed off more than he could spit. He'd fooled them all completely, sneaked right inside the operation, like a chicken sneaking up on a fox. Now all he had to do was keep the fox from having him for supper.

Night was closing in as he made his way down the path to his cabin. Darkness came quickly in the canyon, leaving a ribbon of lighter shadow overhead. He passed two cabins with dim light showing through their windows. A woman's pleasant laughter came from the second. He listened to the gurgling of the creek to his left. Clouds parted overhead and let moonlight dapple the ground through the branches. Ki stopped dead as a thick-trunked maple suddenly split in two shadows.

*"Don't,"* the voice hissed. *"Don't try it, you bastard!"*

Ki's hand froze above his weapon. The man moved a step closer, the rifle steady in his grip.

"I knew it'd come to me," the man rasped. "And by God, it did. You wasn't wearin' chinwhiskers then, but it was you. On the *Texas Star* on the Red River!"

"I've never been on the Red," Ki said quietly. "Afraid you've got the wrong man."

*"Shut up!"* the man raged. "You ruint me, mister, broke

91

me up bad. Shit—takin' up for a nigger that didn't want a whipping. I'm going to kill you for that."

"You don't figure anyone'll hear?"

"Don't give a damn if they do. Now get on down by the creek. *Move!*"

Ki backed off, watching the man's dark eyes, the way he held the rifle. He'd have to try, have to take the chance.

"I never saw you before," said Ki, "but I don't guess you want to listen. Look—I've got about five hundred dollars. It's buried in a sack by my cabin."

"Don't want your goddamn money."

"Five hundred can buy a man a lot of pleasure."

"I told you, mister, I'm going to kill you!"

"I could give you the money," Ki went on, "and maybe you'd change your mind. You wouldn't have to, of course. You could shoot me after that."

The man laughed in his throat. "An' give you a chance to pull somethin', right?"

"Look, now—"

"You goddamn son of a bitch. You hurt me *bad!*" He stopped suddenly, jerking the rifle up fast. Ki moved, knowing he was a small part of a second too late. He threw himself aside, waiting for the quick explosion of pain. Sharp brush tore at his legs and he came to his knees in a crouch, wondering what was keeping the bullet, what the hell he was doing alive. He looked up and saw the man's face, a moon with a hole for a mouth, eyes like pebbles under water. The mouth opened and closed with no sound, and then the head dropped away and Ki saw Peter LaGrange in its place.

"Sorry," LaGrange said softly. "I knew he was tracking you, but I lost him for a minute."

Ki came to his feet. "Don't apologize," he said shakily. "Looks to me like you're right on time. And thanks. I owe you."

"Oh no." LaGrange shook his head. "Other way around. It's me owes you, remember?" Ki saw that his mouth and the side of his face were puffed and swollen from Voegler's fists. "This fella an old friend of yours, or what?"

"Remembers me from somewhere he shouldn't."

LaGrange nodded understanding. "There's a deep hole past the creek. Near the canyon wall. Not far, but you'll have to carry him. I threw a rock down once and never heard it hit." He gave Ki a shy grin. "They won't even smell him for a year."

"That ought to be enough," said Ki. He hefted the dead weight on his shoulders. LaGrange picked up the rifle and led the way. Ki watched the gaunt shadow lope ahead. LaGrange was as clumsy as a day-old colt. He tripped over things, couldn't shoot worth a damn, and couldn't fight. At night, though . . .

A chill touched the back of Ki's neck. In spite of his rigid training, he hadn't seen the man, heard him, or sensed his presence. He was *there*, and then it was over. He'd seen the dead face and then LaGrange with his sad, apologetic eyes. And if the light hadn't hit LaGrange's oversized hands just right, he would have missed it, never seen the thin loop of black wire before it vanished.

*I hope he's got a talent better than shooting,* Ki thought. No wonder Ellie Slate had turned away without an answer!

He walked up the two plank steps of the cabin and opened the door and stepped inside. He stopped at once, backing out of the light, sensing the other presence and smelling the sharp, feral scent in the air. The girl laughed softly in her throat, slid off the bed like water, and came to him. The moon striped her naked flesh as her hands snaked quickly over his shoulders.

"I thought you'd got lost," Cindy whispered. "You and me haven't even had a chance to say hello."

"No. No, we haven't," said Ki. She pressed her body against him, the heat of her reaching him through his shirt. Her wanton animal smell assailed his senses.

"Well, we can sure fix that," she said softly. "Welcome to Group Three."

★

# Chapter 12

They stopped off at five in the evening, finding a young man and his wife in a small adobe house by the river. The man was gaunt and unsmiling, the woman heavy with child. They were scraping out a living raising goats no fatter than themselves, and the baby was nearly due in the heat of summer. The couple was more than willing to share their supper. Jessie left them ten dollars for their trouble, more hard coin than they'd likely seen in some time.

By seven they were on the trail again. Jessie tried to get the girl out of her mind. She was barely eighteen and already dried up like the land, hard days wiping the smile lines away.

"You can't change any of that," said Jeff, guessing her thoughts.

"Yes, I could," she said evenly.

"And everybody else?"

"No. Not everybody else."

They passed another farm after that, and then a small remount station. Jeff said the San Antonio–San Diego stage ran a few miles north of where they were, stopping at Van Horn Wells. The small station by the river served the line.

"You can bet Gaylord Brown's never used it," he said firmly. "Nothin' there but old codgers with time to talk."

Jeff paused several times to inspect a small farm or a collection of adobes off the road. Finally, with shadows growing lean over his shoulder, he paused and leaned out of the saddle and looked at the ground, then got off and squatted in the dirt. Glancing past Jessie, he peered down a narrow, rutted road that vanished over a rise to the north. Nodding to himself, he mounted up again and guided them off a ways, making a wide circle to the northwest.

94

"We'll go off some and come back. Might be nothing, but it's worth looking over."

"What did you see?" she asked.

"Too many wagons using a road that doesn't call for that much traffic. Might be a good reason and might not."

He kept to an arroyo that snaked off to the west, then stopped and crawled up the bank, bringing an old pair of army binoculars out of his saddlebag. A moment later he was back, a satisfied grin stretching his features. "It's a dirt-poor farm, raising chickens and cactus. 'Cept they've got a corral down in a hollow under some trees, with some real fine mules and good horses. That and a couple of fellas wandering around with rifles, doin' nothing. I think we've found Mr. Brown's first station."

"So what do we do now?" Jessie asked.

"We get out of here and get some sleep," Jeff told her. "In the morning we see what kind of tracks lead out."

At dawn they began a wide circle a mile out from the house and the corral, hoping their luck would hold and the wagon tracks would lead somewhere instead of going back to the road. If they did that, Jessie and Jeff would have to follow another day and try to find a second station.

They found the tracks moving south and slightly east, and a little later they had some luck they hadn't expected.

"They camped right here for the night," Jeff told her, sliding off his mount and walking carefully past the damped-out fire. Jessie joined him, and a moment later he called her over to look at the ground.

"There's four of them. Two men in boots. And for some reason, two folks that went barefoot most of the time. Likely one of 'em is a woman or a girl."

"Barefoot?" Jessie came suddenly alert. "I don't know about any girl, but Ki would take off his boots if he got the chance."

"That's his name, huh?" Jeff said curiously. "You know you haven't mentioned it before."

"I'm sorry," she told him. "Yes, it's Ki. He's half Japanese. Show me more of those prints, Jeff. I've got to be sure."

He studied the ground and nodded, and Jessie went to her knees. It was a good, deep print, solid in dusty soil that hadn't been disturbed, and was almost as clear as if it had been made in plaster. She looked at the high arch, the toes, and the outer edge of the foot, which was callused and slightly misshapen. She would have known the print anywhere; it was unmistakably Ki's. There were other prints as well, some of them smaller and more delicate. *Who could it be?* she wondered.

"Yes," she told Jeff, "one of the barefooted ones is Ki. I don't know about the other one, though."

"There's other prints too," Jeff said. "Six mules hauling a big freightwagon. But the wagon isn't carrying any load to speak of at all."

"It's them, Jeff. It's got to be."

He shrugged. "I reckon we'll find out soon."

They rode roughly east, veering farther north with every mile, leaving the Rio Grande far behind. The Finlay Mountains lay to the left, Esperanza and the ruins of Fort Quitman to the south. Jessie counted days in her head, wondering where Ki might be, if he was really with the wagon. He'd come to see her Monday night and returned to Paso del Norte. She'd waited three full days, and gone after him across the river on Friday. She and Jeff had left at dawn the next day. It was Sunday now, which meant she hadn't seen him in a week. If he'd left, say, the very next day after he'd seen her, he was six days ahead. Her stomach tightened in a knot at the thought. Anything could happen in six days. She shouldn't have waited that long to cross the river!

Toward late afternoon, Jeff raised his hand and slid out of the saddle. "They camped here the second night," he told her.

"Can you tell how far they're ahead?"

"Couple of days. Maybe more." He squinted toward the north. "Where they're headed is what's bothering me, Jessie. It's pretty rough country. Not much there except Mescalero Apaches. Or what's left of 'em. We're nearly into the Sierra Diablo. You ever seen it?"

"No. But I know what it is."

"Uh-huh. Well, they don't call it the Devil's Mountains for nothing. Most of it's as dry and hot as a furnace. Not a goddamn drop of water around—unless a flash flood hits it and carries off everything in sight. Just dust and rattlers and rock. Some nicer ground if you get high up, but pure hell down below in the canyons. And that's where a wagon'd have to go. And there's worse when you get past that. Salt flats, until you hit the Guadalupe Mountains." He paused and looked at Jessie. "You still want to do it, I guess."

"If that's where they are, yes."

"All right. We'll try 'er. But we got to take on some extra water. I've been here, and in places like it before. In Mexico and out toward California. It gets kinda dry after the first half-mile in the sun."

They found a lonely adobe just at dark, set in the middle of arid flats for no reason they could see. The old man who lived there carried a sawed-off American Arms twelve-gauge into the yard and looked as if he wouldn't mind using it on Jeff. Jeff kept his distance and bargained for water from the flat brick well. The old man watched while Jeff drew water, eyeing Jessie with rheumy eyes. He stood in the yard without moving, until the two were out of sight.

"What do you suppose he's doing out here?" asked Jessie.

"Probably isn't real fond of people."

"Then he picked the right spot, for certain," Jessie sighed.

"We can stop and camp somewhere, or go on," said Jeff. "Riding the mounts easy most of the night would get us through some of the Sierra Diablo. But then we'd have to face the salt flats in the day, or wait and try 'em the next night. Diablo's not that bad—not when you put it next to the flats this time of year. And we don't know for sure that's where the wagon's heading. I'd still guess the Guadalupes for a place to hole up. There's sure nothing east or west."

"Let's go and see, then," said Jessie. "Get as close as we can and get some rest."

"Fine by me," said Jeff. "We'll pick up the trail south of here and ride till we can't see the ruts."

Jeff picked a spot at the head of a shallow arroyo and hobbled the horses. He thought it best to bed down without a fire.

"I don't think the Mescaleros will bother us," he explained. "The army 'bout drove them to death ten years or so ago. There's still some around, but they won't likely cause us any trouble."

Jessie ate hard dried beef and bread and some dried apples they'd bought on the road south, and washed it all down with a swallow of water.

"Last big Apache flare-up," said Jeff, "about thirty of 'em hit the way station at Van Horn Wells, twenty, maybe twenty-five miles southeast of here. Set fire to some hay in the corral and boxed up the men inside all night."

"And that was ten years ago?" asked Jessie.

"No, that was *last* year."

Jessie gave him a look. "Those are the same Mescaleros that won't likely bother us, right?"

"I said they were pretty much drove off," he said dryly. "Didn't say they were dead."

Jessie sat in silence, then stood and walked up the side of the arroyo. The moon turned the limestone cliffs of the Sierra Diablo a pale and luminous white. The rocks seemed to shimmer and move as she watched. She tried not to think about Ki. Where was he? Was he in some kind of danger right now?

Turning away from the ghostly walls, she walked back down the arroyo and sat down against her saddle. Presently Jeff came back from checking the horses.

"Sit down, will you?" she said solemnly. "I want to talk."

Jeff sat, folding his arms over his knees.

"I've got some things to say. You haven't asked a lot of questions and I'm grateful. But I think you've got a right to know a few things before we go any farther."

"Figured you'd get to it if you wanted," said Jeff. "I'm getting paid good. You don't have to say a thing."

"Stop it," Jessie said crossly. "You're not a hired hand and you know it, so don't give me that."

Jeff grinned. "Go on. I'm listening."

Jessie began at the beginning, telling him briefly about the cartel and who they were, how they'd murdered her father and how she'd taken up the fight, with Ki's help. She told him about Vargas, and how the dying man had revealed what he knew about Gaylord Brown and the school for assassins. Finally she told them there was no doubt at all that the cartel's killers had already murdered a number of prominent men.

For a moment Jeff stared past her into the dark. "By God, lady." He gave a low whistle through his teeth. "You don't spend a lot of time knitting in your rocker, do you?"

"No. Not a lot," Jessie said dryly.

"And that's where you think we're going. Ki's got himself shipped off to this killers' camp."

"I don't doubt it at all, Jeff. I know him pretty well. It's what he'd try to do. Unless Brown found him out somehow and did away with him, he would have come back across the river to me. And I'm not even thinking about something happening to him. I just won't."

Jeff opened his canteen, took a swallow, and offered the canteen to Jessie. Jessie shook her head. "That's one reason you've got a right to know what we're doing," she said. "Another's this, Jeff. If the cartel's camp is really there, it's too much for us to handle. I'd like to get close enough to find it, but that's all. After that, we'll have to find some help."

"Uh-huh." Jeff nodded understanding. Even in the dark she could see him looking thoughtfully at his hands. "You're talking about the law."

"The law, and likely the army to boot. There's not much telling how many men they've got up there. Jeff—is El Rosario wanted north of the border, too?"

"I've, uh"—Jeff cleared his throat—"yeah, I've done a little work up here. Been a while, but the law's real good at remembering."

"Then we'll have to make sure you kind of disappear when the time comes."

"Hey, I'm stickin' as long as I need to," Jeff said firmly.

"I know that," she said gently. "I never doubted it at all."

Jeff was silent a long moment. He looked between his knees and made a circle in the sand with his fingers. "What do you think about me?" he asked abruptly. "I'd kinda like to know."

Jessie gave him a curious look. "Why, I think you're a good man, Jeff. A real good man."

Jeff's face clouded. "Christ, Jessie, don't play games with me now."

"I'm not. What makes you say that?"

"I'm an outlaw, lady. I make a livin' by stealing things. Robbing people. And that's what you call a real good man? Hell, forget it. You've got no reason to give me a straight answer. I don't have a right to ask for one, either."

Jessie sat up and grasped his hand. "Jeff, I *did* give you a straight answer. You don't know me very well or you wouldn't ask. I think you're a good man or I wouldn't say it. And no—I do *not* approve of robbing trains. I think it's a real poor excuse, making a living at other peoples' expense. And I don't think that grandmother of yours would like it much, either."

Even in the dark, she could see her words hit home.

"Yeah, that's the truth for certain."

"Jeff, I'm sorry."

"Don't need to be."

"Well, I am. I had no business saying that. You *are* a good man, damn it. I haven't seen El Rosario. I don't know him. I only know Jeffrey Diego Escobar. And I like *him* very much."

"I tried changing," he said soberly. "Worked on a ranch, then rode with a herd up north on the Goodnight Trail, clear to Cheyenne. Got so bored I damn near came out of my skin. Kept thinkin' how much easier it was to make thirty dollars in about a minute, instead of earning it in a month chasin' the rear end of a cow."

She laughed. "I can see your point." Without thinking, she stretched past his knees and kissed him lightly on the cheek. Jeff looked startled. Instead of moving back, Jessie stayed, her face only inches from his own. Jeff's hands gently cupped the back of her head, turning her face up to his.

"My God, Jessie," he said, "I didn't—"

"Neither did I," she whispered, and then his hands came to her cheeks, framing her face in a veil of strawberry hair. He brought her to him and she opened her lips to meet his touch. Her arms slid over his shoulders and he brought his hands to her waist. Together they slid to the ground, and Jessie looked up into his eyes.

"If the Mescalero Apaches happen by, we're going to be in big trouble," she said. "Anyway, I don't think we ought to talk any more about your career. I don't really want to know, and I don't think you really want to tell me."

"That's for sure," he said. "You got any suggestions as to what we might do instead?"

"If you don't know, mister, I sure can't—"

100

Jeff cut off her words with his mouth. It was a slow, easygoing kiss at the start, but neither of them intended to let it go at that. Jessie closed her eyes as his lips found the soft, pliant flesh at the corner of her mouth. Her lips parted slightly and the tip of her tongue flicked out to find him. Jeff took the offering and drew it gently between his lips. Jessie trembled and stirred against him. The kiss seemed to race through the length of her body, tingle in her breasts, and warm the secret place between her thighs. Jeff drew her closer, kissing the velvet lids of her eyes, the curve of her nose, the soft and downy spot at the base of her neck. Jessie relaxed in his arms with an easy sigh, turning the slender column of her neck to receive his kisses. His mouth found her throat and brushed gently past her chin. When he touched her lips again she let her mouth go slack, let his tongue taste every sweet hollow. She arched her neck beneath him, making her mouth a cup for him to drink. She felt his breath quicken, felt the hard muscles in his shoulders go taut. She let her fingers trail to the corded sinews of his arms. Her hand found the opening of his shirt. She pressed her palm hard against his chest, and felt the rapid throbbing of his heart.

At her touch, Jeff moaned deeply. Pulling suddenly away, he stared into her eyes.

"Well, what do you see there?" she asked softly.

"The finest-lookin' woman I ever hope to see," he said hoarsely.

"Oh, come on," she said. "Better than the girls at Miss Lorna's?"

Jeff flinched. "Damn, lady—you have to remember everything you hear?"

Jessie laughed at his expression, grasped a handful of dark hair in both hands, and brought his head down to her breasts. His lips found her nipples and kissed them through the fabric of her shirt. She felt his fingers tremble as he undid one button and then another, untilt the shirt lay open to her waist. He swallowed a breath and slipped his hands beneath the cloth. She raised her shoulders slightly off the ground and let him slide the garment down her arms.

Jeff wet his lips, marveling at the unblemished beauty of her breasts. His dark eyes devoured her with a hunger that brought a hot flush of color to her cheeks. She felt her nipples harden, swelling into taut little nubs beneath his gaze. She wanted the rough, callused surface of his fingers, the heat of his mouth against her flesh.

"Jeff, Jeff!" With a savage little cry, she grasped the swell of her breasts in her own hands, offering them up to his touch. A deep sigh of pleasure escaped his throat. His hands covered her own, squeezing the rosy peaks firmly together. He caressed the dimpled flesh around her nipples, drawing each pointy nub into his mouth. Jessie trembled with pleasure, twisting her body hard against him. His tongue was like a brand on her sensitive flesh. She arched her back, forcing her breasts deeper into his mouth.

Suddenly, Jeff's hand circled her slender waist and brought her bottom off the ground. His lips left her breasts to brush the satiny swell of her belly. His hands worked roughly at her belt, unbuckling it and tearing at the buttons of her jeans. She moved her hands to help him, sliding the tight fabric past her hips.

Jeff gave a quick cry of pleasure. Peeling the jeans down her legs, he jerked them free and tossed them aside.

"My God," he breathed, "if you aren't some kind of woman!"

"What kind do you figure I am?" Jessie whispered. She rested her elbows on the ground and tossed a thick tumble of hair over her shoulders. The motion veiled her face, leaving the full lips in shadow, the lazy green eyes in half-light. The moon broke for an instant through the clouds, painting her body with creamy light. Molten silver caressed her flesh, kissing every curve and hollow.

Jeff let his eyes wander boldly over her body. He stared at the full thrust of her breasts, the incredibly long legs, the soft patch of darkness between her thighs.

"You never did answer my question," Jessie teased. "What kind of woman do you think I am? You aren't *ever* going to find out by just looking."

"Lookin's not bad," Jeff told her, the words sticking dryly in his throat.

Jessie gave a mischievous laugh. "Lord, I hope it isn't *that* good."

Jeff didn't answer. He lowered his head slowly until his lips touched the thin line of down that trailed from her navel to the proud, silken mound below. His mouth brushed the soft feathery curls, the pale flesh of her thighs. Jessie groaned and planted her feet on the bare ground, arching her pelvis up to meet him. Jeff grasped the firm swell of her bottom, sat himself squarely between her legs, and raised her off the ground until the small of her back rested firmly against his belly.

Jessie squealed with pleasure and scissored her legs around his neck. Jeff held her waist and drew her close until his lips touched the moist and downy hollow. Jessie trembled at his touch, spread her arms on the earth, and clenched her fists. Jeff's eager kisses opened her like a flower, baring the delicate folds of flesh hiding below. His tongue probed gently over the warm and sensitive petals. The sweet taste of her arousal assailed his senses, heightened his desire, and hardened his rigid member even further.

Jessie's breath came in rapid little bursts. Her mouth went slack and her tongue darted frantically over her lips. She tossed her head rapidly from side to side, whipping luxuriant coils of hair across her face. Jeff's tongue probed deeper and deeper into her warm and silken walls, finding every honeyed corner, each soft and lovely delight. Bringing his hands between her legs, he parted the curly nest with his fingers, exposing the delicate shell-pink pearl to his lips. His tongue made a slow and lazy circle, stroking, teasing, caressing, but never touching.

Jessie shuddered uncontrollably at his touch. Her long legs tightened about his neck, trying to draw his kisses deeper, to grind him hard against her. Her hands snaked up to touch her breasts, found the swollen nipples, and circled them with her palms.

"Please, Jeff," she begged, her voice a rush of air between her teeth.

He flicked the tender petal with the tip of his tongue. Jessie's body jerked. He flicked it once more, and then again. Her slender figure writhed, aching for the pleasure he could bring her, the syrupy warmth that would surge through her loins at the whisper of his touch. Just once. Once more . . .

Jeff kissed her lightly and abruptly pulled away. Jessie gasped, her body arching in a trembling bow. His tongue circled the coral bud, flicked it rapidly back and forth. The storm churned within her, an agony of pain and pleasure.

She cried out, begging for sweet release, clenching her fists until the nails bit into her flesh. Suddenly, without warning, Jeff pressed his lips hard against her and drew the swollen pearl into his mouth.

Jessie screamed.

Her body went rigid as the whole world exploded between her legs. A sound like thunder coursed through her ears, the stars reeled drunkenly overhead. An instant before, she'd begged him to let her go, to take her over the edge. Now she pleaded with him to stop, to release her from the pleasure that surged like fire through every raw nerve in her body.

She was dimly aware that the earth had tilted again, lifted her up and tossed her on her belly. The sensitive points of her nipples pressed the ground. Pushing her hands against the earth, she brought herself shakily to her knees. Strong hands grasped her bottom and spread her legs. Jessie gave a startled cry of surprise. She felt the rough fabric of his denims against her hips, and an instant later the cloth sliding away, followed by the exciting touch of his flesh.

"My God, Jeff, I want you bad," she cried, "but you've just about pleasured me out. I'm—I'm nothing but a rag!"

He laughed and gripped her waist. "I'd bet a double eagle there's something left."

"Well, you'd be wrong. I can't even—oh God!"

Without warning, he grasped her hips and thrust his manhood deep inside her. Jessie shrieked and clawed at the ground. His first touch triggered the sensitive flesh once more. She screamed as her orgasm spasmed against his member. Her face contorted with a mixture of pain and pleasure. Jeff clutched her hips and slammed himself against her. Each stroke was an agony of delight. She squeezed her eyes shut, clawing blindly at the earth. Her body moved with a hunger all its own, thrusting up to meet him, urging him deeper and deeper. Once more a savage heat raced through her body. She gasped with surprise at this sensation; he'd drained her dry with his love, brought her to sweet release more times than she could remember. God, it couldn't be happening again—there was nothing left inside, nothing else to give!

She felt him swell inside her, and laughed with joy. His

104

body began to tremble, to harden with the passion that sang between them.

"Now," she shouted. "Now, Jeff—*yes!*"

She thrashed wildly against him, tasting salty sweat on the tip of her tongue. His member grew inside her until she was certain he'd split her apart. The velvet walls within her grasped him hard, stroking him ever closer to the edge. She felt his body stiffen, heard him throw back his head and howl as he loosed his warmth within her, one hot explosion following another, and then another. Her own high-pitched cry joined his, as a fresh wave of pleasure even greater than before swept through her loins and sent her reeling in its fury.

Her legs gave way and she fell limply to her belly. Jeff came to her and took her in his arms. Their bodies were slick with musky sweat. He drew her hard against him, and she wriggled with pleasure into the warm curve of his shoulder.

"That'll teach me," she whispered against his chest. "Give a fellow a friendly kiss on the cheek, and the next thing you know..." She looked into his eyes, shaking her head in wonder. "That was something else, Señor Jeffrey Diego Escobar. *Mucho* pleasure, *muy* good lovin', and—I don't know what all!"

Jeff laughed. "Your loving is a wonder, Jessie—but your Spanish is damned awful. I don't think I can stand it."

"Huh!" she gave him a pouty frown. "Fine thing to say to a lady you just turned inside out and likely emptied forever!"

"You aren't the only one drained and hung out to dry."

"I better not be." She touched his cheek and kissed him, watching him with half-closed eyes. "You know what, friend? You're going to have to get up and find us some blankets. Either that or love me all night to keep me warm. *I'm* not moving an inch."

Jeff groaned and sat up. "I'll get the blankets for now. We'll talk about that lovin' in a couple of hours."

"We'd better not," she said darkly.

He stood and walked shakily to their packs and brought the blankets back. "Listen," he said soberly, "I got to get a good night's sleep. I don't want you wakin' me up and pawin' me all over in the night. Wrappin' those long legs of yours around me and beggin' for pleasure."

"Will you shut up?" she said crossly. "Come here and keep me warm or I'll give you more trouble than you can handle."

He grinned and took her in his arms and pulled the blankets around them. "Sounds to me like something worth staying up to see."

"It is," she told him, moving her head into the hollow of his shoulder. "Too bad you're going to miss it."

# Chapter 13

The sky was the color of slate when Jessie woke and rubbed sleep from her eyes. Jeff was gone, the spot where he'd lain beside her still warm. She sat up and saw him down the gully, saddling the mounts. The horses were lighter shadow against the dark. Tossing the blankets aside, she slipped quickly into her clothes, shivering in the crisp morning air.

"You going to sleep all day or what?" Jeff said from behind her.

"Lord, what time is it?" she groaned.

He grinned and took her in his arms. Jessie nestled her head against his shoulder. The smell of sleep and the musky scent of their love were pleasant reminders of the night.

"Four, I guess, or thereabouts."

"Seems a lot closer to two. I'm *starved*, Jeff. I've got to have something to eat."

Jeff solemnly scanned the darkness. "Ought to be a cafe around her somewhere . . ."

"Real funny, friend." She stretched and walked to their packs and dug out the hard smoked beef and bread and the last of the dried apples. She wolfed down the food and took a long swallow of water, trying not to think about eggs and hot biscuits and coffee.

"You not eating?"

"I'll chew on some beef on the trail."

She caught the slight strain in his voice, nodded, and packed the rest of the food away. "You want us to get moving, right?"

"I think maybe we'd better."

"You worried about something?"

"Not worried," he said, "just cautious. This time of day

107

makes me itchy." He paused and looked at the sky. A thin strip of gray was edging the false dawn aside. Jessie gathered the blankets and rolled them tight. Before she closed her pack she found the ivory-handled derringer in her belongings and stuck it behind her buckle. Then, after hesitating a moment, she pulled a cartridge belt and holster out of the pack and strapped it around her waist, drew the revolver and checked the loads, and slipped the weapon back in the holster. Glancing up, she saw Jeff watching.

"That'a a fine-looking gun," he said. "Mind if I see it?"

Jessie gave him the pistol, and Jeff turned it over respectfully in his hands. It was a .38 Colt on a .44 frame, the metal burnished soft gray, the grips made of polished peachwood.

"That's a real special piece of work," said Jeff.

"It's very special to me," said Jessie. "My father had it made for me and taught me how to use it. Of all the things I have to remember him by, this means more to me than anything else."

"I can understand why."

Jessie shook her head. "I don't think you can. I'm not sure I do, either. Remembering him from a gun's the last thing he'd want me to do. Guns didn't have that kind of place in his life. He didn't like what they stood for—what they came to mean in this country." She looked at Jeff, then past him. "I think I'm carrying it 'cause it'll mean so much when I'm able to put it away. Does that make sense?"

"Makes a lot of sense to me," he said gently. He held her close a moment, then picked up her pack and blanket.

"Trouble is," Jeff said when they'd mounted up, "our timing's all wrong. We've got the salt flats just a couple of hours ahead. Should've kept on going last night and crossed over, except the horses needed a rest."

Jessie sighed. "Which means we're packed up now so we can ride a few miles and stop again. Hole up out of the sun and start off again tonight."

"That's about it. It's eatin' up time, but there's not much for it. It's maybe thirty, forty miles over the flats to the Guadalupe Mountains. I'd sure as hell hate to have a horse drop on us halfway."

The land held its breath a long moment, then the sun exploded with a fury over the high rim of the canyon. Shadow crept down the western wall, turning the wrinkled flesh of the Sierra Diablo brick-red. In an instant, hot winds sucked the cool night air from the canyon floor.

Jeff found the wagon tracks again, still headed north as he'd expected.

"You think they crossed over in the day?" asked Jessie.

"Not likely. Not if they had good sense." He squinted thoughtfully toward the north. There was rain on the far horizon, likely sweeping the peaks of the Guadalupes. "No one in that wagon could make it over the flats during the day. Not 'less they're hunkered in a tub of icewater."

"God, poor Ki," sighed Jessie.

"And the girl. If she's riding in there with him."

"Yes, the girl," Jessie mused. "I wonder who she is."

"Jessie..." Jeff rode close beside her. The brim of his Stetson darkened the upper half of his face. "Jessie, last night was something I'm not goin' to forget."

"Well, you'd better not!" she laughed.

"No, I mean it. You're a woman that—hell, you're a woman puts others in the shade. That's a fine thing to happen to a man. 'Least I guess it is. Makes it kinda rough on the next woman to come along."

"Well, if that's not a *man* talking!" Jessie exclaimed. "Already thinking about the next one, are you?"

"No, I—" Jeff colored, chewing his tongue. "Damn it, that isn't what I meant to say at all."

Jessie held back a smile and gave him a long, solemn look. "I got the perfect answer for your problem, mister. Whenever you get an itch, just keep thinking how good it was with me. You won't have to *bother* with lovin' again." She caught his expression, and exploded with laughter. "That was a fine thing you said, and I wasn't making light of it at all. And I'm *not* going to forget my lovely night with El Rosario himself."

Jeff cringed at the name. "You don't know El Rosario, remember? Now, if you'd like some more of Jeffrey Diego Escobar, I can sure arrange that. We've got a whole day to ourselves, soon as we find some decent shade."

Jessie's green eyes flashed. "You think I haven't thought on it, mister?"

"Lady," Jeff said dryly, "You look at me like that again,

I'll haul you off that horse right here."

"Not in the sun, you won't. You're good, but you're not that—Jeff, what is it?" She stopped as his eyes darted past her, staring intently to the south.

"Something's back there," he said darkly. "On our back-trail."

Jessie turned. Her fingers tightened on the reins as she spotted the low rise of dust on the canyon floor. "What do you think? Apaches?"

"I don't know, but they've seen us," said Jeff. "They damn sure know we're here. Come on, let's make tracks." He kicked his mount hard, cutting sharply to the left for the canyon walls. Jessie followed, jamming her Stetson over her eyes and bending to the saddle. The flat crack of a rifle roared through the canyon. A volley of fire followed the single shot. The riders were out of range, but Jessie didn't stop to look back. Jeff jerked his mount to a halt, shouted, and whipped the animal up a steep rocky draw. Jessie's horse protested as loose rock rattled under its hooves. Jeff stopped, slid to the ground, and tossed the reins to Jessie. She came out of the saddle and crouched low as lead whined off the rocks overhead. Jeff levered a shell into his rifle and went to his belly. The riders spotted him and fired, raising puffs of white dust around him. Jeff answered, squeezing off five measured shots. The mounts tried to bolt. Jessie dug in her heels and held on. Jeff motioned her up the trail, reloading as he went.

"Stopped two of 'em," he said tightly. "That'll slow the bastards down!"

"Who is it?" Jessie asked. "Mescaleros?"

"Hell, no. It's your friend from Paso del Norte. Gaylord Brown."

"My God!" Jessie gasped. "Are you sure?"

"It's him, all right. Maybe nine, ten other riders. Besides the ones I dropped."

"But how did he find us? We—"

"He had a little help. Those two *perritos*, Julio and Hernando. They're down there too. Christ, and I dug a bullet out of the bastard!"

Jessie moaned. "They knew I was looking for Brown. And they figured Brown'd like to know why."

Jeff shook his head and muttered, "I should've known

better. I shouldn't ever have let 'em go!"

"You didn't know my story then, Jeff. Besides, you couldn't just shoot them in cold blood."

"Yeah, right," he said sourly. "And what do you figure they're planning on doing to us?"

Jessie had no time to answer. A slug whined past her head and Jeff jerked her quickly to cover. "We got to get higher," he said. "Come on." He relieved her of the horses and handed her the rifle. Jessie covered their backs. The path led up past high, eroded limestone rocks, jagged teeth climbing the face of the cliff. Jessie saw the imprints of countless seashells, etched forever on a beach tilted crazily on its side. Jeff stopped between narrow slabs of stone.

"It's not good, but it's the best we're going to get," he said tightly. He slapped the horses with his hat and sent them running. The rocks formed a natural pen; the mounts were safe from stray bullets and wouldn't bolt. Jeff bent low and moved back to where he could see down the trail.

"They'll play hell gettin' to us," he said flatly. "But we're not goin' anywhere, either. Looks like we've ridden ourselves into a hole."

Jessie took his hand. "We've got a chance, Jeff. We couldn't have outridden them. You know that."

"Isn't exactly the kind of activity I had in mind for today," he growled.

"Jessie smiled. "I won't argue with that. You want some water?"

"Save it. We'll need it a lot more later, when those— Jessie, look out!"

Jessie went flat as two men suddenly appeared on the trail, levering their rifles rapidly and loosing a withering fire up the draw. Jeff's Winchester roared. The first man threw up his arms and fell away. The second man dove for cover, lead snapping at his heels. Gunmen opened up from the rocks below. Jeff emptied his rifle and turned and ran. Jessie covered his retreat. She caught a man in the open and sent him limping. Jeff rolled to safety, then leaned back and sucked in a breath. His face was covered with dust.

"Stupid goddamn trick, rushing in blind like that." He angrily thumbed shells into his rifle. "Nearly worked, too." He forced calm into his voice. "They wouldn't do that 'less they had something going, now would they?" He came to his feet, searching the canyon walls. "Watch it," he warned her, stabbing his barrel past her head. "Up there. Sure as hell, they're keeping us busy while they send someone up the back way!"

Jessie nodded, brought her rifle halfway to her shoulder, and studied the twisted spires. Heat shimmered off the walls and turned her perch into a furnace. Sweat stung her eyes, but she didn't dare wipe a sleeve across her face.

She could hear Jeff breathing behind her. A man called out. Another answered, farther away. She tried to pinpoint the sound. Below, past the curve in the trail. But the way sound bounced off the rocks—

The sudden blast of Jeff's rifle made her jump. A man howled in pain and Jeff fired again and again. Jessie blinked, then turned away for half a second. The man was nearly on her before she saw him, standing up boldly on the ridge above the horses, the shotgun twisting at his waist in her direction. Jessie fired when her rifle was halfway to her shoulder. The first shot chipped the stock of his gun, the second hit him squarely in the belly. His face contorted in pain. He leaned over the rim, turned head over heels, and dropped at her feet.

Jeff shouted, the words lost in a burst of fire. A man sprang up to her left, firing blindly with his pistol. Jessie squeezed off a shot. The man leaped at her and she jammed the rifle in his face. He knocked it aside with his arm and slammed her to the ground. Jessie gasped for breath, lashing out with both hands. The man hit her hard, snapping her head to one side. Tears of pain filled her eyes. She felt her knee catch between his legs and brought it up with all the strength she could muster. The man yelled and threw back his head. Jessie clawed for the .38, jammed it under his chin, and pulled the trigger. The man went slack, blood pouring from his nostrils and mouth. Jessie rolled free, came up in a crouch, and swept the gun in a half-circle.

"Jeff! Oh my God, *no!*" She ran to him and saw the hot stone under his waist dark with blood. Putting her hands under his chest, she turned him over. His face was white, all the color gone. A shadow fell over her shoulder. She half turned, saw the butt of the rifle coming, and shut her eyes against the pain . .

* * *

112

The water struck her face and filled her nose and mouth. Jessie choked and gasped for air. The man stood above her. When she opened her eyes, he tossed the canteen aside.

"Get her up," someone said harshly.

The man with the canteen obeyed. His hands clutched her roughly under her arms and lifted her limply to her feet. Jessie retched on his shirt. The man cursed and let her drop to her knees. A full canteen fell beside her. She cupped her hands and splashed her face, found her bandanna and ran it over her mouth.

"All right," the voice said. "Get up, Miss Starbuck. I have no more patience with you."

Jessie blinked. Through a veil of her own hair she saw brown lizard-skin boots, hand-tooled spurs. She felt the rock wall behind her, gripped it with her palms, and pulled herself erect. Her head swam dizzily. For a moment she was certain she'd vomit again. She swallowed hard and the nausea faded. The man's face swam into focus. He was tall, lean, in his late forties or early fifties, with silver hair, a full mustache, and weathered skin. He wore a black sombrero, a lemon-yellow shirt, and an ivory vest.

"I'm Gaylord Brown," the man told her. "We haven't met, but I know you."

Jessie didn't need the introduction. Ki had described the man well. "Where—where's Jeff?" the words stuck in her throat. "Is he—he's not—"

"Señor El Rosario is not hurt badly," Brown said impatiently. "Let's talk about *you*, Miss Starbuck."

Jessie gave a cautious sigh of relief. She saw they were back on the floor of the canyon. The high spires above offered a narrow band of shade. Men and horses mingled to her right. She casually tucked in her shirt, feeling for the derringer behind her belt.

Brown gave her a knowing smile and shook his head.

"It isn't there, Miss Starbuck. I understand you're a smart woman. I hope we don't have to go through this more than once. Those two enterprising young men over there came to me with a story about a very pretty woman who went to a great deal of trouble to hide her appearance. They described you well—your splendid figure, the color of your eyes and your hair. On a hunch, I showed them one of your pictures." His blue eyes narrowed in irritation. "It occurred to me then that if *you* were prowling around, that damned Japanese of yours was close by as well. And that's when I remembered the rather distinctive appearance of Mr. Villon." Brown's mouth tightened. "You've made a fool of me, lady. I don't appreciate that. I want some answers from you, and I want them now. How did you find us? What led you to me?" He grabbed her face with one hand, dug his fingers cruelly into her cheeks, and shook her hard. "How! Goddamn you, how did you know!"

"Go—go to hell, mister!" Jessie gasped.

Brown's features contorted in a fury, then just as quickly relaxed. "That is exactly where we're going, Miss Starbuck. Hell. Across the salt flats and the desert. Only we'll have water to drink, and you and your *bandido* will not."

"You wouldn't do that!"

"You know better," Brown laughed. "Your friend's hurt. He won't make it without water. Let me know if you change your mind. I—damn it, what is it?" He turned away, irritation crossing his features. The two men approached, hats held in their hands. Julio and Hernando looked at Brown, then glanced in Jessie's direction.

"We wish to pay our respects to the *señorita*," Julio said, grinning. *"Buenos dias,* pretty lady." Hernando spat in her direction.

"All right, you've said it," Brown told them. "Now leave us alone."

"Señor," Hernando said politely, "we have done as we promised. She is the one, *sí?* You said there would be *dinero* for this. We are in no great hurry, of course."

"No," Julio added quickly. "At your pleasure, Señor."

Brown's expression didn't change. "Francisco," he said over his shoulder. "These gentlemen were promised a reward. See that they receive it, *por favor."*

*"Sí,* as you wish." The tall Mexican nodded courteously to Hernando and Julio, motioning them to follow. Jessie watched as he led them a few yards away. "Wait here, Señores. Please."

Julio and Hernando grinned. Francisco took three steps, turned, drew a long-barreled Colt, and aimed it carefully at Julio's head.

*"Señor, no!"* Julio's face went slack. Francisco fired,

moved the pistol a few inches to the left, and fired again.

Jessie raised a hand to cover her mouth.

Brown smiled. "Now we have two extra horses for our journey, and two more rations of water." He touched the brim of his sombrero. "I have things to do, if you'll excuse me. Let Francisco know if you get thirsty, Señorita..."

# Chapter 14

Ki was awake the instant the man stepped heavily onto the porch. He slid to the floor and crouched by the bed, his Colt aimed at the center of the door.

The man knocked loudly on the panel. "You in there, Villon?"

"What is it?" Ki demanded. "What do you want?"

"Get up and get dressed. Get your stuff packed."

*Get packed?* "Uh—what for?" asked Ki. "Damn, what time is it?"

"Four in the morning," the man said irritably, "and how the hell do I know what for? Come on, mister. You're holdin' up the parade."

Ki cursed under his breath, found a match, and lit the kerosene lamp. It took only moments to dress and toss his few belongings in the valise. Where was he going? he wondered. Hell, he hadn't been here a full two days! Whatever was going on, he didn't like it. Maybe there *wasn't* any trip—maybe Wilhelm Kahr had changed his mind and decided to make an example of him to the others. Maybe they'd found the body he and LaGrange had dumped in the hole . . .

Ki shrugged the thoughts aside and checked the cabin once more for his belongings. The strong animal scent of Cindy Dunne clung to his body like a second skin. The smell stirred his senses, nearly bringing him erect once more. By God, the girl was amazing—as close to mating with a she-cat as he ever cared to experience. Cindy only laughed at soft kisses and gentle caresses. Her hunger was closer to pain than to pleasure—a quick, brutal coupling more like two-way rape than making love. She stirred strange things in a man, hinted at desires that made Ki uneasy. It wouldn't be hard to go over the edge, to give her the things she wanted. There was a savage, elemental nature in every man, things he didn't care to bring too close to the surface.

Outside, Ki's guide led him through the darkness past the creek. He saw at once that they weren't the only ones up and about. Lighted torches flickered through the trees, and men called out to one another.

"What's up?" Ki asked. "What's going on?"

"None of my business," the man said shortly. "And none of yours, either."

The path was one he remembered. In a moment he saw the familiar bulk of the wagon that had brought them to camp. "Damn," he muttered half to himself. "Not that thing again!"

The guide shot him a nasty grin. "Good luck, fella—wherever it is you're going." He nodded and turned back up the path.

Dan Cooper stepped out of shadow, Ellie Slate behind him. Ki glanced at the girl, saw the strain and tension in her features.

"Mark, we've got a job for you," said Cooper. "Time to earn your pay." He wasted no time in greetings. "Ellie here's in charge. You'll do exactly what she says. I need to know right now if you've got any problem with that."

"You say she's running the show, that's the way it'll be," said Ki. "What's this all about?"

Cooper shook his head. "Ellie will tell you all you need to know—when you need to know it." He offered his hand and gave Ki a hurried smile. "This is big, Mark, very big, I'll tell you that much. We're counting on you a lot." He turned and glanced at Ellie. "You ready?"

"Let's go." She edged past the two without looking. Ki followed her into the wagon, and the door shut firmly behind them. The wagon began to roll. Ki gripped the edge of his cot. For an instant he had the peculiar feeling they'd never really stopped at the cartel's camp.

"I'll do the lamp," he said. "Get a little light in here."

"No."

"What?"

"I said *no*, Mark. I don't *want* the lantern."

"All right. Suit yourself."

In a moment a match flared in her corner, briefly lighting

117

up the wagon. He saw her face for an instant as she drew on a slim cheroot.

"I get the idea you don't much care for talking."

"That's right."

"Any reason?"

"*My* reasons," she said sharply. "That good enough?"

"No, damn it, it's not." Ki leaned forward in the dark. "I've got questions needing answers. You're the only one I can ask."

She gave him a bitter little laugh. "That's what bothers you, now, isn't it?"

"What is?"

"That *I'm* the one. You don't like taking orders from a woman."

"My God," he said tightly, "I'm worried about working with you, lady—but it doesn't have anything to do with you being a woman. It has to do with me putting my life on the line for something I don't know anything about, and you being so scared out of your wits you're likely to get us both killed."

Ellie gasped. "Damn you, what are you talking about?" she flared. "You've got no right to—"

"Wait, hold it!" Ki snapped. "Just hold it right there." He stood, gripped the swaying sides of the wagon, and found the kerosene lamp on the wall. He struck a match and lit it, turning the wick up high. Ellie's chin stuck out in defiance, the wideset eyes narrowed in anger.

"Just listen to me, Ellie. Last night after supper you were wound up tight as a drum. It didn't get better when I told you about those horses up at Kahr's, and that Cooper was acting funny. It scared hell out of you 'cause you already *knew* something was up. I figure this hurry-up trip's got a whole lot to do with whoever rode in and set Kahr's tail on fire. Ellie, look—" He let out a breath, releasing the edge of anger in his voice. "Ellie, if what we're getting into's got you worried, I've got an idea I'm not going to like it much myself. Now, do you blame me for that?"

"No, I—all *right*, Mark!" She clamped her lips firmly together. "I know some of it, yes. Dan Cooper said we might have to move a little faster than we'd figured." She stared at the floor of the wagon. "He wasn't supposed to, but we used to be...closer than we are now." Her eyes

118

came up in a challenge. "Don't ask me anything more. That's all you're going to get."

Ki pressed on. "That's some of it, but it doesn't tell me *why* you're not happy about where we're going."

She looked at him with no expression at all. "We're going to *kill* somebody, Mark. What did you think we were going to do?" The pale blue eyes were hard as glass.

"Hell, I already knew it was something like that."

"No. It's not 'something like that.' It's a killing," she said coldly. "We are going to 'take the target out of action,' as Kahr puts it. Doesn't bother you, does it? You've done it before, I imagine."

"When I had to, yes."

Ellie shook her head. "That's not what this is about. You won't kill this man out of anger. He won't get drunk and draw a gun. You'll simply *murder* him, Mark, as quickly and cleanly as you can, and get away to spend your pay."

"You're not telling me anything new."

"Are you sure? Are you?" Her words exploded in a hollow burst of laughter, so quick and unexpected that Ki started. "Because *I'm* not, Mark. I'm not sure you know at all. I don't think I'm the one we need to worry about here. I think it might be you!"

"Well, you're wrong," Ki told her.

"Good," she said sourly. "That is such a load off my mind." She stood, cupped her hand around the lamp, and plunged the wagon into darkness.

Ki let out a breath, stretched out on the cot, and stared at the ceiling, waiting for the dawn. She hadn't answered his question, merely turned it around and used it against him. All he could do was stick with her, and learn what he could about who they were going to kill.

He knew he was setting the thing aside, pushing it out of his mind so he wouldn't have to face it. He couldn't simply let Ellie go. She was a killer, a cartel assassin, the same as Voegler and Strasser and the rest. When he learned who they were after, he'd turn her over to the law. There was nothing else to do. Take her in, and get help backtracking the trail to the camp before Kahr and his people knew something was up.

That, and get a bunch of telegrams off to Jessie. He shook his head at the thought. He hoped she'd had the sense to stay put and not do something rash when he didn't show. She'd be madder than hell, he knew, but there was nothing he could do about that.

At noon, a long eight hours after they'd boarded the wagon in camp, the drivers pulled to a halt for a change of teams. The doors opened on a shallow arroyo. There was nothing at all to see. Bone-dry dirt and prickly pear cactus. They were out of the mountains, in the hot middle of nowhere again.

Ellie wouldn't talk, and Ki didn't bother to try. When the wagon rolled again, he turned his face to the wall and went to sleep. He woke with a start, covered with sweat. Sitting up, he saw that Ellie was asleep. The chemise was pulled up about her thigh, baring her lovely legs and a promising patch of shadow.

For some reason it suddenly occurred to him why the men in camp were out scouring the woods before dawn. They'd finally missed the man that Peter LaGrange had strangled.

While Ki's wagon stopped for the midday meal, a line of riders stretched across the harsh, arid flats some fifty miles to the southwest. Jessie rode directly behind the horse that dragged Jeff on a pole-and-blanket travois that scratched two dusty lines in the parched earth. The man named Francisco rode the horse that carried Jeff. Now and then he turned in the saddle and grinned at Jessie.

Jessie shut her eyes and let her horse follow the others on its own. The sun's reflection off the searing earth burned through her eyelids. Her face was flushed with heat, her lips parched and dry. Opening her eyes to wipe away the dust and stinging salt, she squinted past the flats to the north. The landscape shimmered with heat. A dust devil snaked across their path. The sliced-off tops of far peaks hung crazily upside down. For a moment the inverted ghost of a mountain danced on the horizon, then abruptly disappeared. She wondered where the range might be, or if she'd really seen it at all.

She'd given in quickly to Brown's threats, even before they started over the flats. She could do without water for a while, but Jeff couldn't. It was senseless to make him suffer. There was nothing she needed to hide, no one she had to protect. Brown knew about Ki, and Miguel Vargas was dead.

Brown seemed satisfied with her answer. Something had happened to Vargas, and now he knew what it was. And who else had she told, Brown wanted to know. No one, Jessie answered. Brown didn't believe her, but didn't push her further.

*That's part of the reason I'm still alive,* she told herself. *He's not real sure, and he has to know.*

The rest of it, the other part, was plain enough. She'd seen it in Brown's eyes. He'd made a bad mistake with Ki, a mistake that could damage or destroy the operation. Now, though, he had a card to play that might save his neck with his cartel masters. He had Jessica Starbuck herself.

Ki woke with a start when the wagon came to a halt. The rear door opened and he stepped outside to breathe the cool night air. The sky was overcast, but he figured it was midnight or maybe later. They'd been rolling since four that morning, twenty hours cooped up in the wagon, breathing the same stale air over and over.

Ellie joined him in a moment, wearing denims and a loose cotton shirt. She slipped past him to talk to the driver. Ki stretched and walked around to work the stiffness out of his bones, then retreated to the wagon to clean up. When he returned, thick steaks sizzled in a skillet. There'd been no stops for supper, and the tantalizing smell assailed his senses. Ellie was standing past the fire, looking out into the night. The clouds had scudded away, and the sky was full of stars.

"Real pretty, isn't it?" said Ki. "Even a good breeze coming in from the east."

"Yes, it's nice," she said without turning.

"Ellie, listen—"

"Wait a minute, Mark." Ellie turned to face him. The soft light of the stars made her features more breathtaking than ever. "Let me say it—I'm supposed to be running this show, and it's my place to do it. We both said things we shouldn't—things we should've kept to ourselves. There's

121

no use goin' over it again. We've got to work together. I need you and you need me. It's over, all right? Let's put it all behind us."

"Fine," Ki told her, "I'm for it."

"Good." Ellie granted him a smile. "Let's get some of that steak." She turned and walked back to the fire and Ki followed. He let out a breath between his teeth. If she wanted to pretend, he'd go along. Her eyes, though, told him that nothing at all was settled. The barrier between them was more impenetrable than ever.

He woke at the sounds and sat up. The stars had shifted overhead, and it was still a good hour till dawn. There were two more men in camp. They stood by one of the drivers and talked. The other driver started a fire and got fresh coffee going. Ki saw the two riders' mounts and, past them, four more horses, and a fifth outfitted with heavy packs of supplies.

Nearby, Ellie Slate stirred, sat up, and stretched. She looked at the newcomers and turned to Ki. "Morning. You ready for some coffee?"

"Yeah, I reckon." He nodded toward the wagon. "Guess you know we've got company."

"Uh-huh, I saw 'em." She said nothing more, and went to find cups by the fire. Ki stood and joined her. Without a word, the two new riders mounted up and headed north, leaving the five horses behind. Moments later a driver brought up the mules and hitched them to the wagon. One of the men waved, and the wagon started off slowly to the south.

Ki watched, sipping his scalding coffee. "I figure that pretty soon you're going to tell me what's happening," he said flatly.

"We're on our own," said Ellie. "We're through with the wagon."

"I can see that. What else?"

Ellie motioned him to the fire and Ki sat down beside her. She pulled a folded map from her pocket and spread it on the ground. "We're right here," she said, tapping the map with a forefinger. "In the Tularosa Valley. We're in New Mexico Territory now, Mark. The Sacramento Mountains are right behind us, the San Andres Range up ahead. We're on a place called the White Sands."

"And we're going exactly where?"

"Northwest. Past the San Andres, over the Jornada del Muerto desert. It's not a real nice place, but no worse than the badlands we passed going to camp. Jornada del Muerto means—"

"I know what it means," Ki said solemnly. "'Dead man's journey.' I've been there once. What are we going to a place like *that* for?"

Ellie raised her eyes. "Didn't say we were going there, did I? I said we had to pass it."

"All right. Just asking."

"You know the rules," she said calmly. "When you need to know more, I'll tell you. Come on, let's put some miles behind us before daylight. We've got a lot of bad country to cross." She stood and walked to the horses, leaving him to empty the coffeepot over the fire. He thought about the country past the mountains and the Jornada del Muerto. The Rio Grande curved up from El Paso and the border. To the west was the Continental Divide and wild country. To the north, up the river, was the old settlement of Albuquerque, and the new town growing around it. Past that, Santa Fe. Ki couldn't figure what the cartel would want in that godforsaken country. There wasn't anything there except scorpions, dirt-poor Indians, and rattlers.

When Jeff turned over and groaned, Jessie slid quickly off the bed and turned up the lamp. She held the back of his head while he eagerly grasped the tin cup of water and brought it to his lips.

"Hey, that's enough for now," she said gently, drawing the cup away. "You can have some more later."

Jeff lay back and let out a breath. "This is a dumb question, I guess, but where the hell are we? Last I remember—"

"It's a cabin in the cartel's camp," she explained. "We got here late in the afternoon. The camp's in a high-walled canyon. It's the Guadalupes, Jeff, like you figured. Either just barely in Texas or right over the border in New Mexico Territory."

Jeff frowned. "Late in the afternoon. What time is it now?"

"Nearly morning," Jessie sighed. "You slept clear through.

A man looked at your side and cleaned it up. I watched him bind your wound. It's not bad, but you're going to be stiff. How do you feel?"

"Stiff," Jeff replied. He gritted his teeth, and forced himself to sit and place his feet on the floor. "Christ, Jessie." He ran a hand across his face. "Anything to eat in here?"

"I saved you some cornbread and beans from last night." She got up and brought him a plate. Jeff wolfed it down and finished off the cup of water. When she took the plate, he stood, making himself walk to the window.

"You're right," he said, "it's pretty close to morning. Just the one guard outside?"

Jessie almost laughed. "Right. *Just* one. Take him, and all we've got to do is get past the rest. Jeff, they walked me here through the camp. With just the people I saw, they've got a small army in this place!"

"'Bout what you figured, isn't it?" He stopped and turned to face her. "You don't know about Ki? They haven't told you anything yet?"

Jessie leaned against the wall and closed her eyes. "When we got to the camp," she said calmly, "Gaylord Brown told them what to do with us, then disappeared real fast. You can guess why. He wanted to let them know about Ki, so they could—" Her voice broke, and Jeff came and held her in his arms. Jessie buried her face in his shoulder. She'd been holding back the tears all night, and now she let everything inside her break loose.

"Hey, now, you don't know that they've done anything to him," Jeff soothed her. "You don't know that at all."

Jessie didn't answer. Jeff knew his words were hollow, that they had no meaning at all. If Ki was here, he was dead for certain, and Jessie knew it. He was dead, unless Brown intended to save him, and shoot all three of them at once.

They came for them at dawn, two men with rifles and a third who looked them over curiously, but didn't speak. They led Jessie and Jeff through a thick forest of maple, over a creek lined with cottonwood and willow. The creek was full of immense boulders, stones swept down by the river that had carved the deep canyon centuries before. Jessie saw the strain in Jeff's features. The walk was hurting his side, draining his strength, but he hid his discomfort from the guards as best he could.

The cabin was set well back from the creek, nearly hidden in a thick stand of pines. Brown was waiting on the porch. Beside him stood a tall, middle-aged man with broad shoulders, muscular arms, and a trim, narrow waist. His features were angles and planes, hard stone cut with a chisel. As Jessie approached, he stepped off the porch and gave her a chilling smile.

"I am Wilhelm Kahr, Fräulein Starbuck." He offered a mocking bow. "I am sure there is no need to waste time on pleasantries. You know who I am, and who I represent. And we certainly know you well."

"Yes," Jessie said evenly, "I know who you are."

Kahr looked quickly at Jeff, the jade-green eyes dismissing him with a glance. "I won't keep you in suspense. You are anxious to know about your friend, *nein?*" The sharp features relaxed into a smile. "The man Ki is still alive. He is unharmed, I assure you."

Jessie didn't try to hide her relief. "Where is he? Will I be allowed to see him?"

"Unfortunately, that won't be possible at the moment," Kahr said dryly. He looked at Brown without expression. Brown flushed and stared at his boots. "He left our camp early yesterday morning, with one of the best graduates of our school. He was given a very important assignment. Interesting, yes? Of all the people I could have sent on this particular task . . ." He shook his head and sighed, as if the irony of the situation truly amused him. "Mr. Cooper," he said without taking his eyes off Jessie, "finish this business, will you? I cannot tolerate it longer."

"Yes sir, Mr. Kahr."

Jessie sucked in a breath as the man named Cooper suddenly drew a pistol from his belt. *My God, he's going to do it now—right here!* She clutched Jeff's arm and pressed against him. Her eyes widened in surprise as Cooper turned and leveled the Colt at Gaylord Brown.

Brown paled and turned on Kahr. "Jesus—wh-what the hell is this!" he blurted.

"You made a mistake," Kahr said flatly. " A very bad mistake, Gaylord. "You have put us in grave danger."

Brown looked stricken. "You—you said—goddamn it,

125

Kahr, I found out in time, didn't I? I brought you the woman!"

Kahr turned on him, eyes blazing with sudden fury. "You damned fool! It was an *accident!* You did nothing! The two Mexicans found the woman!"

"Kahr, listen . . ." Brown's mouth quivered.

"Take off your gunbelt and drop it, Mr. Brown," Cooper said politely. "Please, sir, do it." Brown obeyed, tears already streaking his cheeks. "Now. Out of your clothes."

"Wh-what?" Brown looked at Cooper and blinked.

"Just do it," Cooper said calmly.

Brown set his black sombrero with its bright silver conchos on the ground, took off his coat and vest and creamy silken shirt, and laid them beside his hat. Sitting on the steps of the cabin, he pulled off his lizard-skin boots and then his trousers, folding the pants neatly over the boots. He stood then, in his long-handled white underwear. Tears clouded his eyes, and he sobbed deep in his throat.

"All of it," Cooper said quietly. "The longjohns too."

Brown nodded in resignation, stripped off the underwear, and stood naked, the white flesh of his body in sharp contrast to the weathered texture of his face.

For the first time, Wilhelm Kahr turned and faced him. "You will go down to the creek," he said calmly. "A man there will give you a pair of moccasins for your feet. Moccasins and a knife. You have three hours. No one will try to stop you. Only the one man."

"Who's coming after me?" Brown asked dully.

"He is," said Kahr. He nodded, and Brown turned to the grove of trees beside the house. Jessie saw an enormous Japanese standing among the pines. His hair was tied in a knot atop his head. He stood with his arms folded, watching the others without expression.

"Oh Christ!" Brown laughed behind his tears. "Why don't you just get it over with now, goddamn you!"

"Because I wish you to think about your mistake," Kahr said coldly. He turned and let his gaze touch Cooper. "And I want Mr. Cooper here to think about it as well. He will be taking your place." He granted Cooper a smile. "Now, please. You must leave us, Gaylord."

Cooper motioned to Brown with the gun. Brown walked off toward the creek, head bent and hands dangling loosely at his sides. The harsh morning light turned his body the color of chalk.

Kahr turned to Jessie. "The food is good here, and the scenery in the canyons is quite pleasant. In a few days we will have another . . . entertainment for you. A surprise, yes? Goodbye for now, Fräulein Starbuck."

# Chapter 15

At dawn they came out of the desert, the rising sun at their backs. Ki rubbed grit out of his eyes and stared blearily into the west. The first light of morning fired the bleak heights of the Magdalena Range. They crossed the Rio Grande, the sluggish brown water burnished copper by the sun. An hour later they found the small New Mexico settlement of San Antonio, and the freshly laid ties and new rails of the Atchison, Topeka & Sante Fe railroad.

"There's supposed to be a hotel of some kind, and a cafe," said Ellie. "If you'll take care of the horses, I'll get us some rooms. You want anything to eat?"

"I want some sleep," Ki said flatly. "I'll eat if I ever get up."

Ellie nodded and said, "I'll go along with that." She slid out of the saddle and took her pack, and Ki led the horses down the street to the livery. The old man inside gave the mounts a sour look and shook his head.

"Won't promise they'll still be standin' at the end of the day. You come close to wearin' 'em down. You goin' to have to trade up if you want fresh horses."

"We'll talk about it," Ki told him. He took the gear he'd need and the things he didn't want to leave in the stable, and walked into the harsh morning sun. The man was right— the mounts were in sorry condition. They'd started out with four, plus the sturdy packhorse that had carried their water and supplies, and they'd come out of the desert with three. One of the mounts had dropped under Ellie, and they'd let the packhorse go the night before, dividing up what they needed to keep.

Ellie had driven them hard, keeping them in the saddle for close to twenty-four hours, nearly from one dawn to the next. They'd crossed the San Andres and the hell of the Jornada del Muerto, most of the latter in the dark. Eighty or ninety miles, Ki guessed. All the damn riding a man needed, and he had a hunch they weren't finished. Wherever they were going, this likely wasn't it.

Ellie Slate had taken care of his room. He took the key and climbed the stairs, locked the door behind him, dropped his gear to the floor, and fell in bed. *There's probably something I ought to be doing*, he thought wearily. For the moment, though, he couldn't figure out what it was. Ellie had all the cards and she was playing them close to her vest. Until she told him who they were after, who she intended to kill, there was little he could do but go along.

A pounding on the door brought him awake. His body was soaked with sweat, and bright sun streamed through the window.

"Mark, you up?" Ellie called.

"I am now," he groaned. "What time is it?"

"Three in the afternoon. Get something to eat and meet me in an hour. I'm two doors down."

"Ellie—" he called out, but she was gone. He cursed under his breath, then stood and scratched, pulled on his dirty clothes, and stomped down the stairs. At a store down the street he bought new denims and a plain cotton shirt. A few doors away he paid for a bath, put on his new clothes, and threw the old ones away. The bath and the clothes helped. By the time he'd finished a plate of ham and eggs and a quart of coffee, he figured he could give the day a try. In the bath house he'd found some scissors and cut his beard, trimming off the rough edges. He wished he could shave the thing off, get rid of the gun around his waist, and toss the damn boots in the Rio Grande. None of that was possible at the moment, but it was something to think about.

Ellie opened her door and let him in. "Well, you're looking real nice," Ki said politely. "You get a good rest?"

"I'm fine," Ellie said shortly. "Come in, please." She looked at him, the blue eyes distant. Her face showed no expression at all.

"What's up?" Ki asked. "Something wrong?"

"Nothing. We have to talk, is all. I have a great deal to say, Mark, and I'd like to get it done."

"Well, fine." Ki sat on the edge of a straight-backed chair. Ellie walked to the window and hooked her fingers in her belt. The ever-present Colt was on her hip. Her silver-blond hair was freshly washed and looked as fine as spun metal.

"It's time I told you where we're going, and what we have to do," she said evenly. "Dan Cooper told you this job was important, and it is." She paused and looked him straight in the eye. "Mark, we're going to kill the President of the United States."

*"What!"* Ki jerked to his feet, sending the chair clattering against the wall. "You—you aren't serious, Ellie? Christ, you *are,* aren't you? You really mean it!"

"I'm quite serious," she said coolly. "Sit down, please, and just listen. And quit *staring* at me like that. I don't like it."

"Hell," Ki said dully, "what do you expect? It isn't exactly the kind of thing you hear every day."

"Well, you've heard it now, all right?" she said tightly. "Sit *down,* Mark."

Ki pulled the chair upright and sat. Ellie crossed her arms under her breasts and paced the room. "The President's train is coming down from Denver," she explained, "on the new Sante Fe tracks. It'll go through Trinidad in Colorado, and into the territory at Raton Pass, south of there to a little town called Las Vegas, at the foot of the Sangre de Cristos. The line curves up to the west past Lamy, and south down the Rio Grande through Albuquerque, Isleta, Socorro, and San Antonio, where we are now. The track's completed about thirty miles south, moving toward San Marcial. At the railhead, the President will be met by a troop of cavalry and escorted by stage down to Deming. That's the end of the Southern Pacific, a hundred miles from the Santa Fe tracks. From there, he'll take the SP to Yuma and up to San Francisco." Ellie paused and wet her lips. "Only that'll never happen. He'll never leave the Sante Fe line. We'll kill him while he's still on the train."

"My God." Ki's breakfast turned to lead in his stomach. He stared up at Ellie. "Just like that, huh?"

"There's a little more to it, but—yes, just like that. One of the construction engines is making a fast run up north in the morning. I've paid the line foreman to let us hitch a ride. We'll make Las Vegas tomorrow night. Beats riding a horse two hundred miles."

"And then what?"

"And then we wait until the President's train comes through. We get on it and ride back down. We kill him before the train reaches the end of the line."

"And this train," Ki said soberly, "which is likely packed full of federal troops, they just let us hop on, do they?"

"That's been worked out."

"Worked out how?"

"You'll know, Mark. When it's time for you to know."

Ki forced a laugh. "Considering what we're fixing to do, Ellie, it looks to me like you better start trusting me some."

"This isn't a very trusting business, Mark." She smiled then, a quick little expression with a trace of sadness and regret.

"We could give it a try," he told her.

"Do you think so? Really?" She raised a questioning brow. "*I* don't. I don't see how we could do that at all." She shook her head, half turned to the window, and then faced him again. The long-barreled Colt was in her hand, pointing right at his head. He'd never even seen her hand move, her body betray any motion.

"Ellie, what the *hell!*" Ki sat up straight. Ellie backed off quickly; the muzzle of the weapon didn't waver.

"I don't want to kill you," she warned. "I don't, Mark, but I will. You just sit still."

"I've seen you at eighty yards," Ki said wearily. "I don't figure on trying you at two. Now what's this all about?"

"Unbuckle your belt and let it fall. Do it real careful. Then kick it over here."

Ki did as he was told. Ellie sat down on the bed and rested her gun on her knee. When she spoke, her voice was strained. The look in her eyes was one he'd glimpsed for a moment before—a quick, fleeting instant by the cookfire when he'd felt the real Ellie was there.

"While you were sleeping this morning," she said quietly, "I was down at the Western Union. That's part of the operation. We check in at designated points along the way. If anything's changed, they let us know. It's all in code, of course. This morning the messages were mostly about you."

"Go on." Ki let out a breath. Her eyes told him there

was little use pretending anymore.

"They know about you," she said. "Everything. Your name's Ki, not Marcus Villon. They've got a woman in camp. Her name's Jessica Starbuck."

Ki closed his eyes. He felt as if someone had kicked him in the belly. There'd always been a chance they might catch him, trip him up somehow. But Jessie—God, Jessie in Kahr's hands!

"They told me to tell you," Ellie went on, "just so you'd be sure they had her. I'm repeating the words exactly. 'Eighteen carloads of Colorado coal going east.' Does that make sense to you?"

"Yes," Ki said dully, dropping the cowhand's drawl of Marcus Villon, "it makes sense. It's a signature to verify a message. No one else in the world knows it except Jessie and me." He looked narrowly at Ellie. "All right, what happens next?"

"That's up to you," she told him. "At the end of the Sante Fe tracks there'll be a kind of ceremony. Some stands set up, and a band, and some important folks on hand to greet the President before the cavalry takes him to Deming. The Sante Fe and the Southern Pacific are going to join up at Deming next spring, and the line will go on to El Paso in the summer. There'll be railroad people and people from El Paso and a delegation from Paso del Norte across the border." Ellie paused. "This friend of yours, Jessica Starbuck. She'll be in the stands watching."

*"What!"* Ki stared.

"If the President's not dead when the train pulls into the railhead, Kahr kills her. It's as simple as that. If you do anything to try to stop me, if you don't play your part and something goes wrong—he'll do it. He'll kill her if everything doesn't happen just right."

"He'll kill her anyway," Ki blurted angrily. "You know that and so do I!"

"Maybe," she said calmly, "but you won't let yourself really believe it. You'll tell yourself there's something you can do, that you can somehow stop the killing and save her as well." Ellie leaned forward intently. "You'll put off trying to stop it, hoping something will happen. And in the end you'll do exactly as you're told, because you'll tell yourself maybe Kahr won't kill her, and you can't risk taking that chance."

"You've thought it all through, haven't you?" Ki said sharply. "You've got all the answers!"

Ellie shook her head in defiance. Her eyes flashed with sudden anger, then the fire faded and died. "I'm going to tell you something," she said bitterly. "I'm going to tell you because I want you to know where I stand and what I'll do to see this business through. I've got all the answers because I've been there and back again, friend." She looked straight at Ki. "I've murdered for them twice. The first one I killed was from a hundred yards away, with a rifle. It was easy. I didn't even have to run. The second time I smiled real nice and walked right up to an old man coming out of a restaurant. He smiled back and I pulled a .22 pistol out of my sleeve and shot him between the eyes. Then I walked right past him into the restaurant and out the back door."

"You don't have to tell me any more," said Ki.

"Oh yes, I *do* have to tell you," Ellie insisted. "That's the whole idea. I want you to *know* I can do it, and I want you to know why." She paused and wet her lips, the cool blue eyes never leaving his. "I have a brother—he's nineteen now. They have him in Forth Worth. I get a photograph every month and he's always holding up the day's newspaper under his chin. The paper comes along with the picture and he writes a little something on the paper, something about the day's news, and a note about him and me growing up. Something no one else would know."

"Ellie, I'm—"

"No, let me finish." She shook her head, her body already starting to tremble, the tears beginning to cloud the corners of her eyes. "I've been with Kahr over two years now. I haven't seen my brother in all that time. I'll do whatever they want—as long as they want me to do it. Because Billy's all I've got. Do you understand that? I'll kill whoever they want. And I'll kill you or anyone else who gets in my way!"

Ki looked down at his boots. "I didn't know all this. But I didn't think you were one of them. I never did." He looked up and faced her. "Forget what I said just now. That was anger and hurt talking. Fear of what that bastard would do to Jessie. You know what I'm feeling."

"Oh yes, I know." Her eyes blurred, but fierce determination showed through the tears. "Only you're wrong, friend. Dead wrong. I *am* one of them. Just like Voegler and Strasser and the rest. I *have* to be. Don't you see?"

"It's not the same thing," he said.

Ellie stood slowly, pointed the gun directly at his head, then eased the hammer down and dropped the Colt back in its holster. "It's the same," she said softly. "Words don't make it any different." She kicked his gunbelt back across the floor. "It isn't a game you're goin' to like, but it's the only game you've got. Figure out how you want to play it."

He went to his room and stared at the ceiling and tried to think. Anger and frustration tossed reason out of his head and he got up abruptly and left the room, slamming the door behind him. He walked the streets of town, bought a beer he didn't want, and headed east toward the tracks and past the river. A boy was fishing on the bank. A white-haired hound sat by his side. As Ki watched, the fishing pole quivered and bent double. The boy scrambled to his feet and yanked a big catfish out of the water. The dog barked, dancing around the flopping fish.

"Be careful," Ki warned the boy. "If he sticks you with one of those spines, it'll hurt for a week."

The boy nodded, held the fish down with a stick, and extracted the hook with ease. Ki saw that he didn't need advice. Pushing a stick through the gills, he ran from the river and down the road, the dog still barking at the fish.

Ki thought of the boy in Ellie's picture, the one he'd found in her satchel in the wagon. Nineteen, Ellie had said. Posing for a picture every month. He must be half crazy, stuck off somewhere and as worried about his sister as she was about him.

Ki knew all the things he could do.

Like writing it all out and getting it in the mail to Deputy Marshal Long, who'd know he was telling the truth. They could spot Jessie for sure at the ceremony, and get her safely away from Kahr.

Only Ki knew the law couldn't afford to take the chance—even if they got his message in time. They'd never play it out that far, not with the President's life at stake. They'd simply cancel the trip, see that it never happened.

A chill touched the back of Ki's neck. If anything happened to stop that train from coming south—if the President caught a cold, if a bridge went out up the line—Kahr would kill her, no matter who was to blame.

When he walked back to town, the shadows were growing long and the sun was turning the sky fiery red over the mountains. He climbed the stairs and knocked on Ellie's door. She let him in, and he walked past her and stared out the window.

"I can't think of anything to do," he said aloud. "There's no right answer. They're all wrong."

"Yes," she said soberly, "I know."

He turned abruptly and faced her. "How did it happen?" he asked her. "How did they get you?"

She showed him a painful smile. "You really want to hear this?"

"Yes. Yes, I do."

"There's not much to it. We lived in St. Louis. My mother died when Billy was born, and Pa raised us. He'd been a hunter for the army before he settled down and bought a store. He was a great shot, a natural, and I took to it easy. I was better than most grown men when I was seven. Always winnin' prize money at fairs and turkey shoots. Pa died five years ago, and me and Billy ran the store." Her features suddenly clouded. "Gaylord Brown was the one who found me. I was picking up a few dollars at a fair. He saw me, and that was that. I don't think he'd ever recruited anyone who wasn't already outside the law. But the idea of a girl who was, well, pretty, and could shoot like I could, caught his fancy." Ellie paused and looked away. "They—they took the wagon everyone knew belonged to us and left it by the river. There was blood on the driver's seat, and Billy's hat and my bloody dress in the bushes. 'Course, the law must've figured right off we were dead—me raped and killed and Billy cut up, both of us floatin' down the Mississippi. Wasn't any reason to think different."

"Damn those bastards!" Ki slammed a fist into his palm.

"Won't help," she said coldly. "I've damned 'em every night since they took me away from Billy. He's still gone, and I'm still doing what they want."

Ki looked at her. "Have they got the same hold on every-

135

one there? Everyone in the camp?"

"Not everyone, no. They'd like to, but they don't." She gave him a bitter little laugh. "If they don't have you under their thumb, you don't get the big, important assignments. Like me."

Ki studied her thoughtfully a long moment. "But they didn't have a hold over me. Not until they knew about Jessie. Why did they—?"

"Send you out on something like this?" Ellie finished. "I know exactly what you thought. That you were in real hot water when you jumped on Voegler. Only Wolf was in trouble before you ever got to camp. They knew he couldn't control himself. When he tried to kill Pete, that was too much." Ellie shook her head. "That put Kahr in a bind. He and Cooper both wanted Wolf for this job. I told you Dan and I'd been close. He told me something was up on this assignment. It wasn't supposed to happen for another two weeks. Those riders who came in—that's what put me on edge. They came to tell Kahr the President's trip was moved up, that we'd have to move fast."

"That doesn't tell me what I'm doing here instead of Wolf. There were plenty of others Kahr could have picked."

"No, not Kahr. Me. Kahr left Wolf's replacement up to me. *I* picked you."

"What?" Ki stared. "Why, Ellie? Why me?"

"Because you're good," she said evenly. "Better than the others. I saw it right from the start. I have to think like that, you see. Who'll help me with the kill and not make mistakes. So I can keep my brother alive. I didn't know, but I was choosing better than I thought, wasn't I? Now you've got a very real reason to make it work."

"Jessie wouldn't want me to take the President's life to save her own," Ki said harshly. "There's no way she'd make a choice like that!"

"Of course she wouldn't. But it's not her choosing, is it? It's yours. And you won't let her die, any more than I'll risk Billy."

"It's not finished," said Ki. "It hasn't happened yet."

"No!" Her blue eyes narrowed to slits. "Don't start thinking like that, how you can maybe change it. It's no good," she said sharply. "No good at all. It puts us both in danger!"

She caught herself and stopped, staring down at her hands.

"I'm sorry. I used to think about it myself, and it scares me."

"And you don't anymore."

"No. I know better now." She looked up and let out a breath. "Do you hate me for what I've done? What I've gotten you into?"

"You didn't get me into it," he said. "I got into it myself. No, I don't hate you at all, Ellie."

"I'm glad," she said. "It's all right if you do, but I'm real glad you don't, because—" She looked away, color filling her cheeks. "This isn't the right time, but I've got to say it, maybe 'cause there won't ever be a right time for us." Her eyes met his and held them. "I don't know what's goin' to happen. I don't even know what we'll do to each other 'fore this is over. I want to say it now." She stood and came to him, resting her hands gently on his shoulders. "I liked you when I met you, but I put it out of my head. You were one of *them*, and I hated that in you." She snaked her hands about his neck and looked in his eyes. "Only you're not, are you? Turns out it's the other way around. I'm the killer, and you've got every reason to hate *me*. For the same things I hated in you."

"Ellie, I don't hate you at all," he repeated. "I said it and I meant it. I don't know how you could have done any differently than you did."

Her blue eyes softened, filled with sudden warmth. "Would you hold me, then, please? Hold me and kiss me just once, like we weren't who we are, and none of this has happened?"

"Ellie, you must know that isn't hard for me to do at all."

"Are you sure? Really? You don't think I'm—I'm—"

He touched a finger to her lips and brought her closer. "I don't think more talking is going to answer any questions. Not for us, Ellie."

Ellie gave a ragged cry and buried her head against his shoulder. All the sorrow and fear within her seemed to break free at once. Ki stroked her head, then lifted her cheeks gently between his hands and covered her face with kisses. Hot tears scalded his lips. She clung to him fiercely, her body trembling against his. Not a word passed between them. He lifted her in his arms and laid her gently on the

137

bed. Then he eased down beside her, touched her face, and brushed the silver-blond mane from her cheeks. His hand found the column of her throat, the cleft between her breasts. Her nipples grew hard under his touch. She took a deep breath, and the taut little buds stretched the fabric of her shirt.

Ki's fingers found the row of bright buttons and undid them gently. When his hands reached her waist, Ellie sat up and let him slip the garment off her shoulders. Ki's throat went dry at the sight. For an instant the cloth hung precariously on the points of her breasts, baring the tops of her nipples. His hand brushed the shirt down her arms, exposing the full luscious mounds of flesh. Ellie showed him an easy smile. Ki's hands trembled at the buckle of her belt, then eagerly loosed the buttons of her jeans.

A lovely vee of pale, unblemished flesh met his eyes. Running his hand beneath the fabric about her waist, he slipped his hands gently under her hips. Ellie stretched and raised her bottom off the bed, and Ki peeled the jeans down the length of her legs. Pulling her boots off her feet, he drew the denims past her ankles and tossed them aside.

Ki marveled at Ellie's breathtaking beauty. He'd watched her in the heat of the wagon, the thin chemise clinging wantonly to her flesh, the sight bringing him erect more than once. Now this slim and lovely girl lay naked and willing before him. The sight sent a hot surge of longing through his veins. Her body was long and sleek, a sensuous mix of lean, satiny hollows and curves. Her incredibly long legs seemed to stretch out forever. In the fading light of day, dusky shadow kissed the curve beneath her ribs, the dark and secret nest between her legs.

Ellie watched him without moving, her arms stretched above her head in a motion that hollowed her belly and curved her breasts up high and proud.

Ki let a long breath pass slowly between his teeth. Turning around on the bed, he pulled off his boots, stood and tore off his shirt, and pulled his denims over his knees. His erection sprang free, and Ellie's blue eyes went wide. The pink tip of her tongue unconsciously probed at her lips. Ki rested one knee on the bed. Ellie stretched to cradle his hard member in her palm. Without a word she came to her knees, closed her eyes, and softly touched the tip of his shaft with

138

her lips. Ki drew a breath and held it. Ellie pulled him down gently to the bed. Her tongue fluttered delightfully over his manhood. The heat of her touch churned fires deep within him, sang through every nerve in his body. Her lips parted slightly till he could scarcely feel her at all. Her silver-blond hair fell past her shoulders. She shook the heavy mane across his belly, letting the feathery coils whip freely about his erection.

Ki hung on the sharp edge of pleasure, only a touch away from sweet release. Her kiss was as light as a whisper. Her tongue flicked out to tease and stroke him softly. Ki was certain he'd explode at any moment. Sharp teeth nibbled at his flesh. Her mouth closed around him, an agony of pleasure that tightened every tendon in his body. The pressure in his loins swelled to bursting. Her tongue moved faster and faster, darting over his hardness like a snake. The storm thundered within him, threatening to overwhelm him with its fury. Ki groaned, and Ellie slid her hands around his waist, digging her nails into his hips. Her cheeks went hollow as she strained to take him in. She threw herself recklessly against him, her head pounding hard against his belly.

Ki suddenly exploded.

Ellie moaned with pleasure, clung to him hungrily, and refused to let him go. Finally she sank back with a sigh, stretched, and ran her hands through her hair. Ki drew her to him, taking her into his arms and covering her face with kisses. Her mouth went slack, eyes half closed in a sleepy pleasure.

"Thank you," Ki whispered. "That was a fine gift you gave me, Ellie."

"Mmmmm, a real pleasure," she purred.

"But most of the pleasure was mine," said Ki.

"Now that's what you think, friend." She peered up at him through a veil of tousled hair, pursing her mouth in an impish grin. "I wasn't suffering any, either."

Ki's lips trailed past the hollow of her throat to the swell of her breasts. When his mouth found the hard little nipples, Ellie's eyes widened in surprise.

"Oh Lord," she gasped, "that—that went all the way through me!"

"It was supposed to," Ki said, smiling. He kissed her

again and again, drawing the taut buds into his mouth, savoring the sweet, musky taste of her flesh.

"I *love* that," cried Ellie, thrashing wildly beneath him, "but you don't have to do anything for me. Honest. I got an awful lot of pleasure out of lovin' you."

"So did I," Ki told her. "It doesn't mean we have to stop, now does it?"

"No, but—" Ellie's hand found his member and she drew in a quick little breath. "Oh, my! I *thought* that's what it meant. I guess maybe it doesn't!"

She'd drained him dry, left him with nothing more to give. Yet the moment he'd taken her in his arms, drawn her nipples into his mouth, his shaft had gone as rigid as iron. It was as if he'd never touched her, never looked at her naked body.

Ellie Slate bit her lip as Ki spread her long legs and brought himself to his knees between her thighs. He trailed his fingers lazily down her belly, then brushed the moist folds of her pleasure.

Ellie jerked and cried out at his touch. His fingers parted the soft, fleshy petals, triggering a surge of warmth within her.

"Yes, oh, *yes!*" she whispered.

The lovely nest glistened before him like a pink treasure of jewels. He brought his member close, kissed her flesh lightly with the tip, and pulled away. Ellie's legs scissored around his waist to bring him back. Ki laughed and let the gentle pressure of her calves guide him firmly into her warmth.

Ellie gave a deep moan of pleasure. "That's it . . . yes . . ."

"You don't sound like the lady who didn't need any more loving."

"It's not . . . nice to remind a girl of what she said!"

"Reckon you're right," said Ki.

"I *know* I'm right. I just—*aaaaaaah!* Please, more of that!"

Ki thrust his member deep, as far as it would go. Ellie trembled; her breasts pointed straight at the ceiling, the cords in her neck went rigid. She stroked him with soft and velvety muscles. Ki plunged his shaft to the heart of the pleasure. Ellie arched her spine up to meet him, drawing him hungrily to her. Her hands found his back, and slid past his waist to rake the hard flesh of his hips. She caught the rhythm of his love, matching it with her own and the quick little explosions of her breath.

Ki felt himself climbing toward an intense, almost unbearable peak of pleasure. They were both poised and ready, balanced on the joyous edge of release. He thrust himself savagely against her, grasping her shoulders and slamming her breasts against his chest. Ki's loins exploded with a violence that loosed a sharp cry from his lips. His pleasure heightened her own, triggering uncontrollable spasms of delight. She threw back her head and cried out, loosing all the fear and sorrow buried within her . . .

She lay in the shelter of his arms, her head in the hollow of his shoulder.

"I've been calling you Mark," she whispered. "I have to start calling you something else now, don't I? Ki . . . Ki . . ." She tasted the name on her tongue.

She was silent a long moment. In the darkness, her flesh was the color of the moon. "I'm glad it happened," she said suddenly. "Maybe it's wrong, but I *wanted* it to, Ki."

"There's nothing wrong with it, Ellie."

"Yes—yes, there is," she protested. Twisting out of his grasp, she turned onto his chest and looked into his eyes. "It's wrong because—Ki, please, don't try to stop me. Don't try to change what's going to happen!"

He couldn't see her face, but he heard the desperation in her voice. Desperation and fear. She didn't have to put it into words. He could feel it in the fierce grip of her hands across his shoulders, the hot touch of her breath on his cheek. If he tried to stand in her way, stop the assassination, the lovely girl he held in his arms would try to kill him. He didn't doubt it for an instant.

# Chapter 16

Jessie walked back to the cabin with Jeff, the guards trailing a dozen yards behind. They paid little attention to their charges, laughing and trading jokes, stopping on the trail to roll a smoke.

Jessie drew deep breaths of fresh mountain air to clear her head. The terrible image of Gaylord Brown was still with her and refused to go away. He likely deserved what he got, but to go like that, naked, with death right behind you, hunting you down...

"Jessie, you all right?"

"No," she said grimly, "I'm not."

"Don't shed any tears for the bastard," Jeff said darkly. "I don't figure he'd cry over you."

Above her, a golden eagle knifed through the bright blue air, sending a wild cry through the canyon. The path down the hill was dappled with light. Spiny sotol clung to the rocks like big green spiders. Apache plume and yellow columbine painted the clearing with color. None of it seemed real at all.

Half an hour later, a man arrived with breakfast. Dan Cooper followed him in, looked at Jessie, and nodded at Jeff.

"That wound of yours all right? Feel like you got any swelling?"

"It's stiff," said Jeff, "but it's all right."

"One of my people said you were limping. Let me hear if it gets bad."

Jessie shook her head in disbelief. "You folks run a real nice resort here," she said darkly. "Service is good, and the meals are first-rate."

Cooper gave her a look. "I know your friend, Marcus

Villon. Ki, I guess it is. Liked him fine. He's a good man. Well..." Cooper touched the brim of his hat. "You folks make yourselves at home." He nodded to the guard, and the man followed him out of the cabin.

"You suppose the son of a bitch smiles all the time?" said Jessie.

Jeff lifted the cloth off a tray and peeked under. "My God—steak and eggs and a melon. And hot bread and coffee."

Jessie made a face. "They're fattening us up for something. I just don't know what."

"Long as they are, let's oblige 'em," said Jeff. He fixed Jessie a plate and handed her a mug of hot coffee.

"They're not worried about Ki," Jessie said suddenly. "The Prussian made that pretty clear. Brown had to pay for his mistake, but Kahr's not worried at all. That means he's got some way of stopping Ki from—from whatever it is they sent him to do."

Jeff chewed a mouthful of steak. "That's the idea I got, yeah."

Jessie showed her irritation. "And that doesn't bother you any?"

Jeff laid down his fork. "Jessie, it'd bother me a whole lot more if he was *here*. You stop to think of that? I figure we'd all be dead if he was. You heard what that Kahr fella said—how he'd have some kinda surprise for us soon? That's got to have somethin' to do with Ki. It won't be anything pleasant, but it means he's still alive."

"Damn it all, Jeff!" She slammed a fist on the table, sending her tin cup rattling to the floor. "We can't just sit here and wait for it to happen. I can't handle that!"

"We won't, Jessie," he said quietly. "We'll give it the best we've got." He braced his hands on the table and pulled himself upright. His face twisted in pain and he sank back into his chair.

"Oh Lord, it's hurting bad, isn't it?" Jessie shook her head firmly. "Jeff, we're not going to try anything at all— not with you feeling like that!"

Jeff's features relaxed into a grin. He stood easily, with no apparent effort at all, stretched his arms, and walked across the room.

Jessie blinked in surprise. "It hurts some, but not much,"

143

he told her. "Figured if I could fool you, they'd swallow it too. I got an idea I'm goin' to be a hell of a lot worse by morning. Walkin' with a cane, with any luck."

By late afternoon the sky turned black and thunderheads rolled over the canyon, bringing a heavy summer rain that swept quickly through the mountains. The noonday meal, and then supper, arrived on time. Guards came to pick up their dishes. Forks were accounted for before they left the cabin. There weren't any knives. If there was meat on the menu, Jessie and Jeff used their hands.

Jeff had been over their room an inch at a time. There was no metal, and not even a stick of kindling he could use for a club.

The rain returned at dusk and settled in over the canyon for the night. Jessie lay in Jeff's arms, listening to the soft and pleasant sounds. They made love gently and let the rain lull them to sleep.

Jessie woke in the gray hour before dawn. The rain was gone, but the branches outside hung low, heavy with moisture. The idea hit her almost at once. A moment before, there was nothing, and then it was there. She shook Jeff awake and started talking. He rubbed sleep out of his eyes and frowned in thought.

"It could work," he said finally. "It's worth a try, if you're willing to take the chance."

"We know how this is going to end," said Jessie, "unless we do something to change it."

He took her in his arms and drew her close. "All right, by God. Nobody can say we didn't give it a shot."

She asked the guard who brought them breakfast. All they wanted to do was take a walk—anywhere at all, as long as it got them out of the cabin. Jeff's side was aching and he needed to work out the stiffness. The guard said he'd ask, left their food, and walked off through the trees.

"All of a sudden I'm not hungry," said Jessie.

"*Eat,*" Jeff told her.

Half an hour later he was back. He talked to the guard in front of their cabin and came in to take the dishes. "It's okay," he said. "Henry there'll be right behind you. Walk east and stay this side of the creek." He gave them a warning glance. "He says jump, you jump. Understand?"

"Thank you." Jessie gave him a grateful smile. "We appreciate your help."

The man grunted and took the dishes. Jessie squeezed Jeff's hand, picked up her canteen and looped it over her shoulder, then took the tin cup off its hook by the barrel and hung it over the neck of the canteen. Jeff nodded, and she followed him onto the porch. The man named Henry was waiting, the Winchester cradled in his arms. He looked the pair over and motioned them down the path.

"I don't have to say it, do I?" he growled. "Don't try nothin' foolish. It'd be a waste of time."

"All we want to do is walk," Jessie told him. "Lord, it's a lovely day. The rain washed everything clean!" She sighed and spread her arms wide, standing for a moment on her toes. The action swelled her breasts, stretching the taut fabric until a button slipped free, baring a vee of creamy, unblemished flesh. The guard grinned crookedly at the sight. Jessie pretended not to notice, and made no effort to put the button back in place.

They walked down the path through the trees. The sun caught jewels of moisture on every leaf and blade of grass. Jeff set the pace, clearly favoring one side and setting one foot carefully before the other. Now and then he clutched his side, made a face, and stopped to get his breath. At a pile of brush he paused, eased himself down, and poked through the sticks and short branches.

"What are you doin'?" the guard asked warily.

"Thought I'd find somethin' to use for a cane," said Jeff. "Make the walkin' a little easier."

"Huh-unh." The guard shook his head. "You ain't carryin' no stick."

"Christ," Jeff muttered, "what do you think I'm going to do?"

"Nothin'," the guard said flatly. "'Cause you ain't goin' to carry no stick."

"Suit yourself," Jeff said, shrugging. He gritted his teeth in pain, and Jessie bent to help him to his feet.

They came out of the woods and crossed a broad meadow lined with ancient oaks. Through the trees they could see a group of people past the creek, against the high canyon wall. Each had a blue bandanna about his or her arm. They were practicing climbing the cliffs, tossing grappling hooks at the limestone crags. Jessie tried to stop and watch, but the guard motioned her on.

Back under the trees, she saw motion to her right, sucked in a breath, and held it.

"I see 'em," Jeff said quietly. "Edge up a little closer."

Jessie walked on, letting her eyes search the woods. The makeshift corral was some thirty yards away. A dozen or more horses mingled inside. They had to try. There might not be another chance. She looked at Jeff and caught his eye. Jeff took another few steps, let his boot slip, and went down hard, flailing his arms to get his balance.

*"Jeff!"* Jessie cried out, and bent to help.

"Just let me alone a minute," he snapped. "All right?"

The guard stopped behind him. "You okay?"

"Yeah, yeah, fine," Jeff muttered angrily under his breath. "Give me a swallow of that water, will you?"

"Sure. Just a minute." Jessie swung the canteen off her shoulder, went to one knee beside him, and busied herself with the cap. She could see the guard's legs, and knew he was much too far away. Brushing hair casually off her face, she brought her shoulders together, letting the action flare the loose neck of her shirt. The fabric parted nicely. If he moved in another few feet, he could see one nipple fully exposed. *Come on, mister, you're going to miss the show . . .*

She breathed a sigh of relief as he took a step closer, and then another. She filled the tin cup she'd brought along, all the way up to the rim.

"Okay, take a big swallow of this," she told Jeff. She stretched to hand him the cup, then turned quickly on one heel, and dashed the contents of the cup straight up into the guard's face.

The man gasped and cried out in sudden pain as the kerosene Jessie had drained from their lamp caught him squarely in the eyes. Jeff came off the ground and hit him hard, stilling him with a short, wicked right to the jaw before he could utter another sound. Jessie retrieved the rifle and jerked a short-barreled Smith & Wesson from the man's belt as Jeff hauled him off the path and let him roll into thick brush. Jessie tossed the pistol to Jeff and kept the rifle. Jeff stood in a half-crouch, letting his eyes sweep quickly about the clearing.

"All right, let's do it," he told her.

The horses shuffled nervously and blew air. Jeff found a worn rope bridle, searched for another, and gave up. He picked a satiny black mare, sturdy and deep in the chest, and led her quickly through the trees. He pulled himself over the broad back; Jessie held his waist and drew herself up behind him.

"We got to ride double," he told her. "No time to look for any more gear."

"We'll make it," she told him. "Let's get the hell out of here, friend."

Jeff guided the mare uphill, keeping close to the high canyon wall. Ponderosa pines clung to the steep ridge. Wind sighed through the high branches. Jessie watched their back-trail, searching the thick growth below. Finally, Jeff drew the mount up hard and pointed past the trees.

"There," he said softly, "off to the right. There's one perched up in the rocks. He'll see anything that passes down below. And there'll be a couple more to our left." He looked at Jessie and frowned. "Hang on, we don't have any choice. I'm goin' to get a little closer, then ride like hell."

He guided the horse under cover of low branches.

Jessie spotted the guard high above, gazing out over the valley. Jeff felt her hands tighten about his waist. "Easy," he said, "just keep your eyes open. He moves at all, you—"

The sharp crack of a rifle cut off his words. Jeff cursed and kicked the mount hard. Lead clipped leaves overhead. The horse plunged forward, nearly shaking Jessie loose. The shot had come from down the slope to their left. The gunman above opened up, raising dust in their path. The horse leaped a rotten log and tore through brush. Suddenly the trees disappeared. Sunlight flooded the canyon, and the slope leveled off to flat ground. Jessie risked a look over her shoulder. Jeff shouted a warning and the sky tilted up at a crazy angle. Jessie covered her face with her hands and brought her knees up into her belly. She hit the ground and rolled, and saw the horse go belly-up ahead.

"*Jeff!*" she cried out as she swept the rocky terrain with her eyes. She saw him wave her down, come to his knees, and squeeze off shots with the pistol. She still clutched the Winchester in her hand. Lead stitched the ground to her right and she rolled to cover, levered a shell into the rifle, and went to her belly. Riders burst out of the trees—two, three, then half a dozen more. Jessie let out a breath and fired. The first shot missed. The second lifted a rider out of the saddle. Another man dropped and she knew Jeff's Colt had found its mark. Jessie squeezed the trigger again. The hammer clicked on an empty chamber. She dropped the weapon and crawled desperately toward Jeff. The riders were suddenly all around her, towering above her on their mounts. She turned and saw Jeff go down under a gunman's savage kick.

Wilhelm Kahr dismounted, walked toward her, and shook his head in irritation. "If you're finished with this foolishness, Fräulein, come and help your friend back to your cabin." He showed her a thin smile. "We will not be here much longer. Be ready to leave, please, *ja?*" Kahr turned abruptly and kicked his horse away.

# Chapter 17

Whatever Ellie had paid, it was enough to get them a seat on a crowded Santa Fe work train going north. There was an engine, a coal tender, a passenger coach, and a flatcar. Every inch was taken; men squatted in the aisles and clung to the roof. Whatever discomfort there was, it was worth it. At the end of the line was a town where their wages would buy whiskey and a reasonably pretty whore.

More than once, Ki was certain he'd have to fight every man on the train to keep Ellie in one piece. The men were hungry for pleasure, and the lovely young girl in their midst seemed a likely place to start.

"Why don't you just relax?" said Ellie. "You look like you're 'bout to chew someone up and spit 'em out."

"Looking mean is about all I can do," Ki said soberly. "In case you didn't notice, we're slightly outnumbered."

"I'm used to takin' care of myself," Ellie said bluntly. "I can shoot pretty straight—in case *you* didn't notice."

"Fine," said Ki. "I hope you've got a Gatling gun in your belt."

From the town of San Antonio where they'd begun, the train passed Socorro and Isleta, stopping for a hot and humid hour at the trackside settlement of Albuquerque. There were two towns bearing the name: one, the old town, two miles west of the line, had been settled by the Spanish in the early 1700s; the second had come to life that spring when the Santa Fe tracks headed south.

Ki and Ellie got out to stretch, taking in what there was to see in a single glance. The 'depot' was a collection of old boxcars on the siding. The rest of the town site was nearly empty. Scattered signs offered LOTS FOR SALE, $10, but as far as Ki could see, there were few takers. Tents lined the tracks, and the skeletal frame of a single building. The town's first merchant had set up shop right on the ground, digging a hole in the sand to keep his whiskey and beer out of the sun. Each beverage was for sale for two bits a drink. The railroaders swarmed off the train and began draining the merchant's stock dry.

Late in the afternoon they left the Rio Grande and passed Lamy and the spur northwest to Santa Fe. By evening they were in Las Vegas, a booming territorial town. The railroad had put it on the map the year before, when it worked down south from Raton Pass.

Ellie had been there before, and led Ki to a decent hotel. Without asking, Ki checked them into one room. They'd said little to each other on the trip. Now, in silent understanding, they dropped their baggage to the floor and came into each other's arms. Ellie gave a desperate, forlorn little cry and Ki ripped her shirt aside, letting her firm breasts spring free. Her eyes closed and her lips parted as he peeled the jeans down her legs, lifted her naked body in his arms, and carried her to the bed. Tossing his clothes aside, he took her in his arms, entering her almost at once. She scissored her legs about him, forcing him deep inside her. He took her with a fury that brought a cry of pain and pleasure to her lips. With no warning at all, her slender form went rigid and she came again and again. Ki's own orgasm shuddered through his body like a storm. Ellie gave a final hiss of pleasure and went limp. Ki started to release her, but she refused to let him go.

"No," she whispered, "stay inside me. Please."

Ki rolled on his back and she clung to his chest, her moist silver hair plastered against her breasts. "Tell me," she said, "about you. Everything. I want to know where you come from, who you are." Her eyes were narrow slits, her voice throaty and strained.

"Are you sure?" Ki asked. "You might not like to hear all that."

"Yes, yes, you're right," she said intently. "But I don't care, Ki. I want to know!"

He told her about his Japanese mother and his American father, about his youth in the Japans, about meeting his master, Sensei Hirata, and becoming a samurai. When he told her of coming to America, finding Alex Starbuck and the Circle Star Ranch, and becoming Jessie's protector, Ellie seemed to suddenly draw in upon herself.

"I don't care about that," she said absently. "I don't want to hear about her."

"Why?" Ki asked. "If you want to know about me, you've got to know about Jessie."

"Are you that close to her?" she asked coolly. "Don't you have any life of your own?"

He held her cheeks and forced her to look straight at him. "Ellie, I have vowed to protect Jessie Starbuck—though I'm not doing a very good job of it at the moment. She's my employer. More than that, she is a friend. The best friend I have. And that's all. And if she were something more, what would that matter to you?"

Ellie shrugged. "For a man who pure turns a girl inside out in bed, you don't know much about women, do you? You're not mine and you never will be, but you're here, Ki. With me, right now. A woman doesn't like to think about the man in her arms bein' somewhere else."

Ki let out a breath. "Was that all you wanted to know?" he said irritably. "Whether Jessie and I were lovers? Haven't you wondered how we got into all this? What I was doing in Kahr's camp?"

"Oh, I know about that," she told him. "Kahr sent a man to kill Jessica Starbuck. I knew Miguel Vargas. And Dan Cooper told me where he was goin'. When you found out somehow, you came gunnin' after Kahr."

Ki shook his head. "That's what I figured," he said darkly. "You don't have the slightest idea who they are or what they're doing!"

"What are you talking about?"

"Ellie, Kahr and his school for killers are part of something much, much bigger. Bigger and more evil than you can imagine." He held her shoulders and made her listen. Light from a bar across the street painted a dull yellow rectangle across the ceiling. He told her about Jessie, and Jessie's father. He told her what the cartel had done, and what they planned to do—how they didn't intend to stop until they had the whole country in their grasp.

When he was finished, she stood and left him and went

to the window. "Is that true, Ki?" she asked finally. "Yes, I guess it is, isn't it? You wouldn't have any reason to make it up."

"It's true, Ellie. All of it."

She turned to him, the soft curve of her body washed in shadow. "It doesn't change anything, you know. It doesn't stop what I have to do—what *you* have to do."

"Ellie, there's got to be a way—"

"*No!*" she cried harshly. "Don't! Don't start it, Ki!" Her body went rigid against the dark. "You just held me and loved me good, and it's somethin' I'll never forget. But I'll tell you again, friend. You try to stop me and I'll kill you without thinkin' twice. Don't you even imagine it isn't so!"

He held her through the long night, the warmth of her hot against his loins. She cried out once and he stilled her fears. In the morning she woke and kissed him, the taste of sleep on her lips. It was as if nothing but loving had happened between them.

Ki finished his breakfast at the Columbine Cafe and wiped up the leavings with his bread. Ellie watched him and sipped her coffee. He caught her eyes and she looked away.

"I'm sorry," she said. "I'm sorry for all of it, damn it. Except for what we've had. I'm not sorry about that."

"Neither am I," he said. "You ought to know that, Ellie." He wiped his napkin across his face. "What happens now? Do you want to tell me?"

Her smile vanished abruptly. "What you need to know, when you need to know it. Remember? I can't do it any other way."

"I've been wondering about something," he said. "I don't imagine you'll tell me, but it's something I've got to ask."

"Go on," she said.

"Kahr talked a lot about that team business of his, everyone working together. But there isn't any team out here, Ellie, just you and me. On a job like this, he's sending *two* people to do it?" Ki shook his head. "I'm having trouble believing that."

Ellie made a short, disparaging sound in her throat. "That's 'cause you don't know Kahr. He's got a reason for what he does, but it's not the reason you think. You should've figured it out—he worked it on you right off."

Ki looked puzzled. "Worked what? All I did was get myself in trouble."

"Uh-huh." Ellie swept hair off her cheek. "Now you're gettin' close. That's what the teams are really for. To see how people can handle themselves. Kahr *knows* the folks he puts together won't get along. It's like penning up a bunch of fighting dogs. The ones who're *left* are the ones he wants. Whoever's smart enough to survive."

"Nice," Ki said dryly. "You didn't answer my question, though, Ellie. Why is it just the two of us on this job? It still doesn't make any sense."

Ellie shook her head. "It does if you know Kahr. That's the way he works. The fewer people involved, the less likely something will go wrong. You can see that, can't you?"

"Yes, I guess I can," he said. But he still didn't like the answer at all.

She left him at the cafe and said she'd see him later on. Ki wandered around town and then went back to their room. She returned late in the evening, carrying two paper bundles wrapped in twine. Dropping one on the bed, she handed him the other.

"Try it on now, please," she told him. "I think it'll fit, but I have to know."

"What is it?"

"It's what we're going to wear," she said patiently, "when we get on the President's train." Her voice was cold and detached, all business now.

Ki opened his package. There was a U.S. Army trooper's uniform inside—cap, jacket, trousers, boots, the works. He looked up sharply at Ellie. "Are you serious?"

"Of course I am," she told him. "We can't get close enough to kill him unless we look like everyone else."

They left the hotel in the first gray light of dawn, carrying their valises and paper-wrapped bundles. Ellie led them through nearly empty streets to an alley near the new depot. They moved up the narrow passage, and she unlocked a wooden door with a key she took from her pocket. The room inside was small and dark, and stacked with sacks of onions. The strong odor was overpowering.

"We'll change in here," she told Ki, drawing a small gold watch from her jeans. Ki had never seen it before. "It's five-forty now. The Presidential train gets in at six-fifteen."

"You've got it all figured out," Ki said dryly. "Room to dress in, timetable, and everything."

Ellie gave him a look. "I don't like what I'm doing, Ki. You know that as well as I do. But I know how to do what has to be done."

Ki didn't answer. He peeled off his clothes, slipped into the army uniform, and sat down on a sack to pull on the boots. The night before, Ellie had asked him to shave his beard. As Ki had known when he started to grow it, it hid the sharp planes of his face and drew attention from the Oriental tilt of his eyes. Ellie, though, figured a clean-shaven trooper was less likely to catch a critical officer's eye.

He watched her now, stripped down in the small room and drawing the blue trousers over the slender length of her legs. She bound her breasts with a length of cloth, biting her lip against the pressure. When she was through, with the jacket buttoned up and her hair tied under her hat, she turned around to face him.

"How do I look? All right?"

"Just like you did last night," Ki told her. "The only soldier I ever saw that I'd take to bed."

"Don't joke about this, Ki." Her eyes narrowed to slits.

"You'll pass," he said. "No one's going to be looking for a woman on a train full of soldiers." He paused, looked at her, and shook his head. "Ellie, something is bothering me lot more than you in a soldier's uniform. How do we get on that train? Most of the troopers aboard the train know each other. They eat and sleep together."

Ellie smiled. "That's what makes the plan work. The train made up at Denver. Half the soldiers on board will be relieved here at Las Vegas—replaced by a bunch riding in about now from Santa Fe. The new troopers won't know the ones that stay on the train, and the ones already there won't know the new bunch."

"So both will assume we belong to the other group."

"Exactly." She took their valises and the remains of the paper wrappings and stuffed them behind sacks of onions. When she returned, she carried two Henry rifles and two Colt .45s on army belts.

Ki took the rifle and strapped on the belt. "Where's that long-barreled piece of yours? You don't look right without it."

Ellie raised a brow. "You want me to get caught? It's not exactly a regulation sidearm, you know." She tugged on the tail of her jacket. "It's time to go. You ready?"

"I'm never going to be ready for this, Ellie."

"Please, Ki. Just let it happen. Neither of us has any choice. Don't you know that yet?"

Ki nodded but didn't answer. Ellie picked up her rifle, peered out the door, and motioned to him to follow.

The sun came up like molten iron, spilling bright heat across the flats. Townsfolk wandered over to mill about the tracks. The train pulled in from the north, wheezing to a stop in a rush of steam. The crowd waved and cheered, and the President finally appeared on the observation platform of his private car. He was dressed in a coal-black suit and a top hat, and looked as if he didn't much care for getting up before the sun. He waved once and vanished, and the crowd seemed pleased. They waited by the tracks to see if anything more was going to happen.

Ki saw that Ellie was right. They had no trouble at all getting aboard. The troops from Santa Fe waited around in a ragged line until the soldiers leaving the train filed off. Most of the men staying aboard got off to scratch and yawn. There were soldiers everywhere; no one paid attention to two more.

There was an engine, a coal car, three cars full of troopers, and the Presidential car in the rear. Ellie led Ki to the car up front. Ki saw her reasoning at once. The troopers there were a combined platoon from Denver and Santa Fe.

Ellie slouched down in her seat, pulled her hat low to cover her features, and pretended to sleep.

"What happens now?" asked Ki.

"We wait. We've got a long day."

"And that's all you're going to tell me."

She peered out from under her hatbrim. "We've already been through all this."

He said urgently, "Ellie, you don't want to do this any more than I do. Work with me. Help me."

She looked at him with no expression at all. "All right. I'll do anything you want. Show me my brother's safe and it's finished right here."

"I can't do that and you know it."

"You've got as much to lose as I do, friend."

"Jessie's dead, whatever I do," he said harshly. "I *know* these people."

"If you really believed that, you would have handed me over to the law in Las Vegas. You didn't, though, did you? You can't take the chance. Neither can I, Ki."

He listened for a long moment to the clacking of the wheels over the rail joints. The train picked up speed, rushing them swiftly to the south.

"Will you tell me one thing?" he asked her.

"Maybe. If I can."

"I know what you told me—that they left it up to you to pick someone instead of Voegler. I can't accept that, Ellie. As Marcus Villon I was brand new, someone they didn't know. And this is the biggest job they've ever handed out."

"I told you," she said calmly. "They trust me. I've shown them what I can do."

"That's not enough." He leaned in close and looked right at her. "I've got a better answer. They sent me with you for two reasons. First, they assumed that just being near you would keep me in line. And second, after I'm finished with this job I'm expendable. You don't have to bring me back."

"No!" Ellie shook her head, anger and a slight touch of fear sparking her eyes. "That's not true. It's not true at all!"

"Isn't it?"

"My God," she gasped, "what do you think I am? Do you honestly think I could—could give myself to you the way I did—because Kahr told me to? Do you think I could love you like that if I was planning to kill you?" Tears filled her eyes, and she jerked down her hat to cover her face.

"Do you want an honest answer?" he said. "I don't know. I'm not sure whether you could or not. I know you've got a brother who's still alive. I know you wake up frightened in the night, thinking maybe this time something will go wrong. You'll bungle the job and you won't get his picture next month."

"I made love to you, Ki." Her voice trembled as she spoke. "That was *real*, damn you!"

"I know that. You don't have to tell me."

"Well, then?"

"Then tell me what happens when it's over. That message you got, where Kahr told you who I was. What did he say was supposed to happen to me when it's done? Just look at me and tell me the truth, Ellie."

Ellie's eyes didn't waver. "There's a way for us to get off the train when it's over. There'll be horses waiting. It's all worked out. And you're supposed to come with me, Ki. It's like I told you from the start. He thinks you'll do what you're told. He knows you'll figure sticking with me is the only way you'll find Jessica Starbuck again."

Ki studied her carefully as she spoke, trying to read the truth. Her eyes, though, told him nothing at all.

# Chapter 18

When they opened the door of the wagon, Jessie raised her arms before her eyes and shrank from the light. The harsh sun was nearly blinding. The man named Cooper was standing there with a rifle. He glanced from Jessie to Jeff, then nodded to a man out of sight. The man set a keg of fresh water on the wagon, disappeared for a moment, and returned with a basket of food.

"Where are we?" Jeff said harshly. He started for the back of the wagon. "Mister, we're bakin' in this hole!"

"Just stay right there," Cooper warned him. He nudged the air with his rifle. "You two keep quiet, now. Don't give me any trouble."

The door slammed again. Jessie turned up the wick on the kerosene lamp. Her thin chemise was plastered to her skin. Jeff was stripped to the waist, sweat glistening on his chest.

"Bastards," he muttered. "Goddamn bastards."

"See if you can spot anything," said Jessie. "Maybe it'll tell us where we are."

"Not likely," said Jeff, "'less you can tell one patch of sand from the next."

"I don't think so," said Jessie. "I heard *people*, Jeff. I'm real certain I did." She moved past him to the left side of the wagon. Kahr had loaded them in not long after they'd tried to escape. They'd traveled for three nights and nearly three unbearable days. Along the way, Jeff had discovered a small crack in the wooden walls beside his cot, and had spent the dreary hours picking away at it with a bent nail. Finally he had a hole less than a quarter-inch around. It wasn't much, but it gave them something to do.

Jessie leaned down on the cot and put her eye to the

hole. A cry escaped her lips and she turned to stare at Jeff. "My God! Come here and look at this!"

Jeff leaned down beside her. "I'll be damned," he muttered. "Now what do you reckon that's all about?"

"You tell me," Jessie said flatly. "Did you see the booths set up? And the red, white, and blue bunting hung all over?"

"Looks like a—a county fair or something. That doesn't make sense, now does it?"

"It's crazy!" said Jessie. "Why would Kahr bring us to a place like this?"

Jeff looked away from the hole. "It's not a fair, Jessie, it's somethin' else. Hell, I haven't got any idea." He glanced over at the basket. "You want something to eat?"

"No, but I better get something down." She laid her hands on his sweat-slick shoulders. "Jeff, this has got to have something to do with Ki. I *know* it does. I've got a real bad feeling about him."

Jeff looked at her. "Lady, I've got a real bad feelin' about *us*, you know? There's nothing new about that."

An hour later, Cooper opened the door again. "Get some clothes on," he said flatly. "We're going for a walk." He shook his head at Jeff. "Not you. Just her."

"Jessie, forget it," Jeff snapped. "You stay right here."

Cooper gave him a weary grin. "Come on, fella. This isn't your hand."

"It's all right," Jessie said calmly. She slipped a shirt over her shoulders and pulled on her jeans, struggling to get them past her wet flesh. The boots wouldn't go on at all.

"Forget it," said Cooper. "You aren't going far."

Jessie glanced at Jeff, stepped to the ground, and followed Cooper around the wagon. A man shut the doors behind her. Cooper led her quickly to the left, through the entrance of a fair-sized tent. Jessie stopped in her tracks.

"What is this?" she asked warily. "What's going on here, mister?"

"Just a little relief from the heat," said Cooper. "Courtesy of Mr. Kahr."

Jessie walked slowly around the tent. The space was nearly twelve feet square, the sandy ground below covered with clean white canvas. There was a bed in the corner, specially made to fold up for travel. It was big enough for two, and had clearly been slept in the night before. The sheets were of fine-quality Egyptian cotton, the quilted coverlet a burgundy-colored silk. At the foot of the bed was a small dresser and a full-length mirror. On the dresser was a cutglass lamp, a pair of silver hair brushes from Austria, and a tortoise-shell comb.

On the far side of the room was a brass tub, brimming with hot water. Beside it on a bench were thick towels and a bar of Parisian lavender soap. Jessie looked longingly at the tub, then turned away. Her attention was suddenly drawn to the curtained corner of the tent. She walked up and swept the curtains aside, stared, and brought a hand to her breast. Gowns were hung neatly side by side. A selection of hats rested on the rack above. Below, there were nearly a dozen pairs of shoes. Her practiced eye told her that everything there—everything in the tent, for that matter—was tasteful and expensive.

She turned angrily on Cooper. "What is this, mister? Kahr's idea of a joke?"

Cooper cleared his throat. "Might be you didn't notice, Miss Starbuck. Mr. Kahr's not real big on jokin'."

"Whose things are these?" Jessie demanded. "What are they for?"

"Try something on and see. Uh—I'd wait till I got cleaned up, though. No offense meant."

A cold chill touched the back of Jessie's neck. For the past few moments a growing fear had been working at the edge of her thoughts. Now that fear exploded with sudden understanding.

"These things don't belong to me," she said sharply. "What are they doing here?"

"Just take it easy, miss," said Cooper. "I don't want any trouble."

"By God, I'd give you *plenty* of trouble if I could!" Jessie said furiously. "I'll ask you again—what's this all about? What do you want with me?"

Dan Cooper eased himself down on a bench and laid the rifle across his knees. "Miss Starbuck," he said soberly, "I'm sorry. I'm goin' to have to ask you to get in that tub."

Jessie glared. "With you sittin' there watchin' me, right?"

"Yes, ma'am. That's the way it's got to be. And before you get yourself riled up, I'll tell you straight off. Do it on your own or I'll have to get some boys in to help. I don't think you want that."

"Where's Kahr?" Jessie said stubbornly. "I want to talk to him."

Cooper sighed and shook his head. "Which way's it goin' to be, Miss Starbuck? You want me to call 'em in?"

"I don't need any help, damn you," Jessie said coldly. She clamped her lips together and stripped off her shirt, then peeled the jeans down her legs. As quickly as she could, she lowered herself into the tub, covering her nakedness for the moment with steaming water. She hated herself for enjoying the soothing bath, the feeling of mild soap on her skin. Lord, how long had it been? El Paso, at Miss Lorna's place? All that seemed a hundred years ago.

She was keenly aware of the man with the rifle on the bench. At least he wasn't standing right over the tub, eating her up with his eyes. There was something about him, something that didn't fit. She'd noticed it before, back at the camp. He was one of them, and yet he wasn't. A decent man gone bad; a man with some of the good still showing through.

"That's enough, I guess," Cooper told her. "Come on and get out."

Jessie stood, facing him fully this time, making no pretense of covering herself. Droplets of water beaded on her skin, rolled down the curve of her breasts, and clung to the curly nest between her legs.

She forced a smile, taking her time running the thick white towel over her belly and down her thighs. "Help me," she whispered. "Tell me what they're going to do. Please!"

"Miss Starbuck, now you know I can't do that."

"You can if you want to," Jessie pleaded. "Just tell me. Those clothes, all the stuff in here—nothing's mine, but it could be. I know that. What's going to happen? Where's Ki now? Is he alive? You—you said you *liked* him. I remember that!"

"I said it. I meant it, too." Cooper's eyes flicked once over her body. "You might as well cover up," he said solemnly. "You don't like doing this, and it shows. Besides, you're barkin' up the wrong tree."

Jessie felt the color rise to her face. "Yes, I can see that," she flared. "You aren't any different from the others. You don't have the guts to be, do you?"

Cooper's eyes went dark. "Get your clothes on. *Move*, lady!"

Jessie turned away, wrapped the towel around her body, and walked quickly to the rack of clothes. Pulling a robe off a hanger, she slipped her arms in the sleeves and let the towel fall to the ground. Turning again, she stopped and caught her breath. Wilhelm Kahr was watching her from the other side of the tent.

"So, cleaned and refreshed, are we?" He showed her a crooked grin. "Mr. Cooper, bring us some of the good Moselle, *ja?*"

"No thanks," snapped Jessie. "I'm real particular who I drink with."

"As you wish, Fräulein," Kahr said with a shrug. Cooper poured from a decanter and brought a thin-stemmed glass to Kahr. The wine was the color of straw.

"Sit, if you wish," said the Prussian. "I have a great deal to tell you, Miss Starbuck." Jessie didn't move. Kahr eased himself into a chair. "We have come two hundred fifty miles from the camp. West from the mountains, and up the Rio Grande into New Mexico Territory. A few hundred meters past this tent is a railhead. The Atchison, Topeka & Santa Fe line, to be exact." He saw Jessie's surprise, and looked amused. "You couldn't know, of course. It is hard to tell where one is going from inside the wagon, *nein?* Still, there is a railroad, Miss Starbuck. And that is why we are here."

Somewhere close by, a band struck up a rousing march, stopped, and started over.

Kahr smiled and sipped his wine. "It is a military band, and not a very good one, I'm afraid. They practice for the celebration this afternoon."

Jessie's eyes narrowed. "And what is it we're celebrating, mister? I don't understand."

Kahr paused, raised the wine to his lips, and set it down. "Why, the arrival of the President's train, Miss Starbuck."

*"What?"* Something in Jessie's stomach turned to stone. "Oh my God!"

Kahr's eyes sparkled. "I see you understand. The rest of it is this." He leaned toward her, clearly enjoying the impact of his words. "The President's train will arrive, but he will not hear the band and the crowd here to greet him. Your friend Ki will help us kill him—before the train arrives."

Jessie felt her legs turn to water. She sank down to a bench and clutched her knees. "So that's it. That's what it's all about." She looked straight at Kahr. "Ki knows you have me."

"Yes. Of course he knows."

Jessie shook her head firmly. You're wrong, you know. He won't do it."

"He is dedicated to you, Miss Starbuck. The choice between you and a man to whom he owes nothing at all . . ." Kahr stood. "Besides, it does not truly matter what he does. There is someone with him who will see that it happens. Your friend is—what are the words? Yes—the icing on the cake."

Kahr set down his glass and took a step closer to Jessie. "Here are the things you must remember," he said firmly. "You will be in the stands, watching the train come in. You will wear a pretty gown and carry a parasol. There are important people here—businessmen, bankers, railroad men. If you see someone you know, you will smile and say something nice." Kahr's face suddenly went hard. "You will say nothing that might alarm anyone in the slightest. I will be with you at all times."

Jessie gave a harsh little laugh. "I just stand there? That's it? Mister, I've dealt with you people before. I know Ki's as good as dead, and so am I. Just what do you figure I've got to lose?"

"I will trust you to behave, Miss Starbuck."

"What are you going to do? Threaten to shoot me twice?" She looked curiously at Kahr. "What good does it all do, Kahr? All the killings? Will you tell me that? You can't shoot every important man in the country. If one man dies, there's always another to take his place. That goes for the President, too!"

Kahr frowned into his glass. "You are right, of course. It is a question of *who* replaces such men, though, yes? You see, every death brings one of our people closer to power. A man on the board of a bank, the new president of a railroad, a man who will win an election because a senator has expired . . ." Kahr's eyes glistened. "And the President. His death will open political doors that have always been closed to us before."

Jessie's mouth was as dry as dust. The whole thing was suddenly frighteningly clear. It was the cartel's way—bribery, extortion, blackmail. And murder, when murder was the most effective tool for the job. Now they were killing in a savage bid for power. It was a bold and chilling move. And if it worked, Jessie knew, it was a plan that could slice years off the cartel's goal of controlling the nation's wealth.

Kahr seemed to guess her thoughts. "It is closer, Fräulein, closer than it has ever been before. And you will play a small part in bringing it about."

"What? What?" Jessie tried to see through his words, to understand their meaning.

Kahr looked away and nodded to Cooper. "Now, I think, Dan. We must waste no more time with this." Cooper walked to the side of the tent and spoke to someone outside. Suddenly, Jeff appeared in the entry. His arms were bound behind his back, the rope twisted tightly between his legs. The tension arched his back and stretched his shoulders out of shape. Pain widened his eyes above the gag that stretched his face in a cruel grin. Looming behind him was the giant Japanese whom Jessie had seen in the camp.

"*Jeff!*" Jessie cried out, and started for him. Kahr hit her across the face with the flat of his hand and sent her sprawling. Jessie came to her hands and knees and shook her head. She tasted blood in her mouth. "My God, what's wrong with him?" she said angrily. "What have you done to him!"

"Nothing as yet," Kahr said absently. "Mr. Tanaka is merely applying a little pressure to the small of the back." Kahr looked straight at Jessie as he spoke. "Now, Mr. Tanaka. Please break the gentleman's right leg. Just enough to do the job, nothing more."

"*No!*" Jessie tasted bile in her throat. Matsuo Tanaka grinned, tossed Jeff from him, and lashed out savagely with his foot. Jeff fell heavily to the ground. The cords in his neck went rigid; he jerked in pain, and Jessie could hear his cries through the gag.

Kahr looked at Jessie, then turned to Tanaka once more. "Now," he said softly, "put out the man's eyes."

"*Christ, no, don't!*" Jessie screamed.

Kahr held up a hand to Tanaka. "I told you I was certain you'd behave, Miss Starbuck. I think I was right, don't you?" He leaned to the ground and brought his eyes close to hers. "Your friend will be in the stands. You will see him, but you will not be able to reach him." He slapped her cheek lightly with this fingers. "Give me *any* trouble, Miss Starbuck, and I swear to you I'll have his eyes torn out right on the spot!"

# Chapter 19

The Presidential train passed Lamy without stopping, then circled southwest toward the Rio Grande. Close to one in the afternoon, the big Baldwin engine eased to a stop in Albuquerque. Most of the soldiers weren't allowed to leave their seats. They sweltered in the heat while the President made a speech. Twenty troopers got off to guard his special car. They nearly outnumbered the people who'd come to meet the train. Few cared to endure the midday heat of the territory. Ki leaned out the window and watched the ragged line of townspeople drift by.

"Well, shit," one man said to another, "if it was the circus or somethin', that'd be different."

Mess attendants worked through the crowded aisle, delivering cold beans, hard beef, and bread. The troopers cursed and complained, but held out their kits to get what there was.

Ki took the food, but Ellie shook her head. "Aren't you going to eat?" he asked.

"No. My God, you think I'm hungry at a time like this?"

"I'm not hungry either," he said, close to her ear, "but it will look odd if we don't eat."

"No one's even looking at us, Ki," she said calmly. "Just leave me alone, all right?"

Ki had seen it coming and wasn't surprised. The moment the train pulled out of Albuquerque, Ellie had begun to change. Before then they had talked, Ellie letting her feelings show in her eyes and even smiling. Now she was the other Ellie—nerves like steel wires stretched tight, yet everything hidden and under control, masked by icy detachment.

Ki knew exactly what she was doing. Whether Ellie was

166

aware of it or not, her mind had cut itself off from her emotions. Only a cunning, almost animal intelligence guided her now. Ki's samurai training had taught him to will himself into such a state. He could become another Ki, set apart of himself aside, enhance every sense until he could think and act faster than those around him.

He didn't want that now. He wanted to face what had to be done the way he was, to *feel* what he knew he had to do; this was not a thing he could blame on another self.

The soldier in the seat across the aisle was a stocky corporal with thick features and a nose that had been broken and hadn't set properly. He had a bottle under his jacket and sipped from it every few moments. He couldn't take his eyes off Ellie. Either he liked pretty boys, or he had figured out exactly what she was.

"Ellie . . ." Ki pretended to cough and covered it with his hand. "We've got a little trouble."

"I see him," Ellie said coolly. "Just ignore him, Ki."

"Ellie . . ."

Ellie shook her head and drew out her watch. "We can't start back for another fourteen minutes, Ki. If we leave too early, that'll throw us off our—Ki, *don't!*" Ellie sucked in a breath, sat up straight, and stared. Ki smiled as if nothing had happened. His fingers deftly pressed a nerve just above her left elbow.

"Stand up," Ki said gently. "Let's start walking on back." Ellie stood, tension forming a tight white circle about her lips. When she was far down the aisle, he let her go and gently pushed her forward.

"You bastard!" Ellie hissed. "What did you *do* to me!"

"I got you up and moving. There wasn't time to argue."

"You're making something out of nothing," she said harshly. Suddenly her eyes narrowed to slits. "Wait a minute—that's it, isn't it? You're trying to throw me off. You think if you mess up the timing—"

"That's not it at all," he snapped. "Now shut up and get going."

Ellie glared, but let Ki lead her through the crowded aisles. Halfway to the vestibule door, Ki glanced back. The corporal was up and making his way toward them.

"Keep walking," Ki said tightly. "Get to the end of the car and go outside as if you want to get some fresh air."

Ellie protested, but Ki pushed her firmly forward. She opened the door between cars and said something over her shoulder. Her words were lost in a sudden blast of noise, the loud clatter of the wheels and the deep chuffing of the engine up ahead. Ellie gave Ki a puzzled look. He shook his head for silence and leaned against the swaying wall of the car. The corporal stepped out, braced himself, and squinted curiously at Ki. Then he leaned in close to Ellie. Ellie backed off. The trooper's face split in a grin.

"By God, I knew it," he growled. "I'll be a son of a bitch!"

Ki grabbed the soldier's collar and slammed him against the wall. The corporal gasped in surprise and Ki hit him hard on the point of his chin. The man's rheumy eyes glazed and Ki lowered him easily to the floor, making sure he wouldn't fall off either side. Rummaging through the trooper's jacket, he found the half-empty bottle, poured the remains down the front of the man's tunic, and left the bottle in his hand. With any luck, he'd be in a hell of a lot of trouble when he woke. Ki didn't think his sergeant would care for a tale about a fine-looking woman on board.

"Come on," he told Ellie, "let's get out of here."

"Yes, all right." Once more her voice was calm and controlled, her eyes as cool as ice. Ki followed her into the next car. Ellie made her way to the far end. None of the hot and weary troopers glanced their way. At the far end of the car, Ellie touched his sleeve and held him back.

"We've got to talk," she said, "before we go outside. There's one more car, Ki. There'll be some officers there, and some people from the President's staff. I don't think we'll have any trouble."

"And then what? Ellie, you're pushing me into this without telling me a thing. We can't just walk back there and knock on the door!"

"Yes, we can, Ki. That's exactly what we do. The train commander's name is Captain Harder. There's a major named Harris in the President's car. You tell the troopers outside we have an urgent message from Captain Harder for the major. When the guard opens the door..." Ellie let her voice trail off.

Ki frowned. "You go in, is that it? Ellie, there could be a dozen armed men inside."

"There won't be, though. I know exactly who's in there. The President and three or four aides, a man from the territorial governor's office, and a vice-president of the Santa Fe line. The only men with guns are Major Harris and his sergeant. You think they'll stop me?"

Ki let out a breath. "No, Ellie, I don't guess they will."

"It's easy," she said without expression. "And you'll be there to back me up. You're damn near as fast with your hands and feet as I am with a gun. What I need you for is to keep the men in the car before the President's from interfering. That shouldn't be hard. Keep them off me for half a minute. That's all the time I need. Then we simply jump off the train and it's over." She paused, and studied him intently. "You *are* with me, aren't you Ki? This has to happen and you know it." She glanced at her watch again. "Damn—we're right below Socorro. We'll be at the end of the line in twenty minutes. It has to be done by then!"

Ki turned away to hide his expression, then led her out again, toward the last military car. Inside, he let his eyes sweep quickly about. The car wasn't nearly as crowded as the others. Half the passengers were officers, the other half men in black suits and well-trimmed beards. A lively poker game was in progress midway down the car. Cigar smoke formed a blue haze in the air.

A few men glanced up as Ki and Ellie entered. No one moved to stop them till they reached the end of the car. Several officers lounged about, reading or catching forty winks. Two played checkers while another buried his head in the folds of a paper. One of the checker players stood, a young lieutenant.

"What do you want back here, men?" he asked Ki.

"Sir, message from Captain Harder for Major Harris," Ki said stiffly.

The lieutenant looked Ki over and glanced at Ellie. "All right. One of the guards will get the major for you." He turned back to his game, dismissing the soldiers from his mind.

Ki opened the door to the clatter of noise. It wasn't as loud this far from the engine. Less than ten feet away was the door to the President's car. Two troopers with Spencer rifles looked up from the passing scenery and came alert. They saw that Ki and Ellie weren't officers, and relaxed.

"Message from Captain Harder for Major Harris," Ki said absently. "He still back here, you reckon?"

"Yeah, he's here," one of the men answered. He winked at his friend. "That's where the good whiskey is, ain't it?" The other soldier laughed. "I'll get him," the first man said.

*Ki saw it starting to happen . . .*

Between one heartbeat and the next, it was real. One guard stood to his right. The other turned on his heel to knock on the door. Ellie was to his left. He saw her turn and knew her hand was sliding for the grip of the .45. Ki moved. His left snaked out to knock the pistol to the floor. In the same motion, his right caught her shoulder and jerked her around, throwing her off balance and slamming her against the side of the car. Her hat fell away, spilling silver hair down her shoulders.

"What the hell!" The trooper turned abruptly away from the door. His friend brought his rifle up fast. Ellie stared at Ki and gasped for breath.

"Hold it!" Ki held up a hand, palm forward. "I'm on your side," he said quickly. "She was after the President. I'll explain it all to your major!"

"You sure as hell will," the trooper with the rifle said sharply. "Just get your hands up high now, mister!"

"Damn you," Ellie flared. "Damn you, Ki!"

"Johnny," snapped the soldier with the rifle, "I'll hang on to these two. Get the captain or someone out here fast."

"Right." The other trooper moved past Ki. Suddenly the door to the officers' car opened. The trooper stepped back. Ki caught a glimpse of an officer with his hat pulled low over his eyes. A newspaper was folded like a tent over his arm.

"Sir," the soldier began, saluting, "we got us somethin' kinda—Christ, *don't!*"

Ki heard the dull, muffled cough of a pistol. It looked as if a pillow had exploded in the officer's hand. The trooper stepped back, a tiny hole below his eye. The lieutenant fired again and the second soldier died before he could move. Cotton batting and burned powder flecked his jacket. Ki threw himself at the officer. Ellie cried out and leaped on his back like a tiger, pounding his chest and clawing his eyes.

"Hold it right there, you bastard!" The officer's pistol

was inches from Ki's face. "Get back, Ellie. I've got him."

Ellie let go and stepped away. Ki stared. For the first time, he saw the man's face.

Wolf Voegler showed him a crooked grin. "Life's full of surprises, isn't it, Herr Villon?"

"Wolf!" Ellie bit her lip and looked at Voegler. "Wolf, what the hell is going on here!" She bent to retrieve her pistol and jammed it in Ki's back.

"Get his gun," Wolf snapped. "Toss it over here. Quickly!" He glanced warily at the door to the officers' car.

Ellie slipped Ki's .45 from its holster. Voegler caught it deftly and stuck it in his belt. Without taking his eyes off Ki, he wadded up the bundle in his hand in the folds of his newspaper. Ki caught a quick glimpse and knew what it was—a small-caliber pistol wrapped in heavy folds of cotton batting. He had scarcely heard the shots that killed the troopers, and knew no one else had noticed them at all.

Voegler grinned at Ki and tossed the small bundle off the train.

"You haven't answered me," Ellie said tightly. "I don't understand, Wolf. You're not supposed to be here."

"There's no time to talk," Voegler muttered. "We've got work to do, Ellie."

"Wolf!"

Voegler swallowed his irritation. "I am here to help, Ellie," he said calmly. "That is all. Kahr knew this one would behave up to a point, *nein?* You see what he tried to do!"

"Kahr didn't trust me, is that it?"

"Ellie, we can't stand here and talk!" Voegler flared angrily.

"Why don't you tell her the rest of it," said Ki. "Tell her what *I'm* for, Wolf."

"Shut up," Voegler warned him.

Ellie glanced from Ki to Wolf. "What? What are you talking about?"

"I don't leave when it's over," Ki said flatly. "I stay here. A dead assassin. I tried to tell you, Ellie. You wouldn't listen."

Ellie's eyes widened. "No. That's not so! I—" She stopped, and caught Voegler's eye. "My God, that's it, isn't it? You're going to kill him."

171

"Damn you, woman!" Voegler's dark eyes sparked with rage. "Wolf Voegler is dirt, *ja*? But you spread your legs for this bastard!" Without warning, Voegler's pistol swung away from Ki. Ellie squeezed the trigger without hesitating. Voegler's head exploded like a melon. His body hit the narrow railing, twisted over the edge, and disappeared. Ellie's gun moved in a blur.

*"Don't,* Ki!"

Ki froze in a half-crouch. The dark muzzle didn't waver.

"It's over," said Ki. "Put it down, Ellie."

"No, it's over for you, not for me. I have to do it, don't you see?" He read the pain and anger in her eyes. She bent quickly and retrieved Voegler's dropped gun. "Get off, Ki. Jump. Do it now. Oh God!" Her voice suddenly broke. "I love you, don't you know that? I don't want to kill you!"

Ki came at her, his head tucked low between his shoulders. Ellie's gun exploded in his ear, and the muzzle flash singed the side of his face. He flailed out blindly and knew he was going over. His hand found metal and held on. Wind struck his face, and the rails flashed by beneath his eyes. He pulled himself back, heard two shots, and saw lead rip open the locks on the door to the Presidential car. Ellie's boot came up to kick the panel aside.

"Ellie, don't!" Ki brought himself shakily to his feet. A startled sergeant met Ellie with a gun. Ellie shot him in the chest and then fired past him. A portly major grabbed his belly and sprawled over a table. Ellie fired again, and the gun clicked on an empty chamber. She tossed it aside, whipped Voegler's Colt from her belt, and moved swiftly through the car, searching for the man she had to kill. Men cursed in anger and fear and scattered for cover. Ellie fired through an overstuffed chair. A man cried out, slammed against the wall, and shattered a lamp. Bright flame blossomed and spread a tongue of fire over the carpet.

Ki came through the door in a crouch. Ellie spun around and swung the pistol at his head. She stared right at him, but hesitated a fraction of a second. A man in a black suit thrust his arm over a panel of glass. The small silver derringer barked in his hand. Ellie cried out, turned, fired, and hit the man squarely between the eyes. The panel exploded in bright shards of glass.

Ki leaped to his left and rolled for cover, crawling toward

172

Ellie past an overturned table. Fire from the lamp licked at the walls. A thick pall of smoke filled the car. Someone moved to Ki's left, coming directly toward him on his knees. Ki saw the full, spade-shaped beard, the receding hairline, and deepset eyes, and recognized Ellie's prey at once. Ellie spotted motion and loosed two quick shots. Wood splintered the table, inches from the President's head. Ki grabbed his collar and jerked the portly man roughly through the smoke, shielding him with his body from Ellie's fire. A sudden blast of wind swept the choking smoke aside. Ellie stood above him, her legs spread wide, the Colt gripped tightly in both hands.

"Get away!" she cried hoarsely. "Get away from him, Ki!"

Ki backed off, covering Ellie's target. "Go on," he said calmly. "You'll have to shoot right through me, Ellie."

Ellie's hands trembled. Anger and pain filled her eyes. A volley of shots rang through the car.

"Godammit, hold your fire!" an officer bawled. "The President's in there!"

Ellie looked around startled, as shadows moved through the haze. Ki brought his hand up fast and knocked the gun from her hand. Ellie cried out, staggered back, and disappeared.

"Ellie!" Ki started for her. A sudden explosion of flame drove him back. He tried again, felt the heat sear his flesh, and stumbled away. Troopers filled the car, shouting at one another through the smoke. Ki fought his way to the narrow door. He saw two soldiers drag the President to fresh air.

Ki pushed his way through and filled his lungs. He was suddenly aware that the train was slowing. Moving down the vestibule steps, he leaned out away from the side of the car and squinted ahead. Far down the tracks was a splash of color—ladies in bright gowns, tiered rows of seats and colorful bunting. The scene raced toward him with alarming speed.

Ki waited, then leaped to the ground before the Baldwin screeched to a stop. Troopers spilled out of the cars up ahead, rifles at the ready. Ki fought his way toward the stands. Fear seized the crowd as a hot wind swept a veil of smoke from the burning car. A woman screamed as a tier of seats collapsed. A ragged tangle of bunting snapped in

173

the air. A soldier walked blankly past Ki, a trumpet hanging loosely from his hand.

Ki bolted into the stands, fighting against the panic-stricken mass that pushed him back.

*She's got to be here, she's got to be alive...*

"Jessie, *Jessie!*" He shouted out her name, his voice lost in the fearsome roar of the crowd.


The sun beat down mercilessly on the stands. The crowd was in a holiday mood and didn't care. Ladies twirled their parasols and laughed, and sent their men down for lemonade.

Kahr waited until the last moment to take her from the tent. Holding her arm in an iron grip, he guided her through the crowd into the stands. He chose seats four rows up on the far end—easy to reach, Jessie saw, and equally easy to leave in a hurry. As Jessie and Kahr arrived, two of his men rose silently and left, leaving Jessie and Kahr their places.

Kahr wasted no time pointing out Jeff in the stands below.

"You see?" he said softly. "I told you the truth, *ja?* He is here. You can see him all you like."

Jessie swallowed a silent cry. They'd dressed Jeff up in a black suit and stuck a Stetson on his head. His features were pale and drawn. A slender, attractive young woman sat close beside him. Her hair was coal black, her lips full and sensuous. Jessie was taken aback. The girl didn't look like a danger at all.

*I swear to you, I'll have his eyes torn out right on the spot!*

"Who is she?" Jessie demanded. "Who's the girl with him?"

Kahr raised a brow. "Someone you don't want to know at all, Fräulein."

"I don't doubt that. Who is she?"

Kahr's grip tightened on her arm. Jessie gasped and gritted her teeth.

Suddenly the crowd began to chatter with excitement. "Here she comes!" someone shouted, and everyone stood and stared to the north. A plume of smoke appeared in the distance. In a moment the train itself came over the rise. The whistle blew, and a black cloud swept from the high cylindrical stack. The band struck up a march and the crowd cheered.

"Not long now," Kahr said from beside her. "Not long now, Miss Starbuck."

*My God, it's happening—it's happening right now!* Jessie's mind raced, desperately searching for an answer to Kahr's madness. In a few moments he'd kill her—she didn't doubt it for an instant. But *here*—why here? Why did he want her to die in front of hundreds of people?

A murmur of fear began to spread through the crowd around her, a murmur that quickly grew to cries of alarm. "It's on fire!" a man yelled. "My God—the President's car is on fire!"

A woman screamed in Jessie's ear. Kahr went rigid and muttered, *"Verflucht!"* Then he pulled Jessie to her feet. Jessie tried to shake him off; he wrenched her arm and leaped off the platform to the ground. Jessie fell in a heap and he pulled her roughly upright. Kahr started past the stands, stopped abruptly, and stared. His eyes went wide with disbelief. Jessie followed his glance and cried out.

"Ki! *Ki!*"

Ki brushed two troopers aside and bolted toward her through the crowd. Kahr twisted Jessie to her knees, drew a pistol from a shoulder holster beneath his coat, and snapped off a shot. Ki stumbled and went down, then came to his feet and fell back. Kahr laughed and fired again. Sand geysered up at Ki's boots. Jessie gritted her teeth and kicked out hard with her left foot. Kahr bellowed in pain as the blow landed solidly on his knee. He lashed out in fury and slammed her to the ground with his fist, brought the pistol around, and aimed it at her head. A sudden volley of fire rattled behind him on the tracks. Kahr stopped and turned, puzzlement touching his features. A slight figure ran in a crouch atop the train, a rifle clutched in her fist. Lead from the soldiers' rifles splintered wood at her heels. Her silken hair was burned; fire had scorched the sleeve of her trooper's jacket.

*"Ellie!"* Ki shouted.

Ellie stopped, searching the crowd in dismay. Her eyes went right to Kahr. A cry of pain and anger died on her lips. A trooper's bullet struck her and sent her sprawling. She gasped and came to her knees. Kahr cursed and emptied his pistol in her direction. Ellie fired from the waist. Kahr fell backward with a grunt, as one eye disappeared in an explosion of red mist. Ellie looked blank and tried to stand. A bullet caught her in the chest and turned her around. Another tore at her back and puffed her jacket outward. Her body jerked and danced crazily as the troopers' shots found their mark.

Jessie grabbed Kahr's pistol and ran to Ki's side. He waved her away and got to his feet.

"Ki, don't!" said Jessie. "You're hurt!"

Ki ran a hand under his arm. "I'm bleeding a little, but it's not bad." He glanced past Jessie, his face clouded with anger. "Kahr—is he dead?"

Jessie nodded as she checked the chambers of Kahr's weapon. "Sit down a minute," she said, forcing calm into her voice. "I've got to find someone."

"To hell with that," he snapped. "I just got here, Jessie. I'm not leaving you again. Who are we trying to find?"

"A friend," Jessie called over her shoulder. She ducked under the stands and started for the other side. "God, if they've done anything to him—"

Ki grabbed her arm. "Jessie, who else is here, do you know? Kahr's people?"

"A man named Cooper. A big Japanese—"

"Tanaka!" Ki's eyes burned as black as night. Jessie searched the nearly empty stands. A woman had fainted. Her husband fanned her with his hat. A doctor treated people who'd been injured. Squads of troopers raced about, rifles at the ready, not at all certain the danger was over.

"Ki, I don't see him!" Jessie cried. "They've killed him, I know it. Kahr said he'd—" Jessie stopped as she saw Dan Cooper carrying Jeff's limp body in his arms. A cry of rage came from her throat. She brought up the pistol and pointed it at Cooper's head. Ki brought her arm down quickly.

"You don't need that for me," Cooper told her quietly. He laid Jeff on the sand. His head rolled aside; Jessie saw his bloody face and cried out.

"Oh God, Jeff!"

"It's not as bad as it looks," Cooper told her. "He's out, but that's because of the pain." Cooper looked up at Ki and said disgustedly, "Cindy Dunne cut him up bad when things started popping. She likes that kinda stuff. Crazy as hell. I stopped her soon's I could."

"Where is she?"

"Right where she's likely to stay," Cooper said flatly. He looked straight at Ki. "Ellie—she got Kahr, and those goddamn bluebellies gunned her down!"

"I know," said Ki.

Cooper turned to Jessie. "Get some water for that bandanna, and keep him from losin' more blood. His eyes are all right. She didn't get to that. There's likely a doctor around."

Jessie gave him a curious look. "I'm—I don't know what to say to you."

"Nothin' I want to hear," he said bluntly. He stood and held Jessie's eyes. "What you said about me back in the tent was close to right, I reckon. That doesn't mean I thank you for it." He faced Ki again. "Most of these bastards will make tracks without Kahr. I don't know about Tanaka. Miss Starbuck, you want to turn me over to the law or something, you do what you got to do. But you're going to have to use that thing if you figure on stopping me from walking." He nodded to Ki, turned, and started away from the stands.

Ki followed the horse's tracks away from the railhead, letting his own mount move at an easy pace. There was no great need to hurry; the way the man was punishing his horse said he wouldn't be riding very long. Even if the animal was big and sturdy, it would drop. Its rider was simply too large a man to sit in a saddle for long at more than a walk. At the pace he was setting now . . .

The horse lasted longer than Ki had imagined it would. He didn't find it until dawn, in the foothills of the San Mateo Mountains. He swung out of the saddle and led his mount over the dry, parched earth, across a deep arroyo, and up a rise. From the rise he looked down and saw the man waiting. He was standing against the trunk of a stunted tree, arms folded across his thick chest. He was bare to the waist, and wore the loose black trousers and red sash he'd worn at the camp. The two blades of the samurai warrior were stuck in the sash.

Ki stopped twenty yards away. He wore denim trousers

177

and a light cotton shirt. The boots he despised were gone, and his bare feet welcomed the touch of the earth.

Matsuo Tanaka looked up at Ki and laughed, a rumble that came from deep within his chest. He spoke to Ki in the language they shared. "Ah, the pupil comes to challenge the master. You have ridden a long way to die."

"Master?" Ki spat on the ground. "You dishonor the name of my master! You are no samurai. You are a man who would use the *katana* blade to clean a fish."

Tanaka's face clouded, then relaxed in a crooked grin. "And you follow the code of *bushido,* do you, mongrel?" He looked Ki over with scorn. "Who is your mother—a whore who pleasures white men in an alley?"

Ki's eyes didn't waver. "Put your weapons aside. I will show you what my mother's son can do. You should welcome death. Your white master is gone. You will have to beg for scraps."

Tanaka's eyes narrowed. He drew the two swords and tossed them aside. Flexing his great arms, he stalked toward Ki like a bear. Ki let his arms hang loose, as if the ritual strutting meant nothing to him at all. Tanaka moved closer, feinting with his arms while he shifted his massive legs for an opening strike.

Still, Ki made no move at all to meet the attack. Tanaka's dark eyes said he didn't understand this at all. He knew now what he hadn't known before, when Ki was Marcus Villon, that the man he now faced was a samurai. Why didn't he use the classical stance? What was the use of pretending now?

Tanaka suddenly feinted with his left hand, drew back and twisted on one leg, and struck at Ki's chest with his heel. Ki leaped aside and let the murderous kick go harmlessly by. Locking his fists together, he swept them like a hammer at the base of Tanaka's thick neck. Tanaka grunted and staggered away, shook his head and turned to face Ki again.

It was just as Ki had guessed from watching the man before. Tanaka was fast enough for a man his size, but his true danger lay in his awesome strength. Ki knew the strike he'd delivered should have cracked the vertebrae in Tanaka's neck and killed him at once. Instead he had shaken off the blow like a dog coming out of the water. *I'll have to wear him down,* Ki told himself grimly. *There's no other way.*

Ki waited, leaving the attacks to his foe. Tanaka tried to draw him in, but Ki knew better. Tanaka feinted with a kick, pulled his leg back, and swung at Ki's chest with the side of his hand. Ki let the blow graze his shoulder, stepped aside, and kicked Tanaka twice in the ribs. Tanaka spun about in a rage, and Ki kicked him solidly in the face. The giant bellowed and backed off. Blood ran from his nose into his mouth. Tanaka wiped a big arm across his face and struck out at Ki once more. He backed off, letting the killing blows hammer nothing but air.

The morning sun already baked the land with murderous heat. Sweat glistened on Tanaka's chest and shoulders. Moisture beaded his brow and ran down his face. He was breathing hard, already slowing down. It had been some time since he'd needed to use his strength to stop a foe. Now the heat and exertion were telling.

Tanaka rubbed sweat and blood away and lumbered toward Ki once more. This time he made no effort to mask his intentions. He came at Ki with his arms spread wide, fingers bent in stubby claws. Ki knew exactly what his foe intended to do—catch him and crush out his life with those killing hands.

Ki backed off. Tanaka grinned and motioned him in, daring him to come a step closer. Ki let him come, watching the heat drain moisture from his body. Suddenly, Tanaka raised his foot and slammed it to the ground, turned in a half-circle and stalked Ki from the other direction. Ki waited. When Tanaka repeated the move, Ki darted in quickly and drove his heel into the side of Tanaka's throat. Tanaka bellowed in rage. He came after Ki, his great arms swinging like hammers.

Ki moved away, twisted, and kicked Tanaka three times in the chest. Tanaka feinted, pulled his left hand back at the last instant, and threw a fierce right at Ki's head. Ki turned in a full circle and kicked Tanaka solidly in the groin.

Tanaka bellowed in pain and lowered his guard, bending to clutch at his vitals. Ki rushed in, cocked his arm like a bow, and drove his fist at Tanaka's face. Tanaka moved in a blur, and Ki's hand found nothing but air. Too late, he knew Tanaka had deliberately drawn him in. He felt the great fists coming up from between Tanaka's thighs. He tried to pull away. The blow caught him full in the face and lifted him off the ground.

Ki hit the earth and gasped for breath. He wanted to scream with pain, but the muscles in his face wouldn't work. Through a pale curtain of red, he saw the giant blot out the sun, towering above him and lashing out savagely with his foot. Ki rolled frantically away, fighting to get to his feet. Tanaka's foot struck his shoulder and numbed his arm. Ki fought the nausea that threatened to pull him under. He came to his knees, forcing leaden muscles to work. Tanaka's foot found his ribs and sent him sprawling. Ki flailed out blindly and brought himself erect. Tanaka's fist caught him in the belly and sent him reeling. Ki retched through his broken mouth, but refused to fall. Only his will was keeping him on his feet. He knew that if he went down again, he was dead.

Tanaka came at him, dark eyes narrowed to murderous slits. Ki staggered back. He knew what he had to do, but wasn't certain he could bring it off. He had to *let* Tanaka get to him once more, draw him in the same way Tanaka had done to him. If he didn't, Tanaka would play with him like a cat with a mouse and finally kill him. He had to get past those massive arms, take his punishment, and strike.

Ki stumbled back, fighting off the pain that threatened to pull him under. Tanaka grinned. He knew exactly how much damage his blows had done. He raised his big fists, bent in a half-crouch, and leaped off the ground. His right foot came at Ki like the bole of a tree. Ki moved desperately aside, and the blow glanced off his thigh. Tanaka came on without stopping. His left fist lashed out, missing Ki by inches. Ki ducked and let the big right hand pound his shoulder. At once, Tanaka struck again, his left driving up like a wedge for Ki's throat. Ki brought his right up to block it, took the punishment on his arm, thrust out his left with stiffened fingers, and hit Tanaka solidly in the eye.

Tanaka roared in pain, lumbered rapidly away, and shook his head. Ki came at him relentlessly, the hard edges of his palms before his face. Tanaka raised his arms to fend him off. Ki's left drove past the guard, crushed Tanaka's nose, and opened his cheek. His right drove through the mouth, thrusting flesh and teeth into the throat. Tanaka gagged and

180

gasped for air. Ki pounded the ruined features until his fists were slick with blood. Tanaka flailed out blindly to keep him off. The massive legs stumbled, swayed, but refused to give way. Ki drove his fist into the man's throat, closed his other eye, and lashed out at the bloodstained mouth. Tanaka's arms sagged. Ki brought his right hand back to his shoulder, hit Tanaka once at the base of his nose, and drove a wedge of bone into his brain. Tanaka went limp and fell heavily to the earth.

Ki looked down at the man and staggered back to his horse. Opening his canteen with a shaky hand, he soaked his bandanna and pressed it gingerly to his face. With luck, he decided, he could get back to the railhead before he passed out and fell off his horse.

Ki walked back to the stunted tree. He retrieved the blades, dug a small hole, and buried them in the sand. He let Matsuo Tanaka lie in the sun. There was honor in the blades, despite the one who'd worn them. Ki could find no harm in the man . . .

# Chapter 20

Ki opened his eyes and saw her sitting beside the bed. Jessie smiled and reached out to touch his hand. "You going to sleep all day?"

"Have you been here very long?"

"Couple of minutes, that's all."

"Jessie," he said wearily, "you don't have to come and see me every day."

"Maybe you're right." She bit her lip in thought. "Guess I could just leave you in El Paso and go on home."

"Sounds like a good idea to me," he said solemnly. "I could catch up wi—" Ki flinched and raised a hand to his face.

"Listen, will you shut up?" Jessie said firmly. She leaned in close and gripped his hand. "The doctor says you're not even supposed to *try* to talk for another week."

"I've been lying here for a month already," Ki muttered.

"Ten days."

"What?"

"Ten days. Not a month, Ki."

"It feels like a month," he muttered.

Jessie pressed her fingers against his lips. "Hush, will you? Just listen to me a minute. I got word this morning that the army found Kahr's camp. It was empty, of course. Just a bunch of cabins and no people. Like we figured, enough of Kahr's men got away from the railhead to warn 'em. And there wasn't a scrap of paper in the camp. No documents, no letters, nothing at all." Jessie let out a sigh. "The newspapers are saying Kahr was some kind of 'mad foreign anarchist' linked up with a well-organized bunch of outlaws. Nothing at all about the cartel, naturally."

Ki made a sound through his teeth.

"Don't talk," Jessie said flatly, "just listen. I'm not finished. All that stuff in the tent, Ki. I knew I had it right, that it was supposed to belong to me. That's the way the law would have put it together. The President's assassinated and you're found dead on the train. With a gun in your hand, of course—and it wouldn't take long to link you with me. And *I'm* dead up in the stands. A suicide, after I've watched my plan succeed. Who'd notice another shot in all that confusion?"

Ki blinked in surprise. "What plan, Jessie? No one who knows you would figure a thing like that. Kahr must have been out of his mind to think they would!"

"No," Jessie said soberly, "you're wrong, Ki. Kahr didn't leave any loose ends at all. He moved real fast when he caught me, and saw a way to make the assassination work even better. You were already on the way. A telegraph message to Ellie Slate simply told her who you were; she was to tell you that you had to go along or I'd be killed. Then Kahr sent this Voegler to wind things up the way he wanted."

"It didn't matter," Ki said darkly, "one way or the other. I was dead either way. As Marcus Villon or as myself." He looked up at Jessie. "Ellie Slate didn't know, Jessie. She didn't know what Voegler was supposed to do."

"I know," Jessie said gently. "Don't talk, Ki, please."

Ki shook his head. "She didn't guess Voegler would kill her too. I'm sure that was the way it was supposed to be. That was his job—to make sure no one was left when it was over. Kahr probably had a big surprise planned for Voegler if he made it through alive."

Jessie sat back and brushed a wisp of hair off her cheek. She looked past Ki at the bright El Paso sun outside the window. "I didn't tell you the rest," she said evenly. "I didn't know myself until a few days ago, and you weren't feeling all that good at the time."

"What?" Ki tried to lift his head. "Didn't tell me what?"

"You said no one would believe I was involved in all this, Ki. That's not so, I'm afraid. Three days ago, a maid in a hotel here in El Paso cleaned up a room and turned over what she found to the manager. The rent on the room was up, and he'd told her to see what was going on." Jessie paused and looked at Ki. "The room was rented to Jessica

183

Starbuck of the Circle Star Ranch. A lot of clothes and things that could've been mine were in the room. There was a packet of papers and a letter. The letter was in handwriting a lot like mine. It talks about my anger at the President, and how I think he's a danger to the country. There's a lot of rambling on that doesn't make much sense. I sound like a pretty disturbed person. At the end of all this, I say I'll happily take my life, knowing I've played a part in destroying this evil man."

Ki stared. "My God, Jessie!"

"He could have brought it off," Jessie said distantly. "No matter what folks believed about me, there it is. I'm a suicide, you're a dead assassin, and there's the letter. And no one around to say it didn't happen that way."

Ki was silent for a long moment. Jessie seemed lost in thought. "It's over," he told her finally. "It didn't work, Jessie."

"Yes, you're right, I guess. It didn't work."

Ki tried to clear his throat, flinched, and saw that it was a bad idea. "That friend of yours, is he doing all right? Is he still recovering over at Miss Lorna's?"

"Too quickly, if you ask me," Jessie said dryly. "Some of those gals there think his scars are real cute." She grinned wearily and shook her head. "He's going to be all right. But he still looks too much like his poster. I think it's a good thing we didn't risk a hospital. And Lorna's doctor can be trusted." Jessie smiled. "He's a friend of hers from Paso del Norte. And a good customer of the house." Jessie pulled back her chair and stood. "Anything you need? Anything I can get you?"

"You can get me out of here. And bring me something to eat besides mush."

She bent to kiss his cheek. "I'll barbecue you a whole steer personally," she promised. "As soon as you can chew it."

"Jessie . . ." Ki paused and looked away. "I've had a lot of time in here to think. Maybe I should have handled it all differently, I don't know anymore. I couldn't risk trying to stop the assassination earlier, before it even got under way, by calling in the law. And Kahr was smart, up to a point; he knew I wouldn't try anything until I knew whether or not you were safe. I almost hesitated too long."

"You didn't, though, did you?"

Ki sighed and shook his head wearily.

"Get some sleep," she said as she leaned over and kissed his cheek again. "I'll see you the first thing in the morning."

She left, and he watched until she was gone. He couldn't tell her that sleeping was the last thing he wanted to do, that sleep brought dreams of silver-blond hair against his cheek, and the touch of satiny flesh. He didn't want to sleep and find Ellie there again . . .

Watch for

**LONE STAR ON THE TREASURE RIVER**

thirty-first novel in the exciting
**LONE STAR**
series from Jove

*coming in March!*